A SPORTING MURDER

A SPORTING MURDER

LESLEY A. DIEHL

TORONTO • NEW YORK • LONDON
AMSTERDAM • PARIS • SYDNEY • HAMBURG
STOCKHOLM • ATHENS • TOKYO • MILAN
MADRID • WARSAW • BUDAPEST • AUCKLAND

Recycling programs
for this product may
not exist in your area.

A Sporting Murder

A Worldwide Mystery/April 2019

First published by Camel Press, an imprint of Epicenter Press Inc.

ISBN-13: 978-1-335-45537-6

Printed in U.S.A.

As always, to my cowboy and biker

ONE

"SHARKS? YOU'RE WORRIED about sharks?" I leaned back in my chair and let the wind blow the sweet smell of salt water into my face. I sat with Madeleine, my best friend and business partner, on deck in the stern of the cabin cruiser, the sun warming us as we headed down the mangrove-lined waterway.

Madeleine moved her head from side to side, gazing into the water rushing past us. Droplets of ocean spray in her hair caught the sun, creating prisms of tiny lights in her red curls.

"We're here to relax, not worry about some big ol' fish. Besides, sharks usually only come out at dawn and dusk. To feed. We'll keep an eye out." I reached for the sun block and stretched out my legs to apply it. My legs were fish white. I needed to get outside more often. Both of us did, but that was the downside of owning a retail business. You worked six days a week, and exhausted, slept the seventh.

Out of the corner of my eye, I saw a break in the mangroves. "Take a look at that boat. Grandy and Max said it's been there for years and that someone lives on it."

My words had the desired effect. They took Madeleine's attention off her fears and focused it on the beaten-up sailboat that lay anchored in a small canal to our left. It looked as if it had been wedged there for decades.

Alex, a private investigator and my current squeeze—and he really was a man any woman would love to squeeze and often, towering just a bit over me and blessed with intense deep-set azure eyes and a full head of sun-bleached hair—turned his head to look and nudged David Wilson, our captain and Madeleine's new boyfriend, to take a look at the wreck.

"Yep, it has been there for a while." David backed our craft off plane, and we drifted by at idle speed. "I heard they're trying to remove it, but as long as she floats and someone lives on her, there's not much that can be done."

I raised my binoculars to my eyes and caught a glimpse of movement on the sailboat. "I see the guy. He's pretty scrawny. He looks about as bad as the boat." I handed them to Alex to take a gander.

The guy on the boat looked in our direction. I waved and smiled. He gave us the finger. I guess he thought we were invading his privacy. David pushed the throttle forward and we sped off, back on plane and down the waterway to the bay beyond.

We were on our way to Nest Key, one of the small islands near Key Largo, to meet my grandmother, her husband Max, and some of their friends for an afternoon of swimming and sunbathing. David kept his old Chris Craft cabin cruiser docked in the same marina where Grandy and Max's boat was moored. Since David's boat slept four, we decided to spend the afternoon on the island, stay for dinner cooked on the boat, then return to Key Largo. We'd anchor in Sunset Cove and do an overnight there.

It was Sunday, the only day Madeleine and I closed our consignment shop, Second to None, in Sabal Bay. We would have to return early tomorrow to reopen, but we thought it was worth giving up our one day of rest, since we rarely got out of rural Florida and almost never found the time to visit Grandy and Max, who ran a fishing charter in Key Largo.

David and Madeleine had only been dating for about a month, but it looked like she'd finally met her man—one who wasn't afraid of her. Not that she's so scary, but my friend is unusually clumsy, and she's been known to wound her dates in the first few minutes of getting to know them. Not on purpose, of course. So far David had been lucky. Or Madeleine had. We were both lucky, I thought. David was not only very fit and handsome in a Brad Pitt way—on the short side for me, but tall next to Madeleine—but he also had this great old boat, and we got a ride in it. How much better could a Sunday be? Sharks? Forget it.

A cigar boat approached us from the opposite direction. On the weekends, the wealthy from Miami drove their boats south to Key West to dock at the bars along the way. On their return north, the boats' pilots were too often drunk, although the bikini-clad girls alongside them didn't seem to worry about their driving, only about whether the sun was deepening their tans and streaking their hair. The men drove full throttle ahead, throwing out a rooster tail of water and swamping every small craft unfortunate enough to try to share the waterways with them. Canoes and kayaks were particularly vulnerable.

Although this channel was marked at idle speed, the boat continued racing down the waterway, throwing a wave of water toward us. It would have inundated a smaller craft or one not piloted by someone as expert as David. He steered toward the oncoming waves, and our bow cut through them.

Madeleine jumped out of her chair and headed for the side of the boat.

"What you doing? Get back here. You'll fall overboard." I grabbed for her and missed.

She leaned over the side for a few minutes, then straightened up. "I thought I was going to be sick."

"I thought you said you liked David's boat?"

"Shush. I don't want him to think I don't. I like it when it's smooth, but I hate that bumpy feeling."

Oh, great. That "bumpy feeling" would probably continue if there were other craft on the water. On the weekend there were lots of them, and many would be as discourteous as the last one.

"What are you looking for, Madeleine?" asked David after he rode a second wave caused by yet another boat.

"Hmm? I was looking at some fish." She shot me a look, warning me to silence.

Our afternoon of pleasure threatened to turn into a landlubber's disaster. But once we were out of the channel and into the open waters, fewer boats came near us. Or perhaps, suspecting Madeleine's problem, David gave them a wide berth.

When we arrived at Nest Key, other boats were already anchored off the island. We had to anchor farther out because David's boat was an inboard and needed a draft of several feet of water under the rudder and propeller. The others, all outboards, were steered by moving the prop right or left, which meant they could be tilted out of the water to avoid the bottom.

"Do we have to swim ashore?" asked Madeleine. She bit her bottom lip as her eyes took in the expanse of blue water separating us from the island.

"*We* don't, but you might." I thought she'd catch my joke. She was so short she'd have trouble keeping her nose out of the water unless she did swim. I was doing it again—being insensitive. She didn't think my little joke was funny. Ever since someone pushed her into the rim canal that circled the Big Lake, she'd been uncomfortable around water, even water as warm and inviting as the azure blue of the Keys.

Fear filled her blue eyes.

"I'm sorry." I reached out to pat her shoulder, but before I could, David took her in his arms.

"I'll carry you in," he said.

Alex and I grabbed our cooler and basket of food and toted it all onto the island, careful to keep everything out of the water. After depositing Madeleine on the sand, David went back to the boat for our chairs. Max and Grandy waved at us through the crowds of people talking in groups, lounging in beach chairs, or sitting in the shallow water. A volleyball game was about to begin. Alex and I joined in while Madeleine and David set up the chairs and flopped into them. Someone handed them each a beer. The party was on for the afternoon.

Grandy and Max introduced us to their friends, some of whom were fellow boaters living on board at the marina; others were from a campground in Key Largo. With the mix of nationalities—some from Canada, others from the U.S., a smattering of Germans and English—the island became its own tiny world community.

After the game, Alex and I walked into the shallows and sat in the water. I glanced down at my arms and legs. Despite having a fair complexion—who am I kidding, my spiky blonde hair comes out of a bottle—I tan up easily. I hadn't had this much color in years. I wiggled my toes in satisfaction and scared away a school of tiny silver fish. As the sun began to slip lower on the horizon, people gathered up their picnicking articles and began to leave.

"Why don't you stay and have dinner with us?" David asked Grandy and Max. "I brought plenty. I've got a barbeque grill on deck and we're doing steaks. Stay. I know Eve would be thrilled to have more time with you."

I nodded. It would be great to catch up with them. It seemed that lately Grandy and I only got together when someone was killed, and then we were often joined by my mob friend, Nappi Napolitani, who knew his way around murder and could lend a hand bringing the bad guys down.

Grandy must have been thinking the same thing. She hesitated for a moment, then shook her head. "I've had enough food for one day. Besides, we came with our friends, who have a smaller boat than ours."

"We'll take you back. You can just eat salad or have a piece of key lime pie," David said.

"We've got two charters tomorrow," Max said. "One in the morning, the other in the afternoon. We should get the boat ready."

I waved them goodbye and watched the boat move

away from the island then gain speed as it raced for deeper water.

"You know, I'm with Grandy," I said. "I'm so full I don't feel like eating now." I continued to stare at the boat as it turned into a tiny speck on the calm water.

"So let's stay here for a while and relax. Then we'll take off for the bay and grill our steaks there. How about you, little girl? You hungry yet?" David put his arm around Madeleine and squeezed her to him.

"I think I'd like to get all this sand off me. I need to take a swim," said Madeleine.

"Are you okay with that?" asked David. "Not afraid of the water now?"

"Of course not. I'm fine." Madeleine walked out into the shallow water, then farther out and began to do the breast stroke. She was a strong swimmer, but not as comfortable in the water as I am. I'd grown up in Connecticut and spent my summers on the shore. She teased me that I had gill covers. Madeleine had recently been tossed into the dark waters of the Rim Canal with her hands tied behind her back, an experience that would traumatize even the best swimmer. As I watched her confidently cut through the water, I gave a silent cheer. It looked like she'd put that horrible experience behind her.

While David watched Madeleine swim back and forth near the boat, Alex and I wandered down the shore, wading in the warm water, holding hands, and talking about nothing in particular.

The sound of an engine drew my attention away from Alex. A fishing boat pulled up near ours and anchored.

"That's an outboard," Alex said. "He could come in closer. I wonder what he's doing."

Madeleine paid no attention to the boat, but continued to swim, turning over to slowly backstroke near our boat.

David waved to us and called out, "I think he's ruined the romance. Let's pack up and go."

A man with long black hair and dark skin came toward the bow of the boat with a bucket in his hand.

"What the…?" said Alex.

"He's throwing something into the water. It looks like—"

"It's bait. That idiot is tossing bait into the water. Doesn't he see Madeleine?"

David threw his hands into the air and yelled, but the man seemed not to hear him and continued to toss chunks of bloody fish into the water. Then he upturned the bucket and poured out the remaining slurry.

David finally gave up trying to get the man's attention and directed his yells to Madeleine.

"Get out of the water, Madeleine. That guy's dumping fish bait. It'll attract…" The last of David's warning was carried off by the wind, but I knew what he'd said. It would attract sharks.

TWO

DAVID BEGAN RUNNING toward Madeleine, his heels kicking up the sand. Once he was in the water and it was deep enough, he dove in and began swimming.

"Oh, good. Now the sharks will have two people to dine on," I said.

Alex grabbed my arm and turned me toward him as if to reprimand me for such an insensitive remark, but when he saw the expression on my face, he knew my comment was my clumsy way of dealing with the horror of what could happen.

"Let's go," I said. "We might as well make it a four person stew." We both ran in and began swimming for the boat. Maybe more people would frighten the sharks off or confuse them. Who knew how their fishy little brains, if they had any brains, worked?

Madeleine, seeing the water turning bloody near her, panicked and began to flail her arms around as if trying to beat off whatever was causing the blood. When she spotted David swimming toward her, she must have assumed he had been injured and she began to paddle in his direction.

"No, no. Back the other way. To the boat." David continued to stroke toward her. Alex and I were not far behind.

A gray fin cut through the water nearer the fishing

boat. A sandy-haired man had joined the other one, and a cheer went up from them when they spotted the fin.

David and Madeleine collided in the water. He grabbed her and began swimming her toward the boat. They reached the dive platform and pulled themselves onto it. Now Alex and I were the freshest items left on the dinner buffet. The fin swept past the fishing boat and toward ours. A huge mouth with rows of sharp teeth erupted from the water, grabbing a large piece of bloody chum. It then submerged and was lost to our view.

"You think he's full?" I asked Alex. I was breathless, not from the exertion of swimming but from the fear that he and I might end up in the shark's belly— or at least parts of us. "Where the hell is it?" It was frightening enough seeing the fin, but terrifying when I couldn't, imagining the creature sneaking up on us from behind. Or below. *Dun, dun dun, dun*. The theme from *Jaws* ran through my head.

A dark red piece of chum floated toward me, and the fin surfaced behind it, narrowing the distance between eater and stuff to be eaten. I stopped swimming for a moment, reached for the bloody piece, and flung it back toward the fishing boat. The fin turned and followed. The dive platform was now only a few feet away. We pulled ourselves out of the water.

Safe. We were all safe.

The platform was still too close to the water for my comfort. I sprung into the stern of the boat and grabbed Alex's hand to drag him after me. We were all shaking. I knew my trembling was from fear, not from the cold, even though my teeth were also chattering. Madeleine looked like a ghost. Even her freckles faded into the grayish color of her skin. Her lips were blue.

After throwing us towels, David began yelling at the men in the fishing boat. "Didn't you see there was someone swimming in the water by our boat? What's wrong with you throwing all that bait out here?"

This time the sandy-haired man heard him. "Hey, we didn't see anybody but the three of you on shore. We figured it was safe. We wanted to get ourselves a shark."

"There's one here now." The man who dumped the bait spoke nonchalantly and turned his back on David.

"You almost killed one of us. How can you be so irresponsible to toss bait around a boat people have to swim to?"

"We weren't going to be here long," the man said, his tone dismissive. "We'd get our shark and clear out. We figured it would be safe for you to swim out then." He never turned his head in our direction but continued to play the fish on the line.

"It's not going to be safe around here for a long time. Now the sharks think this is a feeding ground. I ought to—"

"What ought you to do, Mr. Wilson?" The man who was fishing handed his rod to the other man and came around to face our boat.

"I should report you." David spoke calmly, but I could tell by the red flush beginning to work its way up his neck that he was furious.

"Really? You think you have a private claim to these waters, do you? It was a mistake. Like my man here said, we thought you were safely on shore. No one got hurt. What's your problem?"

"Ah, damn. He got away, boss." The other man began to reel in the line.

"Then we go. Have a nice day." The dark-haired man's lips twitched into a crooked smile.

They hauled anchor and started their twin outboards.

I was so angry at their casual attitude that I wanted to bite them. A chunk of chum bobbed toward us. I grabbed it out of the water and threw it at their boat. It landed in the stern.

"Lucky toss, Eve," said Alex.

I smiled. "You don't know how lucky. The top was open to the box where their deck cushions are stowed. It landed in there with them." I pointed to the gory mess as it slid down into the box between the cushions.

As the boat moved away from us and its captain opened the throttle, the surge forward made the cushion box slam closed.

"That should smell pretty ripe in a few days." Alex chuckled. "That's my Eve."

David didn't laugh with the rest of us.

"He knew your name," I said. "I get the feeling this wasn't a chance encounter. Does he have some kind of a grudge against you? Tossing out that bait wasn't a mistake, was it?" David nodded, and for a moment I thought he wasn't going to say more, but finally he spoke, the anger in his voice barely under control. "I know him. I don't like him, and he doesn't like me. We're competitors. He owns the other hunting ranch in the area and part of it abuts my land. His name is Blake Reed."

Seeing David's distress, Madeleine put her arm

around his waist as he leaned against the cabin near the wheel.

"Can I tell them the rest of it?" she asked.

"Go ahead. It's no secret."

Madeleine fussed with the towel, pulling it tighter around his shoulders and placed her hand on his.

"I think we all could use something to drink first," said Alex. "How about a beer? There are some left in the cooler. Oh damn."

"What?" I asked.

"It's all on the beach. We had to leave it when we swam out here. You think it's safe to go back in the water around here? Should we chance it?"

"I wouldn't," David said. "I wasn't exaggerating when I said sharks will think this is a feeding ground for a while." David looked up at the sky. "And it's getting late. The sharks like to feed now. We'll leave it. I can come back tomorrow after you've left and see if our stuff is still there."

"I don't want you going back into that water." Madeleine hugged him tighter. "It was just a Styrofoam cooler, and I think there were only four beers left."

"What about the picnic container and the chairs?" asked Alex.

"The beach chairs were bought at a yard sale and the picnic container came from a thrift shop in Stuart. We can replace them, but we can't replace you." I walked forward and put my arm around David, who became a hug sandwich between Madeleine and me.

"Hey, okay. I'm covered in women here and can't see to drive this boat. I'll leave the stuff." David smiled a weak smile which soon erupted into a wide grin.

Alex grinned as well. "You can bet if it was Eve's

shoes left on the beach, we'd go back right now, sharks or no sharks." He ducked as I reached out to slug him on the shoulder.

Madeleine nodded in agreement.

"So, is everyone still up for steaks and anchoring out tonight?" David asked. "We either take the turn to Sunset Cove ahead or we head straight for the Cut and the marina and call it a day."

"I'm not going to let some nasty, mean-spirited jerk ruin my dinner and evening," I said, heading below to fetch one of the bottles of red wine we had in the galley.

"What if he follows us there too?" Madeleine sounded worried.

"Then we'll send Eve over to his boat with more chum to stash away." David chortled at the idea.

I emerged from the cabin with the bottle and four glasses in my hand. "We don't have any bait."

"Let's pull in at Louis' and buy some. We go right by there." Alex pointed to the marina up ahead.

Of course we didn't pull into the marina, but we were all in good spirits as we sped past. Madeleine went below to get the corn for our dinner, while Alex and David had their heads together over the fish finder screen in front of the wheel. I was the only one to see the fishing boat docked at Louis' for refueling. The man David identified as Blake Reed looked up as we sped past. Our eyes met for a moment. His predatory gaze reminded me of what I'd seen in the shark's eyes when it surfaced to take the bait this afternoon. Hungry. Evil. A killing machine. I shivered and shook myself free of those thoughts. I was overreacting. Wasn't I?

THREE

THE BARBEQUE GRILL was designed to use alcohol as fuel, a safety precaution on boats so that gas didn't seek its lowest level and collect in the bilge, potentially causing an explosion. It attached to the side of the boat and hung over the water.

"If I blow it with these steaks and they catch fire, we can dump the whole thing overboard," David said.

"And dive after the steaks before the fish get them." I was famished from the earlier adrenaline rush of fearing I'd be on the menu myself.

David smiled. "There's peanut butter in the galley, but I've gotten pretty good with this grill. I don't think we need to worry."

I sighed with relief. There's no worse romance spoiler than peanut butter breath.

We sat in the stern and watched the sun set, taking bets on the exact time it would slip below the horizon.

"We could be betting for some real money at a bar on the bay, you know," Alex said. He put his arm around me and squeezed me tight, letting me know he was happy here rather than in some crowded dive, jockeying with the tourists for a view of the water.

I leaned my head on his shoulder. "Yeah, and we'd be paying real money for the drinks too."

A flock of roseate spoonbills flew overhead, their wings flashing gold in the setting sun. The cormorants nesting in a nearby mangrove gave their final pig-like grunts for the evening, then settled down. Quiet crept over the darkening waters.

Our dinner was perfect. Potatoes roasted on the grill, medium rare steaks, salad, and more wine. After stuffing ourselves, we cleaned up quickly; then, coffees in hand, we hurried out to sit on the deck in the stern.

"Look down there." Madeleine pointed and leaned nearer the water's surface. It glowed with a green-blue light that shimmered and undulated in the water.

"Phosphorescence from plankton. Beautiful, isn't it?" David sighed, a sound of contentment and of relief. We hadn't heard the entire story about Blake Reed, and I was curious, but not curious enough to want to break the spell of enchantment we all were experiencing. A chorus of sighs joined David's.

And that's the last thing I remembered until Alex shook me awake. "Get up, Eve. You'll get damp and cold out here. Let's go in and hit the blankets."

David pulled the plastic side and rear curtains down around the open stern and zipped them up to keep out the chill and mosquitos. We all stumbled down the stairs and into the cabin. David and Madeleine took the king-sized V-berth in the bow. Alex and I removed the seat and back cushions from the banquette and lowered the table to seat level, using the cushions to create a double bed. We opened our sleeping bags, zipped the two of them together and were soon cocooned inside. Some giggles and a slight snore from the other bed and soon Alex and I drifted into sleep.

I awoke sometime near dawn, thinking I heard a boat engine, followed by voices. I slid out of the sleeping bag and tiptoed up the cabin steps to the deck.

With the plastic curtains in place, it was difficult to see anything outside. I crossed to the back and unzipped one side. I stuck my head out and saw only still water. The boat swung on its anchor so that I was facing the mangroves.

Something broke the surface of the water between the boat and the mangrove where the cormorants nested. A fin. I shuddered then jumped when a hand gripped my shoulder.

"You're letting in all the mosquitos." It was Alex.

"I didn't mean to wake you, but—"

"I heard something, too, but there's nothing out there."

"You're wrong about that. Look." I pointed to the movement in the water. Another fin joined the first and then two more. The group moved toward us.

"They can't get us in the boat," said Alex. But I could tell just the sight of them made him uneasy.

David and Madeleine joined us on deck.

"We're surrounded," I said.

"They couldn't have followed us here, could they?" There was fear in Madeleine's voice.

David poked his head farther out of the curtains, then laughed.

"They're not sharks," he said. "It's a pod of dolphins. And it looks as if they have some young with them."

The sun broke over the mangroves, stirring the cormorants into activity. The dolphins moved closer to our boat. One stuck its head out of the water only a few feet from my hand. I reached over and touched its nose. It made a clicking sound and retreated.

"It's as if they knew we needed to get going early. Our special alarm clock." Madeleine was back to her usual happy self, all earlier fears swept away by the appearance of these friendly creatures.

"And now we need to put on the coffee, get dressed, and hit the road," I said. "We'll just make it to open at eleven if we leave here in an hour." I pushed Madeleine back down the steps.

We got back to the marina in time to wave at Grandy and Max as their boat left for a day of fishing.

"I'll give you a call tonight." I hoped Grandy could hear me over the sounds of the engines. She must have, because she nodded and smiled.

We docked David's boat and left him to finish securing her for the week. Alex had driven me down to Key Largo and Madeleine had come with David, but since she and I needed to open the store today, Alex offered to drive us back early. David would follow later.

None of us was happy to be leaving for rural Florida. Not that it didn't have its appeal, but when you're in the retail business and trying to stick to your budget, the store owns you six days a week. On the seventh, we often went in to check inventory, clean, do the books and generally worry about our business. Taking off this Sunday for a trip on David's boat meant we'd have to make up for our fun later in the week, probably one evening. We usually spent the time after we closed the store heading to the coast to pick up merchandise from our wealthy West Palm clients who couldn't take time off from their charity events to bring us their clothing, jewelry and any other items they no longer wanted. We counted on these high end items to set us apart from the other consignment shops in Sabal Bay and even those on the coast in Stuart.

Some of our consignors did make the trip to Sabal

Bay because they thought it had "charm," meaning they found the miles of pasture with cattle an oddity to gawk at. But most of all, they enjoyed staying late into the evening and hanging out in the cowboy bars because, well, there were cowboys there. And there's nothing as handsome as a long lean man, face tanned from riding herd on those cows, and wearing tight jeans, colorful Western shirts, and cowboy boots. Sometimes they even chose to wear their spurs into the bars. I think they did it to show off to the gals from the coast. Jangling spurs upped the charm factor.

And, of course, some of them could dance and sing. I agreed with my clients. These guys were yummy. Not that I didn't already have a yummy guy of my own. I did wish he would consider losing the polo shirts and khakis once in a while.

"OUR LEASE IS up the end of this month and the owner sent us the renewal." I'd picked up the mail when I ran out to the nearby fast food place to grab burgers for lunch. We'd only had toast and coffee on the boat and hadn't stopped once on our way up here from the Keys. I was starved.

Madeleine was in the back, assembling a mannequin we'd purchased from a consignment shop on the coast. Actually it was one of their old mannequins they were replacing.

"Isn't that some kind of violation of consignment shop ethics, buying a new mannequin?" I'd said to Madeleine when we'd picked it up several days ago.

"Shhh. Don't let them hear you. We only paid five bucks."

We'd hustled it into the back of our van feeling better than if Manolo Blahniks were half off at Macy's, but this morning Madeleine was having trouble with it.

"I can't get this damn arm to stay on." Madeleine sat on the floor of our shop leaning over the mannequin and looking as if she was in a women's wrestling competition. "I don't think it fits."

"I guess we could leave it off. Our other mannequin only has one arm. We could place them next to each other and dress them in similar clothing, like they're Siamese twins or something."

"That's just gross." Madeleine sat on top of the recalcitrant model and pushed the arm into the shoulder with a grunt. "You try." She held the arm out to me.

"Oh, crap. Will you look at this," I said.

She got up and dropped the arm. "Be back in a minute, Cheryl."

"You named the mannequin?"

"I thought it might be more cooperative. Maybe she doesn't like the name."

Madeleine took the paper I held out to her and read through it quickly. "We can't afford to sign this lease. They've doubled the price. We're barely covering our expenses now."

"I'll call them and give them a piece of my mind. This is Sabal Bay, not City Place in West Palm."

"I wouldn't tell them that, Eve. Let me handle it." Madeleine took the phone out of my hand and punched in the numbers. As she wandered across the room to talk in private so that our landlord wouldn't hear me yell obscenities, Madeleine tripped over Cheryl's arm and almost fell.

"Damn you, Cheryl. Stay out of my way." She put her hand over the phone for a moment, kicked the offending arm, then plastered a charming smile on her face and continued to speak with honey in her voice. "Mr. Roland? About our lease…"

"She didn't mean to take it out on you, Cheryl," I said. Now she had me talking to the mannequin. I went over and picked it and the arm up and joined the two with no effort.

"I hate you," Madeleine mouthed at me from across the room. I blew her a kiss and took Cheryl into the store to have her choose a dress to wear. I mean, I chose a dress for the mannequin.

Madeleine ended her call and crossed the room with an expression on her face that said the negotiations had not gone well.

"Roland won't budge from his position. I reminded him that we paid on time and that we are good tenants, but not only does he insist on twice as much, he says he has a prospective client who is interested in buying the entire building."

"I didn't know Roland wanted to sell."

Madeleine gave Cheryl a glance. "I see the surgery was successful."

"I'm stronger than you are."

"Right. I know that. Do you think that skirt and blouse are right for her though?"

"Skirt's a little long. I'll pin it up." What was I doing? Who cared how Cheryl looked in the skirt? She was a mannequin, for heaven's sake. I removed the skirt and selected another one. "So Roland wants to sell, does he? Maybe we should consider buying."

"I don't think we can afford it right now," Madeleine said. She was the one who always worried about the money, while I always assumed things would work out somehow.

"I know. Unless…" I paused.

"What?"

"We could get a loan."

"The banks wouldn't go for it. We're stretched too far already with the renovations we had to make to the space."

I stared out the front window.

Madeleine grabbed a bathing suit off the rack. "Here. Try this. Show off her legs."

I thought I saw Cheryl's lips curve upward a fraction of an inch as I slipped her into the red suit.

"I don't mean a bank loan," I said.

Madeleine's smile seemed to slide off her face like an egg off a greasy frying pan. "Oh, no. No, no, no. I refuse to go into business with a mob boss."

She was talking about Nappi Napolitani, who had come to my rescue on several occasions. I was aware of his connections to the mob, but I considered him my friend anyway even though Alex and Madeleine didn't trust him. I did, and so did Grandy. Her support was good enough for me.

"He's a friend. And I'm certain the money would be clean."

Madeleine continued to shake her head so vigorously that I thought it might fly off. "No. Of course the money would be clean. It would have been laundered through some other legit business and then through ours. Are you crazy?"

I gave in to her reasoning. It was one thing to have Nappi's support in the way of errands or backup if I needed it, but he had broken into a house for me and that was about as far as I wanted to go stretching the boundaries of what was legal.

"We have no choice but to look for another location. I guess we could begin by making a few calls now, then follow up after we close the shop this afternoon." I grabbed the local newspaper and flipped it open to real estate listings.

"You want to cancel our tour of David's ranch? We're scheduled to meet Alex there after we close. Did you forget?" she asked.

I had forgotten. "Let's see if I come up with anything for us to look at."

As it turned out, there were two places available in town, but one was beyond our budget; the other we couldn't see until the next day.

THE LEASE ISSUE was still on my mind when Alex, Madeleine, and I headed out to David's place after we closed up shop in the afternoon. I knew Madeleine was thinking about it too. She was gnawing on her thumbnail, something she did when she was worried.

"That's Reed's place. You know, the shark guy from yesterday." Alex slowed the car as we drove by the entrance.

The letters spelling out "The Reed Ranch" were burned into a piece of cypress hung by two chains attached to large metal statues of horses on either side of the drive. The horses were stallions and reared up, big as life.

"Does he let his clients hunt horses as well as game?" I asked.

"Huh?" said Alex.

"Why the horses?"

Alex shrugged.

"They sure are impressive. Big," Madeleine said.

"He should have put life-sized sharks out front," I muttered under my breath.

"He should have put pants on them," Madeleine said.

I was surprised at her. "I never knew you to be a prude."

"I'm not, but I think it's kind of..." She searched for the word.

"Ostentatious, crude, tasteless?" I offered.

"Like the owner, I guess," said Alex.

"Then I think it's perfect." I wondered how easy it would be to come out here some night and paint pants on them. I looked at Madeleine and saw a tiny smile lift one corner of her mouth. Childish, yes, but making fun of the man would send him into a rage. I had seen enough of him to know he wouldn't take our joke well. I nodded and Madeleine winked at me.

AT DAVID'S RANCH, we found he was out with a client and hadn't returned yet, but he'd told his foreman Dudley Thomas to take us on a tour in one of the swamp buggies. David would join up with us when he finished with the client.

"The boss told me to steer clear of the west side of the ranch near Reed's property. He let me know about your encounter on the water yesterday. That guy is a real bad one, and that goes double for his foreman. From what David said, it was the foreman who was on the boat with him. Big guy, bigger than Reed, looks real harmless with his twinkling blue eyes and all those freckles, but he's mean as a bull alligator in mating season. He has an appetite for settling arguments with his fists. Or so I hear." Dudley maneuvered the big-wheeled buggy into a swampy area and out again with ease. "We'll stop and take a walk over toward that field. No one's around here right now, and if we're real quiet we might sneak up on some quail nesting out there."

This was the first time I'd met Dudley, but he seemed like a knowledgeable fellow, intelligent and friendly. Dudley was short and wiry, his face deeply lined with wrinkles from years in the sun. When he smiled, dimples formed and the cleft in his chin became more pronounced. David's old foreman had retired and Dudley had taken his place only weeks ago.

Alex and I had jumped down from the buggy, and Dudley, seeing the concern on Madeleine's face, helped her off the behemoth. With those huge tires, the distance to the ground must have looked like jumping off a precipice to tiny Madeleine.

Dudley held up his finger. "Okay, let's move quietly and…"

A thunderous bang sliced the silence followed by another.

"That's from a large caliber weapon," said Alex.

Dudley's face darkened. "Yep. And that's something we don't use on this ranch."

FOUR

"I THINK I'D better go see what's up with that shot. I'll run you folks back to the office." Dudley's expression was grim.

"I'll come with you after you've dropped Madeleine and Eve," Alex said.

Dudley hesitated a moment, then agreed. We all reboarded the swamp buggy.

We hadn't gone but half a mile when we heard another vehicle behind us. A Jeep with the ranch's logo on the side pulled up beside us. David was driving.

"David, are you all right?" Madeleine leaned out of her seat and reached for him. He grabbed her hand and gave a quick nod.

"One of you got a cellphone on you? Mine's dead."

Alex handed his over to David.

"We heard a shot. Did you?" asked Dudley.

David nodded. "Yup." Into his cell, he said, "I've got an emergency on the Cypress Plantation. Someone's been shot." He listened for a moment on the cell, then said, "I believe he's dead." He ended the call.

Dudley frowned and said, "This is the first accident we've had on this ranch since your father started running it twenty years ago. What happened? I'm not accusing you of anything, boss, just saying what's true."

Sure, Dudley, but now's not the time, I thought to myself.

David drew Dudley away from us and spoke under his breath. I couldn't catch his words.

"I'm just glad it wasn't David." Madeleine chewed on her thumbnail. "I wonder who got shot."

Blake Reed, I thought for a moment, but I knew I was just wishing and the wish was unkind. Well, nobody ever accused me of having generous thoughts about those I didn't like.

"I need to get back there." David started up the Jeep. "Dudley, you can bring the authorities out there. You know where it is—in the west section, near that big bog."

"You mean on the border with Reed's place? I thought you told me not to go near there, boss."

Gee, Dudley, could you lay off the nagging?

"I know, I know." David sounded impatient. Were good old Dudley's reminders getting to him, too? "Now I wish I hadn't gone over there with Mr. Jackson, but we caught sight of a wild pig and Jackson got curious. He's from up north, and he'd never seen one before, so I thought, why not show him? I told him we didn't have the weapons to hunt it, and we'd have to be careful, but he was determined, so we trailed the pig through the field. When we hit denser brush, we got out of the Jeep and circled around the bog area. I took the lead, and I thought Jackson was right behind me, but when I turned around to signal him that we'd lost the pig, he wasn't there. That's when I heard the shots. I found him face down near the bog and… Look, I've got to get back there."

I realized there was something David wasn't telling us.

"And what else?" asked Alex.

"There was a dead oryx not twenty yards from him."

"What's that?" asked Madeleine.

"An exotic from Africa, sometimes brought onto hunting ranches for specialty hunting. They're large and gray, with two long, straight horns." David shifted the Jeep into gear.

"I'm coming with you," said Alex.

"I don't want anybody near there."

"Look," Alex said, "you just found a guy dead on your ranch. I think it would be better if I drove you back there. That's quite a shock and the authorities might—"

I interrupted. "My detective friend here is saying the authorities will be suspicious. Alex wants to be sure you don't say what you shouldn't."

What I didn't say was that Alex wanted to make certain David didn't contaminate the scene any more than he had already. David could also use a witness when he returned to the scene. He guessed what Alex and I were thinking.

"I wouldn't kill my own client." David's tone was angry and his face flushed.

"No, of course not, honey, but they're right. It's best to be cautious." Smiling, Madeleine reached out to touch David's cheek. I guess that was all the encouragement he needed because he agreed. Leave it to my pal Madeleine to take suspicion and make it sound as good as a Sunday picnic.

Alex climbed into the Jeep, and I jumped into the back. For a moment David didn't notice he was now carrying more than a lone passenger, but Alex called me on my maneuver.

"Get out of here, Eve."

I crossed my arms over my chest. "Make me."

"You are so childish—"

David turned to look at me. "From what Madeleine told me, she's a pretty damn good little sleuth. I can use all the help I can get—one PI and one business-woman with attitude."

"Exactly," I said.

"And one load of trouble." Alex shook his head.

"I am not." Not everyone thought that. Just Alex and Madeleine and… I knew my friend Frida, a Sabal Bay homicide detective, would probably be assigned to the case. She would consider me trouble with a double barreled T. Yes, she would.

When we arrived at the spot, I could see the body of a man lying near a swampy area and the carcass of a large, gray and buff colored animal with long horns nearby.

"You wait here," Alex said. I assumed he meant for David to wait in the Jeep, so I followed Alex over to the body.

"Ugh." I wasn't crazy about viewing dead bodies, although in the past I had seen several.

"God, Eve, you're worse than Velcro. Get back in the Jeep."

"But I want to help."

"That's what I mean. Help by getting back in the Jeep."

I crossed my arms again and stuck out my lower lip, but Alex didn't notice. He focused on the body.

"Did you touch him?" he asked David.

"I had to find out if he was dead. Or if I could help him in some way."

I walked away from the body and stopped at the dead animal. I'd never seen such long horns. What a shame. It was a beautiful beast. I took a few more steps toward the water.

"Eve, what are you doing now?"

"Nothing." That wasn't true. I was looking at the edge of the bog, churned up with animal tracks. "I think that pig you were chasing was here. The shore is all torn up and muddy, and there's junk all over here."

"You're about to step onto Reed's property. I'd stay out of there," David said.

"Are you using this swamp as a dump?" I was shocked that David would be so careless of the environment.

"No. Why?"

"There are cans, plastic containers, and other junk here. I..." I stepped on a hard object that rolled under my foot. I began to slip and reached out to catch myself as I fell. My hand touched the other end of the object that I'd stepped on. I pulled it out of the muck and took a good look at it. A rifle. Oh, oh. Frida would have my head. Messing with the crime scene.

"WHAT WERE YOU THINKING, EVE? You handled what will probably turn out to be the murder weapon. And, you, Alex. You let her just trample over the area."

"Sorry, Detective, but I thought Eve had gotten back in the Jeep."

"Because you told her to? When has she ever followed anyone's orders?" My friend Frida, almost as tall as I am, has sparkling brown eyes and dark hair. She has to be the most attractive police authority in rural Florida and one of the most competent, too.

Frida was steamed. I knew she would be and with

good cause. I knew better than to compromise the scene, but sometimes I get carried away.

"I was trying to get away from the dead body," I said. "That's all. How did I know I'd find the weapon in the muck over there?"

Frida wasn't listening.

Her partner, Linc Tooney, newly appointed to the position of detective, stood over the rifle where I had dropped it—leaving prints, of course.

"I should just arrest all three of you." Frida strode back and forth near the Jeep and the swamp buggy that Dudley had used to lead her and Linc to the scene. The Sabal Bay Police SUV stood behind them and behind it, the crime scene technicians had arrived driving the department's van. Muttering to herself, Frida walked around all the vehicles. Finally she said, "I'm going to let these guys and Detective Tooney finish up here while all of you come with me back to headquarters."

She got in her SUV and was about to back up when she rolled down her window and yelled, "Where's Madeleine?"

"At the ranch's office," I replied.

"I guess I should be grateful for that." Frida drove off. I could see her head moving from side to side. She was still talking to herself. Suddenly she stopped the vehicle, then turned it around and drove back to us.

"One more thing."

I thought I knew what was coming. And I was right.

"Yes?" I used my most innocent tone of voice.

"Don't even think about bringing in any more friends to help on this case. I've got this. Understand? I'm on top of it."

"You don't have anything to worry about. I can't

see any reason for asking my connections to help out. You've got it. But in case you find you need…"

The window went up, and she drove off again.

Now why would she think I'd ask my old buddy the mob boss Nappi Napolitani to help out? Why would I do that? Just because I'd done it twice before…

Dudley came up to me. "Your friend wasn't happy being left at the ranch."

"I know."

Madeleine would be furious, and since David was her boyfriend and Alex mine, the only person she could hold responsible for excluding her from the excitement was me. What are friends for?

Before we could leave, I saw another Jeep approach from the west. Tooney ran up to it and waved his arms. "That's far enough. Back off."

It was Blake Reed who jumped out of the Jeep. "That's my oryx. Who shot it?"

I wondered at someone who could drive up to a crime scene, see a human corpse, and remark only on the dead animal lying nearby. The guy was a piece of work.

"What's with you, David? Stealing my exotics for your clients?" Reed asked.

"The client's dead," I said. "Probably the oryx shot him then committed suicide. Isn't that how you figure it?"

"You've got a smart mouth on you, don't you?" Reed said.

Yes, I do. "And you know nothing about this, I suppose?" I was once again stepping on Frida's territory, but the man so infuriated me that I couldn't help myself. "I think you should arrest him," I said.

Tooney arched one eyebrow in curiosity.

"He tried to kill Madeleine yesterday. He tried to kill all of us," I told Tooney.

Reed laughed. "It was a mistake. Miss Appel, isn't it? Eve Appel. I told you that." He looked around the area. "Someone's been dumping junk. It's not on my land, but I'd think you'd take better care of your property, David, old fellow."

"Okay, now this is getting more interesting. Why don't you accompany us down to the station, Mr. Reed?" Linc said.

"Are you arresting me?" asked Reed.

"Not now, but I could arrange that if what Ms. Appel says is true, about you trying to kill them."

"I'll be glad to talk with you at the station, but I want my lawyer with me. So, if you'll excuse me, I have business to attend to." Before he got back into his Jeep, he glared at David. "I'll send you the bill on my oryx. It'll be pricey."

BACK AT THE STATION, after calming an angry and worried Madeleine, I explained to Frida what had happened out at the boat yesterday.

"It could have been a mistake," said Frida.

I could tell from her dubious tone that she doubted it. "You've had run-ins with our Mr. Reed before, I gather?"

"Yes, I have," she said.

I tapped my foot and waited. I was dying to hear what she had to say.

"I've had complaints that he abuses the Guatemalans he employs. And not from them. They don't like to make waves with the law. I heard it from some of the Anglos that work at his ranch. He's—"

"A mean SOB," I finished for her.

"I can't prove anything. By the time I get any names of the men he's mistreated, they're gone—off to some other work, I guess. You know how these farm workers move around, going where the jobs are. I haven't been able to track down a single one of them." Frida sounded frustrated.

"I'll need your fingerprints, Eve," Frida said. "They'll be on the rifle. Linc will take them."

Linc led me off to another room, but not before I heard David say, "I'm sure this involved Reed in some way."

While Frida interviewed David, Alex, Madeleine and I hung out near the station's coffee machine. An hour later, David emerged from the interview room, looking worn and exhausted.

"Not only is a man dead, but he died on my property. This won't help my business."

"Did you know the client well?" asked Alex.

"No. He simply showed up this afternoon saying someone had recommended my ranch. I didn't have any other clients scheduled today, so I took him out. I wish I hadn't let him talk me into tracking that pig. You know, I think he was bored with looking for quail. He gave me the impression that he was after something more exciting."

"Like an oryx?" I asked.

"Maybe," David said. "I can't think why he thought my place would provide him with that kind of game."

"So who recommended your place to him?" asked Alex.

"It could have been Reed," I said.

"Why would he do that and lose a client?" asked Alex.

"He recommends David to the client, follows them

out to the area, then shoots the guy and the animal and conveniently shows up back at the spot when the cops arrive."

"You really don't like this guy, do you?" Alex smiled. "I don't either, but why shoot someone just to make trouble? That's a stretch."

"Was it a stretch to believe he purposely dumped chum into the water to attract sharks? You know that was intentional." I tossed my empty coffee cup into the trash and stood up. "I don't care if you don't agree with me, but there is something seriously twisted about that man."

"And you are the judge of who is seriously twisted? With all your crime fighting experience." Alex winked at me to take the edge off his assessment of my lowly status as an amateur snoop.

"I agree with her," said Madeleine. "I think she knows plenty about bad guys."

David pulled himself out of the chair he'd sunk into. "I have to agree. Reed Blake has been a thorn in my side since he bought the adjoining ranch two years ago. That was about the time Dad turned our place over to me to run full-time. I think Reed doesn't like the competition. We've been in the business for years, and we've got a good reputation. We do mostly birds, but we also offer hunts for wild pigs. They're growing in numbers around here, and they're pretty destructive. They churn up waterholes like the one you saw today. But we don't do exotics, and we never will. I only want indigenous species for hunting."

"So you and Reed really aren't competitors, are you?" asked Alex.

"No, but I think Reed wants everything. He'd like to buy me out."

"What makes you think so?" asked Alex.

David didn't answer but started toward the door. "Let's get something to eat. And drink. Mostly drink. We can stop off at the Burnt Biscuit. It's Monday, and they have their rib special."

Alex and Madeleine indicated they weren't too hungry, but I'm always up for a rack of ribs. Besides, we'd just grabbed a few small sandwiches for lunch. "Let's go. I'm starved."

"I don't understand how you stay so skinny and eat so much," said Madeleine.

"I've got a runaway metabolism."

"This could be my last meal before Frida arrests me," said David.

"Now why would she do that? You didn't kill the guy," I said.

David paused before he got into his Jeep. "No, but she doesn't know that. And the rifle you found in the swamp? It was mine."

FIVE

THE BISCUIT WAS crowded as always on Mondays, when they featured their all-you-can-eat ribs. We'd been lucky to get a small table in the corner near the entrance to the kitchen. I didn't mind the wait staff hustling back and forth past our table. What I did mind was the smoky, spicy, yummy smells emanating from the kitchen each time the door swung open, and the wait. I hated the wait.

"So now you've had two toxic doses of Blake Reed. I told you there was history between the two of us, but I never got to finish the story." David moved his water glass around in circles, leaving a trail of moisture on the table top.

I was surprised that after being interviewed by the authorities for over an hour, he chose to discuss his feud with Blake Reed. I wondered if he was trying to avoid talking about the murder of his client, or the fact that it was his gun found at the scene.

Madeleine looked distraught. Her usual open expression and sunny smile were gone, replaced by a pinched look. The skin around her thumbnail was red and bleeding. I handed her a napkin and began searching the depths of my purse for a Band-Aid.

"You think Reed is behind this murder, don't you?" asked Alex.

"Of course. He's been trying to buy my place since

he came here. The man doesn't like me on top of his land. And I think sportsmen should come here to hunt what Florida has to offer. I'm not setting up the African plains in Sabal Bay."

The waitress arrived with our drinks and took orders for dinner. I ordered a rack of ribs.

"A whole rack?" she asked.

"I'm starving. It's after seven at night and I only had a small sandwich for lunch. That was hours ago."

She took a look at my long, lean figure and shrugged. "Well, whatever you can't eat, you can take home in a doggie bag."

I shook my head. "There will be no need for a doggie bag."

"If I didn't know better," Alex said, "I'd say you were eating for two." He held up two fingers, signaling the waitress that he too wanted a full rack.

I looked at him, seemingly terrified.

"What? I can eat as much as you," he said.

"No. The other."

"I'm right, aren't I? You don't have a tapeworm, do you?"

Alex and I were trying too hard to make funny. Our antics didn't help erase the looks of anguish on David and Madeleine's faces.

I reached out and gave David's hand a pat. "Tell us about Reed. What's he done so far?"

"That waterhole today? That's not junk I dumped there. That had to be him. And he runs his Jeeps through my fields when I'm not around, scaring off the quail and disturbing nesting birds and water fowl, as well as other animals. Just the other day, I found that about ten of the palms in my field to the north had been cut down. My client numbers have gone down in the past two months. When I contacted some of my regulars, they said Reed was giving them a better deal and offering the possibility for gator hunting too."

"It's illegal to take gators," said Alex.

"The man doesn't care about legal or illegal," David said.

"I'd sic Frida on him. I think she's just looking for a reason to arrest him. If she can't pin this murder on him, then maybe she can get him for these other violations." I tapped my spoon on the table in frustration.

David leaned back in his chair and sighed. "It really doesn't matter. I'm going to sell the place anyway."

"You're letting him run you off?"

"Not everyone is as eager to take on the bad guys as you, Eve," David said.

Madeleine had been silent until now. "It's not Reed. Although he's making the decision easier."

"You knew about this and didn't tell me?" I thought Madeleine and I had a pact. Gal pals told each other everything.

"I asked her to keep quiet about it," David said. "In fact, I'm not going public with putting it up for sale. I know who would buy it. Blake Reed. I'd rather keep it and close it down than have him own it."

The waitress slapped the platters of ribs down. "Getcha anything else?"

David held up his glass. "Another of these."

"Go slow, honey," said Madeleine.

I was hungry and wanted to tuck into the ribs, but food took a back seat to my curiosity. "Why are you selling a place that's been in your family for years?"

"Because I hate guns. I haven't picked one up for two years."

"So, you see, there's no way David could have killed that man," Madeleine said.

"HE HATES GUNS? Some people are born with silver spoons in their mouths. He had to have been born with a rifle in his hand. Who's going to believe him?" I was going over the events of the evening with Alex as he drove me back to my house.

"I believed him."

"It was pretty clear Madeleine did too, but why this sudden dislike of a sport he was raised to love? Something had to have happened to create his abhorrence of guns."

Alex pulled up in front of my house and gave me one of his let's-get-friendly looks. "How about it, hon?"

"'How about it?' Isn't that romantic."

"Okay, how about, 'I love you and will for all time. You are my moon, my stars, my...'"

There was a rap on the car window before he could finish.

My ex-husband, Jerry, stood beside the car. Alex rolled down the window.

"Hi, kids. What's up?" Jerry smiled one of his cheesy smiles, so I knew his presence tonight meant he was up to no good and likely wanted something. Jerry was a great looking guy, but I was immune. Having an ex who cheats will do that to you.

"Whatever you want from me, Jerry, you can't have it. Go away. Alex was trying out some wooing, and I'd like him to finish."

Alex didn't look too happy to see Jerry either, but

I figured that was due to Jerry's poor timing and not because he disliked the guy. For reasons I didn't understand, the two of them got along well. Like most women, I didn't understand male bonding, other than that it involved a lot of burping, watching ball games on TV, and slapping each other on the butt.

"Uh, Mr. Napolitani wanted me to handle a sale for him in West Palm, and here I am."

"This is not West Palm. It's Sabal Bay. You know that, so why are you here and not there?" Why did I bother to ask? I knew I wouldn't like the answer.

Jerry worked for Mr. Napolitani, running errands, doing odd jobs, nothing illegal. Before we divorced, Jerry had had a relationship with one of Nappi's daughters. It had ended badly, so badly that, instead of roughing him up, Nappi made him a kind of indentured servant. Jerry seemed happy to have gotten off so easily.

"I came over here to go to the casino and play a little Texas hold 'em," Jerry said.

"And you lost." I couldn't help myself. He was so predictable.

"Yep, and then—"

"You decided to try to recover your losses by getting into a private game with the good ol' boys who took your money off you and you lost again. And now you have no money. Right?"

Jerry looked insulted. It's a look he must have perfected in front of the mirror when he shaved in the mornings, along with the I'm-so-innocent look, the I-didn't-do-it smile, and the who-me grin. Jerry had a repertoire of faces he could put on when he was caught at something he shouldn't have been doing. None of what anybody saw there was the true Jerry. Underneath, there was no underneath.

Not that Jerry didn't have his appeal. He was close to six feet tall with brown hair, thinning a bit on top. He dressed well and might be considered a catch if a gal could overlook his inability to commit in a relationship and his propensity for making bad life decisions. After overlooking these negatives for ten years, I'd finally become convinced he'd never change and divorced him. Since going our separate ways as husband and wife, we'd been thrown together more often than before the divorce. I seemed to always be bailing him out of sticky situations.

"That's not how it went." He paused and looked at his feet. "Uh, it wasn't a bunch of good old boys. It was a gang of four women, all around fifty or so. I figured it had to be blind luck for them to win at the tables, so when they took pity on me... I mean, Eve, one of them looked like your grandmother, Grandy. I thought to myself, I can get my money back with just a few hands, so we took the game to one of their houses. They fed me apple pie and milk. They were so friendly. And so naïve, I thought. And that's when I lost the car."

"You bet your car?" I had misjudged him. He was even more of an idiot than I thought.

"I got no transportation. And there's a bass tournament in town, so there are no rooms. And I have to be at the real estate office by nine tomorrow." He hung his head like a naughty little boy, another ploy to play on my sympathies, but I wasn't having any.

Male bonding to the rescue. Alex, riding in on his white horse, said, "Eve—"

"Do you understand what he's asking?" I asked.

Alex nodded.

"Right. Then you let him stay at your place and you give him a ride to West Palm bright and early tomorrow. I'm going to bed." I got out of the car, slammed the door with as much force as I could, and stalked to my front door.

"Did I ruin your night?" I heard Jerry say to Alex as he opened the passenger door.

Alex rolled down his window. "If I had finished my romantic appeal, would it have done any good?"

I didn't hesitate. "No."

"Then, no, you did not ruin my night, old chum," he said to Jerry.

I MET MADELEINE at the only retail space available that we could afford Tuesday morning, early, around seven. I'd had only one cup of coffee, and I wasn't in a hopeful mood. I never was when Jerry showed up. You'd think the man would have the decency to leave me alone once I'd divorced him, but he was always popping up, usually at the worst times.

The building housing the space for rent was too far out of town, but we had no other choice. If we could sign a six-month lease, maybe something else would come up closer in, and we could move. The store was in a small strip mall that yelled shabby with no chic. The mall housed only two businesses. The other one was a bar called T 'n A. There were no T's or A's in sight this morning, but there were two motorcycles in the parking area in front of the bar and the lights were on inside.

"Kind of early for beer, isn't it?" I asked the landlord, who stood in front of the rental flipping a set of keys back and forth in his hand.

"Not if they serve bacon and eggs with it." He was a big-bellied man wearing motorcycle boots. He inserted a key into the front lock and stood to one side, gesturing us into the room. "Take a look around, ladies. I'll be with you in a second." He let the door slam shut, and we turned and watched him walk next door to the bar.

"Probably his bacon and eggs were getting cold," said Madeleine.

"And his beer warm." I flipped the light switch by the door and nothing happened.

"Well, there's enough sunlight coming in through the windows. We can see all right, I guess." Madeleine walked slowly through the space and headed toward the backroom.

I looked around at the walls. Some kind of beige. Probably "ick beige," I thought, one of your less popular decorating colors. Well, we could change that, and there was more square footage here than in our present space.

I thought of a new advertising campaign. Come to Big Lake Country to shop and you can share the dressing room with a biker.

"Eeeeech!" yelled Madeleine.

I rushed into the backroom. "What's wrong?"

"Look." She pointed at a table in the corner of the room. Large golden-colored bugs crawled among the crumbs there, joined by small black ants whose backpacking buddies carried food down one of the table legs across the floor, disappearing under the woodwork.

"Roaches." She gave a shudder of disgust.

"Actually, I think they're palmetto bugs."

"I really don't need a lecture on entomology, Eve. They're bugs. Let's get out of here."

I glanced around the room. Aside from the table and a pile of rags in the far corner, the place was empty. It had potential.

"We can call a fumigator and paint. The space is more than adequate. What else can we do?"

"You can pipe down and get the hell out of here. I'm trying to sleep." Madeleine and I both jumped. The voice came from behind us, out of the rags, which began to quiver and move. A hand emerged from the pile, followed by a head of greasy hair.

Madeleine would have sprinted across the room if I hadn't grabbed her.

"Who the hell are you? And what are you doing here? We were considering renting this place, but—" I was interrupted by the landlord, who strode into the room.

He stopped and put his fists on his hips. "Get up, ya bum. You've got work to do. You can't take all day to sleep it off."

"You know this guy?" I asked.

"Yeah. He's my cook next door. I let him sleep here sometimes when he's had a few too many. Don't want him to take his bike out on the road and kill himself."

"Or someone else," I said.

"Huh? Oh, right. Well, I take care of my people. He's a damn good cook. Now, get up and skedaddle over there. I keep breaking the yolks of the eggs. Folks are getting pissed."

The rag man Madeleine and I had taken for a vagrant crawled out of what turned out to be an old khaki-green and purple sleeping bag. Once he got to his feet, he staggered a moment, got his balance, and walked from the room in less than a straight line toward the front door. The landlord, Madeleine, and I followed. I stopped a moment. Now the front room smelled like bacon, eggs, coffee…and beer. It made me kind of hungry.

"You gals are welcome to come next door. Breakfast's on me." The landlord smiled, flashing several gold teeth. "He don't look like much, but Donnie's the best short-order cook in the county."

"Would we be expected to provide him accommodations next door on those nights he overindulged?" I asked.

"Up to you. I could consider a break in the rent if you did."

"Uh, we'll have to give this some thought." I gave him my best businesslike smile.

"Don't wait too long. Somebody will snap this up. It's a prime location."

"What are we going to do?" asked Madeleine as we drove back to our shop to open. "There's nothing in town we can afford."

"Buy a lot of paint, hire a fumigator, and find Donnie a better sleeping bag." And, I added silently, change our advertising campaign to read, *Come to the Big Lake Country to shop. We sell used sleeping bags.*

Madeleine stared at me for several minutes, then turned her attention to the herds of cattle outside the window. "I'd rather wrestle an alligator than rent that place."

"Be careful what you wish for. I understand the Miccosukee tribe is looking for a girl gator wrestler. I heard it from my friend Sammy Egret. Maybe I can get you an interview."

SIX

WE WERE LATER than usual getting to the shop because all the food smells from the T 'n A made me hungry. We used the drive-through at Burger 'n Bun. Madeleine was still grossed out by Donnie and the bugs, so she only got a latte.

As I pulled into our parking lot, I saw our landlord Roland and a woman standing in front of the store. Both of them looked impatient.

"I thought you opened at eleven," Roland said. He was a short, stocky guy who favored brown suits several sizes too large. When we met, I thought he might be simpatico with us since I assumed he bought his clothes from secondhand stores and hadn't had the suits altered. But no. He told me he bought new and couldn't understand how anyone could wear clothes worn by someone else. I guess he liked his clothes roomy.

"Had to grab breakfast." I selected a key from my ring while I tried to juggle my purse and my coffee in my other hand. Where to put my breakfast sandwich… I stuffed it into my mouth and inserted the key in the lock. It stuck, as usual. Madeleine was unloading some consignment items from the car, so she was no help. Roland held papers in one hand and a keychain in the other. You'd think the man would notice and lend a hand, but he rolled his eyes and shook his head. I took the sandwich out of my mouth and handed it to the woman at Roland's side.

"Hi ya. Would you mind holding this for a sec? I need two hands to do this. Oh, and here, my coffee." I slipped my purse back onto my shoulder, and now that my hands were free, unlocked the door, reached around and turned the sign to "Open."

"Thanks." I took my coffee and sandwich back. "I'll have coffee brewing in a minute. In the meantime you can browse."

"Does the lock always stick that way?" she asked. "It should be fixed."

I gave Roland a glance. "Not our problem anymore, is it, Roland?"

I eyed my customer. I'd never seen her before in the store. She was shorter than me and much curvier. She dressed well. I loved her shoes, which had to be Ferragamos. Purchased new, I wondered? But the hair and that awful makeup… If she smiled, which she hadn't done yet, she'd crack the veneer. Her brown hair was medium length and looked as if she had set it with hot rollers. Who used hot rollers anymore? For a moment I thought about giving her some fashion advice, but I bit back my words, which showed unusual restraint on my part. I looked at my coffee. Maybe I should have gotten the ten-gallon-hat size to get me started on being more like the Eve everyone expected.

Roland stopped me from heading for the coffee-maker in the backroom. "She's not a customer, Eve. She's the person who might rent the space when you move out. I assume you've found another location?"

I thought back to the space in the strip mall and our resident drunken cook and nodded.

The new lessee walked through the store, but seemed to be less interested in the space than our merchandise. She ran her hands over some of the silk blouses, took several cocktail dresses off the wall and held them up to her body in front of the mirror, fingered one of the boots perched on a rack and then wandered toward the backroom.

"So what are you thinking of putting in here?" I asked.

She turned and smiled at me, and I didn't like the smile. It seemed arrogant.

"A consignment shop."

I tossed a haughty smile back at her. "I'm not certain that's such a good idea. Sabal Bay has a number of consignment shops. The only reason ours can compete is that we take in designer merchandise from the coast and sell to women who come from as far away as West Palm. The merchandise is high end, as is our clientele."

She fixed me with her odd eyes, almost an opalescent blue or green or gray—very pale, but luminous. I thought of the phosphorescence in the water when we were in the Keys and wondered if her eyes glowed in the dark.

"Yes, I know what you do. I intend to do the same."

Not good, I thought. If she tried that and took over our location, she'd win over our customers. Why drive out of town to a place that smelled like booze and fried food unless you liked rubbing elbows with bikers? I didn't think that would be the case.

Madeleine struggled through the front door with dresses slung over her arm. "I could have used some help."

She dumped her load of clothes on the top of one of the skirt rounds and gasped.

"Elvira Reed. What are you doing here?"

"I'm about to put the two of you out of business." She tapped Roland on the shoulder. "I'll take it. Make sure these two are out of here by next Monday."

"They still have two weeks to go on their contract," Roland said.

"Not if you want me in here. I'll offer three times what they're paying."

Madeleine and I stared after her as she strode out the front door and got into a Mercedes convertible.

"You heard the lady," said Roland. "You can hand me the keys on Saturday. I'll be by to pick them up. Good luck to you. I think you're going to need it."

MADELEINE AND I had little time to discuss Elvira Reed. We were busy inventorying the clothes we'd gotten in on consignment last week and waiting on customers. At lunchtime there was a rush of women from the coast, led by one of our most faithful customers, Marjorie Sinclair. She was the most unpretentious of the West Palm matrons. She dressed well, but in an understated way. As with many of the wealthy West Palm women, she'd had work done on her face, but the doctor who'd done it took away some wrinkles and sag but left all her character and charm. She still looked fifty, but it was a healthy and realistic fifty. She liked rural Florida, and she and her husband had purchased some land over by the Kissimmee River. They ran cattle there, and I knew some of the cowboys they'd hired—not only knew them but had danced with them at the Biscuit.

I told Marjorie we were moving and I had no idea

where. I also confessed that another shop with the same high-end concept was coming to this location.

"Don't you worry, Eve dear. I'll spread the word among my friends. I love you and Madeleine. We all do. You know your business. What background does this other woman have, anyway?"

I admitted I didn't know if she had any background or business experience. "But her husband owns one of the hunting ranches around here."

"Don't you worry. You'll find another location and go on as before. I just know it. And if there's anything I can do to help, just say the word." Marjorie waved one of her friends over, a tiny woman with blonde hair. "This is Susie Clarin, Eve. She's been dying to visit this place."

"Thanks for coming."

"Oh, you do have nice things, but I really came to see the cowboys."

I laughed. "Sorry. We don't stock them here."

"I told you, Susie. You'll have to wait until later at the Burnt Biscuit."

"What are all of you going to do until then?" I asked.

"We'll have lunch out at the restaurant at the park, drop by to see how the bass tournament is going, take an airboat ride, and drop by the casino. It's going to be a full afternoon."

I gave Marjorie directions to the airboat ride run by my Miccosukee friend Sammie Egret.

"He's a real Indian?" asked Susie.

"Yep. He and his grandfather run the airboat business."

"There will be alligators?" asked another woman.

"Sure. Lots of them."

I figured I'd better stop talking or I'd get them so worked up they'd head straight for the airboat ride and forget about buying anything here. "I've got some Ralph Lauren Western shirts over there on the rack. That way, next time you come here, you'll be dressed for the experience." I wondered if Ralph even knew what cows looked like. I loved his clothes but doubted he had any knowledge of the real West—and especially of authentic Florida swamp wear.

THAT NIGHT MADELEINE and I met our guys at the Mexican restaurant, the one where last year my car had blown up like popcorn in a microwave bag.

"You nervous?" Madeleine slid into a booth, leaving room for David. I took the seat across the table.

"If you mean about the possibility that someone might take a run at my Mustang and turn it into toast, the answer is no. I'm not superstitious. Lightning does not strike twice." I looked out the window at my car, parked just beyond the handicapped spots.

"You couldn't have parked it any closer. I was worried you'd try to drive it into the bar area just to keep an eye on it." Madeleine perused the menu as if she didn't eat here so often she had it memorized.

"It doesn't hurt to be cautious." I ordered a margarita from our waiter.

Madeleine held up her fingers. "Make it two."

"Make it a pitcher," Alex said. He and David arrived together and settled into the booth.

We exchanged pleasantries for a few minutes until our drinks arrived.

"Guess who we ran into today?" I licked the salt from the rim of my glass.

"Maybe we should choose another topic of conversation for the evening." Madeleine shot me a warning look across the table.

I didn't think now was the time to hedge about our visitor and I said so. "Elvira Reed is up to something. I just know it. It wasn't a coincidence that she's going to rent our space."

"If she's anything like her husband, I'd have to agree with you." David twisted the stem of his glass around and around.

"She could give him lessons in nasty." I decided on the carne asada and closed my menu.

"Now, you don't know that," Madeleine said.

"I don't know it like I don't know the brand names of designer footwear, right?" I said.

"I hate to break up this fashion discussion, but I need to have you come with me, Mr. Wilson." Frida had approached our table without our noticing. She was accompanied by her partner, Linc Tooney.

I worried at her use of "Mr. Wilson," so formal, like she might be— "Are you arresting me?" David got out of the booth.

"Just come with me, please. I have a few questions for you." Both Frida and Linc had official cop business looks on their faces.

"I'll come too." Madeleine slid over and grabbed David's hand "We all will." I pushed Alex out of the booth.

"Our business is with Mr. Wilson. I can't prevent you from coming to the station, but you may have a long wait ahead of you." Frida seemed uncomfortable and eager to leave the restaurant. She was doing her duty, but I knew she wasn't happy to be doing it in front of a roomful of people.

"Fine," said Alex. "We can wait." He threw enough money on the table to cover the cost of the pitcher of margaritas. The three of us followed David and the detectives to the door. Every eye in the place must have been on us. Just as we were about to exit, I saw Blake Reed and his wife sitting at a booth near the door.

"Trouble, Wilson?" Reed asked. Try as he might to plaster a look of concern on his face, he couldn't hide the smile that lifted the corners of his mouth. David ignored him. I started toward the booth, but Alex grabbed my arm and steered me out the door.

"You'll tell them the whole story, won't you, David?" Madeleine continued to hold his hand with both of hers as if she could prevent the detectives from putting him into the backseat of the police car.

At Madeleine's remark about "the whole story," Frida stopped and turned toward Madeleine. "What story would that be?"

Madeleine ignored Frida, her grasp on David's hand tightening to a white-knuckled hold.

"You'll have to let him go, Madeleine." Frida's voice was kind. She had to know how difficult this was for Madeleine, who had finally found a man she cared for and who loved her in return.

By the time Madeleine, Alex, and I arrived at the police station, David had been taken to an interview room.

"I've got a bad feeling about this," Alex said.

I began to pace back and forth, intent upon wearing a path in the station's floor.

"You're making me crazy, Eve. Sit." Madeleine was on the verge of tears.

"Sorry." I began to chew my thumbnail, a habit I'd obviously picked up from Madeleine. "I think it's time you came clean with us, Missy."

"What do you mean?" Madeleine tried for her best innocent look, but I spotted the deception in those baby blue eyes.

"You know something about David, something that says he's not guilty of the killing."

"We all know he's not, Eve," Alex said.

"That's because we know the kind of man he is, but Madeleine knows more. Don't you?" I asked.

"It's kind of a long story, but since David alluded to it before with you and Alex, I don't see why I can't tell you the rest," she said.

I took a seat on the bench, sinking back into Alex's shoulder. "We may have all night. Tell away."

Madeleine leaned forward, her elbows on her knees. "David was married, you know."

I nodded, as did Alex. David had made no secret that his wife had left him several years ago and that she had custody of their only child, a girl, now about twelve years of age.

"Angela, his wife, is from Boca Raton. She hated living here. She considered the school system substandard and didn't like their daughter growing up on a ranch with no close neighbors. I guess there was nothing about living in the country that appealed to her. David bought a house in Sabal Bay and commuted every day to the ranch, but Angela was still unhappy. She missed her family and friends on the coast."

"So she took the daughter and left? How does that

prove him innocent?" I was growing impatient with the story, which seemed unrelated to the shooting. And besides, I was getting grumpy without my dinner. I thought of my unordered carne asada and my stomach responded with a growl.

Madeleine shook her head. "She left, but not for those reasons only. Something happened."

"Go on," Alex said.

"One night, an intruder broke into the house and entered the daughter's room. David heard him and sneaked down the hall to confront him. The guy turned when he heard David. In the moonlit room, David could see he was carrying a gun. He told the guy to drop the weapon, but he fired at David—"

"And David had his gun, right?" Alex said.

"Right. The intruder missed David, but David fired back and hit him. Shot him dead."

"He was defending himself and his family. The cops couldn't have found fault with that," Alex said.

"They didn't. It was self-defense. That's not the issue."

"I don't get it. David can't hate guns because he defended his family, can he?" I asked.

"No. Of course not. It's not that simple." Madeleine hesitated, then added, "The intruder was a thirteen-year-old boy."

SEVEN

"THIRTEEN? DAVID MUST have been horrified." Now I understood why David loathed guns and how difficult it must be for him to continue running a ranch where he found himself constantly around them. It was one thing to use them for hunting and quite another to kill someone, especially a kid. He certainly could make a compelling case for not shooting that client, especially since there was no apparent motive.

Frida walked through the door and into the waiting area. Her usually carefully coiffed hair was in disarray, strands of it sticking out from behind her ears. "You might as well go home. We'll be keeping him here."

I jumped up and confronted Frida. "*Keeping* him? You mean you've arrested him, right? What are you thinking? That's absurd." I knew I sounded argumentative and couldn't be helping David with my tone of voice and pugnacious attitude, but it was late and we'd just heard a story Frida should take into consideration. I wanted this whole misadventure wrapped up and soon. If she hadn't heard the tale from David, I was going to tell her. "You don't know the whole story."

"No, Eve, I do. You're the one who doesn't know the whole story. David had motive to kill that client. He and the man had a fight about hunting that oryx. The client wanted to take it down, but David told him no. So he shot him to prevent him from killing the animal."

"He confessed?" Madeleine's voice was filled with disbelief and fear.

"He needs a lawyer. The best you can do for him now is to get him one. A good one. He'll be arraigned tomorrow. That's all I can tell you. Go home. That's what I'm going to do." Frida turned her back on us and headed toward the door to the interrogation rooms. She stopped, and keeping her eyes on the floor, said, "I'm sorry." Then she was gone.

Madeleine burst into tears and Alex and I, both shocked at the arrest ourselves, gathered her in our arms and tried to comfort her. But what comfort is there to be had when the man you love is being held for murder? Had we misjudged David?

MADELEINE REFUSED TO stay home from the shop the next day. "I called Barton Hall. He's the best attorney around here." She seemed to have gathered her courage overnight. I admired how she'd wiped away her tears and leaped into action on David's behalf. I was determined to support her insistence that he was innocent. Although Alex and I discussed the possibility that David had killed the man in a fit of rage, we weren't about to share that conversation with Madeleine. We'd keep our doubts to ourselves.

"We have to face it, Eve. We've got to take that crummy place next to the bar or we're out of business."

"We have until this weekend to find another place. Let's sit on it until this thing with David blows over."

Madeleine gave forth a bitter laugh. "It's not going to disappear, you know. There's nothing we can do for now. His lawyer will get him out on bail. I hope. Until then I need to focus on something else, something I can control. Like where we're going to sell our merchandise. His hearing isn't until this afternoon. I want to work until then." She chewed on her thumbnail. Despite her brave words, she would be thinking of David every moment. But she was right. There was little we could do for now.

"I just can't face renting next to the T 'n A," I said. "There has to be something else." I fired up my laptop to check ads in other papers. "We may have to relocate to the coast."

"We can't afford that, and besides, if we take a shop on the coast we'll lose our edge over the other consignment shops. We're here because it works, has worked for the last year." Madeleine continued to gnaw on her thumb and gazed out the front window.

I turned off the computer. She was right again. We had to stay put here in Sabal Bay and fight it out with Mrs. Reed.

"We could apply for a small business loan. That would give us the money to rent in a better location."

"What?" Madeleine continued to stare out the window. "I'm sorry, Eve. I can't keep my mind here."

I walked over to her and put my arm around her shoulders. "I know, honey. I'm sorry."

She seemed to shake herself back into the present. "A loan? But that could take months. What do we do until then?"

"We could—"

"No, you don't. We can't do business with your mob friends. I will not do business with Nappi Napolitani."

The thought of working with Mr. Napolitani distracted her enough that she stopped biting her nail. There was very little left of it.

"I'll start the paperwork for a loan. In the meantime, I think we need a large van or two and some help to move all this stuff out of here. We only have until next Saturday."

"Who can we call?"

"I have an idea."

Madeleine shot me a look and shook her head.

"I meant I'll call Sammy Egret and see if he's willing to lend a hand. Maybe he can get a couple of his cousins to help also."

Madeleine smiled. "You are such a bad liar. You did not mean you were going to call Sammy, but it is a good idea."

"Alex would help, but he's tied up in a case in Miami for the week and he's spending nights there."

I punched Sammy's number into my cell and got a busy signal. Over the next half an hour the phone continued to ring busy.

"I'm going out there. I'll stop at the deli and buy us sandwiches for lunch. Are you okay to mind the place for an hour?"

"Go. I'm fine." She looked down at her thumb and sighed, then started her brutal manicure on the other one.

WHEN I ARRIVED at Sammy's airboat business, I saw the boat was gone. The parking area was filled with cars and women stood in line in front of the tiki hut. Grandfather Egret was behind the counter, holding court with stories from the past that the women seemed to find entertaining.

I waved at him as I got out of the car. He returned the wave but continued on with his story. I walked close enough to hear. Ah, he was telling about the time he captured a couple of kidnappers. I smiled. I'd been in on that caper. The version he was telling his audience was a bit exaggerated.

"There she is," he said, pointing to me, "the woman who helped me take down those bad guys."

In the distance I heard the airboat. As Sammy turned the boat toward the landing I could see it was full. Something was going on. Business was booming.

The women waiting to take the tour turned their attention to the boat's arrival. I overheard one of them say to another, "Wow, he's even more handsome than we heard. Look at those muscles."

Grandfather Egret came out from behind the counter.

"What's going on here? I couldn't get through to Sammy's cell, and it looks as if you're chock-a-block full with customers," I said.

"It's your doing. You sent us that group of women from the coast yesterday, and word has spread through West Palm, it seems. We're all the rage with your wealthy lady friends." Grandfather's impish smile said he liked being surrounded by all these women as much as he liked taking their money for tickets.

Grandfather addressed the waiting customers. "If you'll just step to one side and let them off the boat, you can find your seats, and we'll be off again." He directed them down the path toward the landing, where Sammy was refueling the boat. Sammy looked up and saw me and waved. He set the gas cans down and started up the path. When he got to where I stood, he put his arms around me and hugged me close. The women watch-

ing swooned in envy, and I almost lost my footing as
he lifted me off the ground and spun me around. *Wow*.

"I haven't seen you much lately." He set me back on
my feet and held me at arm's length. "You look good."

"Is he your boyfriend?" asked one of the women.

Before I could answer, Sammy nodded.

"Sammy," I said so only he could hear. "What are
you saying?"

"You could be my girlfriend, you know." He gave
me a roguish grin.

"Alex might protest."

"Yeah, but he's not my worry. You are."

Sammy was in a mood I'd never seen before—flir-
tatious, something I didn't know he did.

"What's got into you?" I asked.

"Oh, I don't know." He looked around him, at the
sky and then the river beyond the landing. "It's a beautiful day, and I've got more customers than I can handle."

"Oh, I get it. All this money is making you horny."

The words had leaped out of my mouth. It was the
kind of sassy, sexual teasing I might say to some of my
cowboy friends from the Burnt Biscuit, but I'd always
been careful around Sammy. We'd spent a night alone
in the swamps, and had never talked about the feelings that had developed out there. It seemed to make us
both self-conscious. Besides, Alex and I were a couple.

"Sorry, Sammy. I didn't mean that."

He gave me one of his soul-searching looks. "Didn't
you? Too bad for me."

Both of us stared at the ground; then the uncomfortable moment passed. Sammy broke the spell.

"Well, you did us right, woman. Sending all these

folks our way. I may be able to buy a new shirt for the first time in five years."

"Keep that one. It looks great." I liked Sammy's understated handsome looks and rugged style—the faded pink and turquoise Miccosukee-pattern long-sleeved shirt, which pulled tightly across his broad chest, and the jeans bleached almost white from too many washings. The clothes did not make the man. Not in this case, anyway. This man—tall, dark-skinned, with long black hair—made the clothes. On anyone else they would just look worn. On him, they looked like a very attractive second skin.

"So if there's anything I can do to repay you, let me know," he said.

Boy, was this easy. "As a matter of fact, there is. Can you help Madeleine and me move out of our shop?" I explained to him about the loss of our lease, David's arrest, and Alex's job in Miami.

"So I'm what, third best in your choice of movers?" His black eyes twinkled with good humor.

"Yeah, something like that." Good. Sammy and I were once more on familiar, friends-only footing. I was relieved and he seemed to be at ease as well, the earlier discomfort gone.

"And before you get a big head, I wondered if you could bring along some of your good-looking cousins to help out. We can't afford to pay them, but we could provide pizza and beer afterward."

"You know you're not supposed to give firewater to Indians," he said. Yep, Sammy was in a good mood.

"When are you free?" If all this activity continued, Sammy might not be able to help us for a while.

"It will have to be tomorrow evening. I can't do it

during the day, as you can see, and I've got tribal meetings the rest of the week. You say you have to be out by Saturday?"

I nodded.

"Where are you moving to?" he asked.

I had no idea.

I RETURNED TO the shop with our sandwiches. Madeleine, having dined on her thumbs and fingernails, ate only a little of hers. I put it in the fridge for a snack later. We agreed that she would attend David's hearing while I kept the shop open. We couldn't afford to close the shop and lose a half day of revenue, not when we might have a drought in income coming soon.

Several customers came into the shop, not to buy but to check on the rumor that our store was being taken over by another owner. I set them straight on that matter, but when they asked where our new location would be, I couldn't tell them anything. We were going to lose customers before we even closed down. We had to find a place and soon. I could apply for all the loans I wanted, but until they came through, we were in danger of losing the momentum and clientele we'd gained in the past year. I hated to think that this could be the end of Madeleine's and my business together.

I had Sammy and his cousins lined up to help us move our merchandise, but no place to move it to. We were screwed.

The bell on the shop door rang. I looked up and groaned to see my ex, Jerry. But then my mood lifted. Right behind him walked Mr. Napolitani.

"Nappi! Oh, it's so good to see you."

He wrapped me in the scent of expensive male cologne and a more expensive silk suit as he hugged me to him. Today wasn't so bad, I thought to myself. I'd been hugged by two very sexy men—first Sammy, now Nappi. The anxiety over the shop must have been getting to me. All I seemed to think about other than my business was sexy men. I wished Alex wasn't gone this week.

"How are things, Evie?" No one ever called me Evie except for Jerry, and I hated it when he did. I gritted my teeth and tried not to growl out loud at him. I was wrong. Not all the men today were sexy. There was Jerry, whom I once thought sexy but now only considered annoying.

"Don't call me—" I began.

"Sorry, babe," Jerry said.

"Or babe."

"Sorry." Jerry would have said something else equally aggravating I was certain, but Nappi placed his hand on my ex's shoulder and squeezed. Jerry's face turned a color between green and puke.

"I hear things are difficult around here." Nappi perused the shop as if the merchandise might be creating problems for me.

"We're having some ups and downs," I said.

He gave me a look that seemed to penetrate my brain.

So I told him everything. How could I not? Dealing with Nappi Napolitani was like taking truth serum. You couldn't leave anything out.

He was silent for a moment.

"Hmmm. I could float you a loan."

"We're getting a loan from the small business administration. I think."

"That takes time. Until then, where will you operate?"

"From my living room, maybe?"

Nappi smiled. "You're not zoned commercial, are you?"

"No. I guess we could rent space at the weekend flea market."

"Limited income."

We both nodded.

"My loan would come through today. No waiting for paperwork to go through," Nappi said.

"I know, but…" I shrugged.

"Madeleine doesn't like the idea of mob money," he said. Nappi looked hurt for a second, then recovered. "I have an idea."

Before Nappi could spell out his idea, Madeleine rushed into the shop. Her face was blotchy from crying. She threw herself into my arms, almost knocking me over.

She could barely speak but managed to get out the bad news between sobs. "No bail. David's been charged with first degree murder."

EIGHT

"FIRST DEGREE MURDER? Why?" I was stunned by Madeleine's pronouncement.

Nappi and Jerry got her a chair, and I rushed for the bathroom and a glass of water. As I filled the glass, I wondered why water was considered such a comfort. What did it do, really?

"Here. Drink this." I held it out to her as if I thought it would erase all her troubles.

She sipped at it and seemed to recover her composure. "David admitted to fighting with his client—"

I didn't let her finish. "He shouldn't have admitted to anything. He should have kept his mouth shut. If he'd had a lawyer with him, he would have known that."

Madeleine gave me a look filled with frustration. "Do you want to hear this or give your paralegal critique?"

"Sorry." I waved my hand to signal her to go on with her story.

"They argued about the oryx, and then David followed the client as he stalked the animal. According to the DA, that gave him enough time to plan out what he was going to do. Premeditation. And because David has no family here, he's considered a flight risk."

"His ex-wife is on the coast, not far from here." I was offering a weak argument, and I knew it.

"They allowed me some time with him after the

hearing. He'd like you to get in touch with Alex. David thinks someone is setting him up to take the blame for the murder, and he wants Alex to do some PI work for him."

"I can't believe Frida would think David did this."

Madeleine shrugged her shoulders in a gesture of helplessness. "It isn't about what Frida believes, according to David's lawyer. It's what the DA can prove. Do you think Alex can help him?" Madeleine's voice was quavery, and I was certain she was about to lose control again, but she took a deep breath, looked at Jerry and Nappi and shifted gears.

"Eve didn't make any deals with you about this shop, did she?"

"Madeleine, how could you think I'd go against your wishes? See here. I've been working on the loan application." I moved the laptop screen around so she could see the form.

Nappi took Madeleine's hand in his. "Eve wouldn't betray you. But there is the problem of what you're going to do with the store contents until the loan comes through. You're at a critical point in your business."

She looked up at him with curiosity in her innocent blue eyes.

"I think I can help." He held up his hand to prevent her from speaking. "Hear me out." What he had to say wasn't going to make everything perfect, but it went a long way toward repairing the damage and staving off complete business disaster.

After he finished telling us his plan and before either of us could react to it, the phone rang. I was glad I was the one who answered it and not Madeleine.

"It's Elvira Reed. You know you must be out of the

shop by Saturday. I'm picking up the keys at five, and I expect the place to be empty and clean by then."

Before I could deliver one of my clever and sassy replies, she hung up.

Harassment, pure and simple. The bitch.

Seeing the thunderclouds in my expression, Madeleine asked, "Who was that?"

"Uh, it was our landlord reminding us we needed to be out by Saturday afternoon."

"We already know that. He's harassing us. I should call Frida." Madeleine reached out to grab the phone.

"Let's not do that now. You only think if you give Frida another case, it will take her mind off David. She's a homicide detective, and unless we're willing to kill someone, she's not interested in us." I'd goofed again. The minute the word "kill" was out of my mouth, I wanted to call it back. Madeleine's eyes filled with tears, and her lips trembled.

I sprang into action. There's nothing like work to take your mind off murder. Well, there are other things too, like sex, food, dancing…

"We've got to get organized," I said. "We need to get everything in here ready for our move. Sammy and his cousins will be here to help us, so no more boohooing." I opened the laptop to make a list.

"I can help too," offered Jerry.

No, no, no. The last thing I needed right now was Jerry to screw up everything. And he would too. The guy had a way of not getting anything right.

Nappi interceded on my behalf. "Jerry, you have work to do for me. You bungled that real estate deal, and now you need to make it right."

See? Told you. Jerry messed up everything. Sometimes I wondered why Nappi kept him on. It had to be because Nappi's daughter was still sweet on him.

Jerry hung his head and didn't make eye contact with anyone.

"And it looks like I have work to do also. I will see you later." Nappi took my hand and kissed it then did likewise with Madeleine.

"Thank you," she said. "I may have misjudged you."

That was quite a concession, for her. I couldn't believe it wasn't temporary—the outcome of her concern for David.

ON THURSDAY MORNING, Madeleine was in the backroom wrapping breakable items and boxing up lamps, jewelry, hats, scarves and other smaller pieces of merchandise. We'd put a sign in the window saying "We're moving. But you can go with us." Madeleine nixed the next line I wanted to use, which was "Find us on Facebook and follow us on Twitter." I thought it was cute, but Madeleine was so practical. She suggested we insert what details we knew of our move on the line below.

Sammy slammed open the door around eleven in the morning, and from the look on his face, I knew what he had to say wouldn't be good.

"What's wrong?" I reached out and touched Sammy's arm and maneuvered him toward the dressing room area. I decided that Madeleine had more than enough bad news right now in her life, and I didn't want her to hear Sammy's.

"My nephew, Bernard, the one who went to college in Orlando? He's missing."

"Missing? For how long?"

"His folks hadn't heard from him this weekend. He usually calls. They waited until Monday morning and then put in a call to the college. He missed all his morning classes. His roommate said he left their room on Friday night and never returned. He thought Bernard went home for the weekend. He said Bernard was depressed over the grade he got on a math test and thought he might have wanted to spend time with his family. No one's seen him since Friday around five. His car is gone too. Campus security says it's nowhere on campus. He has a parking permit for one of the student lots near his residence hall and usually parks there."

"I'm so sorry. Do they have any leads?" I asked.

He shook his head. "I'm sorry, Eve, but I need to get out there and search."

"Isn't that the authorities' job?"

"They are less than interested in an Indian boy."

"You can't mean that," I said.

"I do. If he were white, they'd be all over the place. But a poor Miccosukee… Get real."

I sighed. I'd seen it before around here. Indians were second class citizens. The prejudice was subtle, but it was there.

"Do you have any idea where he's gone?" I asked.

Sammy shuffled his feet back and forth and then looked up at me. In his eyes was fear and anger. "I have some ideas. Did you know that a number of farm workers have gone missing around here in the past few months?"

"No."

"And you know Grandfather and I spotted the Hardy brothers, who used to own the other airboat business, travelling into the swamp with people on board then coming back out alone?"

"But they're in jail. And they were transporting illegal aliens. I thought the authorities put a stop to that."

"They put a stop to the Hardy brothers' work, but there are others who would take their place. Anglos can't tell an illegal alien from a Mexican farm worker from a Miccosukee college kid."

"I don't know what that means," I said.

"It means that these people are disappearing for some reason. I intend to find out why. And I will find Bernard too." He clapped his beat-up cowboy hat onto his head and started to leave.

At the door, he stopped. "Sorry I can't be here. I'll send a couple of my cousins to help with the loading. Will tomorrow night work for you?"

"Sure. Say, who's going to run your airboat business meantime?"

"Jerry said he'd help Grandfather."

Oh, just great.

He pushed open the door and left before I could express my concerns.

"His nephew is missing?" Madeleine stood in the doorway to the backroom.

"I was hoping you weren't listening. You really don't need any more bad news."

"You get a hold of Alex yet?"

"I left a message for him to call me. He didn't get back last night or this morning. I think he had a late night doing surveillance and slept in this morning. He'll get in touch soon. Don't worry."

Madeleine swept the curls off her forehead with a sweaty hand. "Here's more bad news. The air conditioner in the back room cut out, and it won't go back on. We've probably overloaded the circuit somehow. That's been happening often lately."

"What do we care? We're moving," I said.

Madeleine and I looked at each other for a moment. Then we burst out laughing.

"We'll see how fast the landlord fixes it for Mrs. Reed. She might find it mighty hot moving in here." I pictured all that makeup cascading off her face. That image made the work of moving our merchandise easier. I shared the vision with Madeleine, and she shared in my levity.

We worked late Thursday evening to ready the shop for our departure.

I looked at the shop clock. It read eight. "I'm starving. Let's stop and get a pizza and take it to my place." I wiped away the beads of sweat from my forehead.

Madeleine nodded at my suggestion and tossed several cardboard boxes into the corner. "We'll finish in the morning."

Both of us agreed we were too tired and hungry to shower first, and if we didn't, no restaurant would serve us. We sat on either end of my couch. We were so exhausted from the day's work and all the emotional upheavals of the past few days that we each ate only one slice of the pie, but finished off the half gallon of iced tea I had in my fridge.

"Want to watch the evening news?" I asked.

"Sure. I'll just pick up our plates and put them in the dishwasher first." She got up from the couch.

"Leave them."

We both slid back onto the couch pillows and put our feet up on my coffee table. I hit the TV remote.

The next thing I knew my phone awakened me. It was Alex.

"Sorry I couldn't get back to you sooner."

As I suspected, he'd been out late and had slept in this morning before he again took up surveilling a target.

After explaining that David had been denied bail, I asked if he'd be free to handle some PI work for our poor friend.

"Glad to do it. I'll be out of here by this weekend. I'll visit David then, and we'll see if we can come up with any leads."

"I can think of one." I couldn't keep the smug tone out of my voice.

"Could it be the same one I'm thinking of? Maybe he's been set up by the parents of the kid he shot?" he asked.

Dang, the guy was good.

"I was just testing you to see if you were listening to the story Madeleine told us."

"No you weren't. You were trying to one up me. I didn't get my PI's license out of a cereal box, you know."

A name on the television news diverted my attention away from Alex.

"The missing man's car has been found on the county road leading to the casino outside of Sabal Bay. There is no sign of the man, but authorities suspect foul play."

"I've got to run, Alex. Bye." I made a kissing sound and ended the call.

Wide awake, Madeleine was sitting forward on

the couch, intent on the newscaster's report. "Poor Sammy."

I punched in Sammy's cell, but it went to voicemail.

"I'm going out there to see if there's anything I can do."

Madeleine jumped up off the coach and grabbed her jacket. "I'm coming with you."

WHEN WE ARRIVED at Grandfather Egret's house next to the airboat business, the place was surrounded by trucks, cars, and police vehicles. I recognized the SUV that Frida usually drove, so I wasn't surprised to see her when I entered the house. Madeleine and I each gave Grandfather Egret a quick hug. I approached Sammy, who stood among a group of Indians surrounding Frida and Linc, her partner. If these two were on the case, the news couldn't be good.

Frida was speaking with a man who looked like he could be Sammy's older brother, but when she saw me, she left the group and came over.

"Is he…?" I asked.

"We haven't located him yet, but there was blood on the seat of his car."

Sammy joined us. "You think he's dead, don't you?" He sounded more agitated than distressed.

"I don't know yet, Mr. Egret. We don't know what happened. The blood may not even be his." Frida didn't react to Sammy's anger. From the expression on Sammy's face it was clear he was looking for someone to strike out at, and Frida was right in front of him, an easy target for his feelings of impotence and worry.

"We all need to remain calm while we try to put the pieces together. Bernard was supposed to be at college in Orlando. Can you think of any reason why his car would be out near the casino?" Frida was so smart. She'd solicited Sammy's help, making him feel useful rather than confrontational.

"According to his roommate, he got a bad grade on a math test. It's possible he wanted to come home to talk with his family about it."

"The casino is hardly on his way home," Frida said.

One of the young Miccosukee men moved over to us. "Detective? I'm Edward Smith. Bernard was my cousin and best friend. He wasn't coming home to talk to his family about a test score. He told me on the phone he was heading home, but not to talk about a bad grade. He was going to tell them he had quit college."

NINE

"BERNARD WAS SUCH a good student, and we all thought he loved college. Why would he just up and quit?" Sammy looked shocked at the news.

The man I thought resembled Sammy, only older, turned out to be Bernard's father, Bill, and Sammy's half-brother. He had overheard what Edward said to us.

"That can't be true, Eddie," Bill said. "We talked to him last week and he said he intended to change his major from computer science to sociology. He wanted a course of study more people-oriented."

The woman at his side introduced herself to me as Bernard's mother, Angela. "I'm so confused by all of this. I felt like there was something he wasn't telling us, but I thought maybe it was about a girl."

The young man who introduced himself as Bernard's best friend Eddie shifted his weight from one foot to the other. His glance moved across the room to the people on the other side then back again to us. He did not look happy, more like he'd prefer a sinkhole to swallow him up rather than remain here.

Frida caught the fight-or-flight look in his eyes and put out her hand to restrain him. "You have something else you want to tell us?"

"No."

"Are you sure? You're not hiding anything that might help us find him? He could be in danger. It looked to me as if someone hijacked his car and attacked him too. You could help him. Maybe save his life," she said.

Eddie's eyes widened, then filled with tears.

Sammy put his hand on Eddie's shoulder. "We're not blaming you. Tell us what you know."

Eddie drew in a breath deep enough to suck the oxygen out of the room; then he let the air out of his lungs, and with it, an avalanche of words.

"Bernard went to the casino with some friends the first week of school and won a lot of money. They all went back the next weekend. He admitted he lost that time, but he kept going back. He told me he knew it was just a matter of time before his luck turned, and he'd make back his book money—"

Bernard's father interrupted him. "He gambled away the money we gave him to buy his books?"

Eddie nodded and continued, "Then he heard about a private game."

"From whom?" Sammy asked.

"I don't know," Eddie said. "I think it was one of his gambling friends, but I don't know. He was supposed to go there, then come home. He thought he'd be coming home with a lot of money. I told him that was crazy, but he wouldn't listen. I think he was in too deep to pull out."

Frida, who had been scribbling notes, interrupted him. "Maybe he did win, and someone followed him home to rob him of his money. We need to talk to these college buddies. Do you know their names?"

Eddie shook his head.

"Well, I guess we're going to need to find out." She sighed, and I knew she was thinking of the footwork she and Linc would have to do trying to find out who had befriended Bernard then led him astray.

After speaking a little longer with Bernard's parents, Frida and Linc left. Sammy stopped them on their way out.

"I assume you'll be visiting Bernard's college tonight?"

"Not tonight, Sammy, but first thing tomorrow, when the offices are open and we can get access to records and information about Bernard's classes and the full name of his roommate. No one is answering the phone in his residence hall right now. All we know is that the roommate's first name is Oscar."

Sammy nodded and followed them out the door. I followed Sammy and caught him standing on the path to the airboat business.

"You're going up there tonight yourself, aren't you?"

"Let me go with you, Uncle Sammy." Eddie had joined us on the pathway.

"No. Go home." Sammy started to walk toward his truck, which sat near the tiki hut.

Eddie caught up and danced in front of him. "There's something I didn't tell the cops."

Sammy paused and I could read his expression by the light of the rising moon. He was not happy, but willing to let Eddie speak.

"His roommate's name is Oscar Bundy. He was the one who introduced Bernard to the guys who hooked him up with the private game. Bernard told me Oscar works the nightshift at the convenience store just a block south of the campus' west entrance." Eddie grinned. "So, how about it? Can I go now? I gave you the best lead, didn't I? Better than what the cops have."

"No." Sammy continued to walk toward his truck.

Eddie watched him, then hung his head and walked back toward the house. But Eddie had given me an idea. I ran up to Sammy as he started to open the truck door.

"Eddie's right. You could use some help."

"And what use would you be?" he asked.

I could have been insulted by his question, but I decided it was better to put my ego aside and make my case.

"What college kid is going to talk to some huge Miccosukee Indian who appears out of the dead of night and wants to know about another missing Indian? You'll scare the bejesus out of him. When you're in a good mood and smiling, you scare the pants off most folks. Let me talk to him."

"I might as well let Frida at him tomorrow."

"No, no, no. She's a cop, and if he's in any way involved in Bernard's disappearance, he'll be covering his own ass."

Sammy's black eagle eyes pierced my sassy Eve armor, but I returned his look with one promising simple friendship. He must have seen the truth of what I was saying.

"Go back and make up some story for Madeleine. I'm leaving here in five minutes with or without you," he said.

That would be *with* me.

"So what did you tell Madeleine?"

"I told her we wanted to be together."

Sammy almost ran the truck off the road. "What? Are you out of your mind?"

I chuckled. "Naw. I told her you were upset and wanted to talk."

"That's almost as bad."

I thought about it. He was right. Alone with a handsome Indian. Talking? Who would believe that? I hoped Madeleine's naïveté would allow her to buy my excuse. And I hoped she would keep it to herself.

"Madeleine will believe it."

"Why should she?"

I didn't want to examine that question too closely. Did he mean Madeleine would be unlikely to believe we were only talking because she had picked up some attraction I had for Sammy or because she'd picked up on Sammy's attraction to me? I looked over at him. We were attracted to each other, but we'd danced around that feeling, never talking about it. I decided it was better not to think about this complication too deeply. Now was not the time to have a conversation about "us."

"Madeleine will believe me because she knows I wouldn't get sexy with any guy tonight—not smelling the way I do. I just spent the day in ninety degree heat packing up the store. Neither Madeleine nor I had time to grab a shower. I'm not romance material right now."

Sammy gave a barely perceptible sniff. "I wondered."

"Do I smell that bad?" I lifted my arm and smelled myself. Kind of stale, but that might have come from Sammy's truck.

"You smell different from the way you usually do." He gave me a quick look, then peered ahead into the darkness of the road leading north.

Sammy was a true gentleman.

We stopped at YeeHaw Junction, where I ducked into the ladies' room. Removing my shirt, I splashed cold water on myself and used a bit of the strong-smelling yellow soap in the dispenser to do a quick wash-up.

There. All better. Now I smelled like truck stop restroom.

WE DROVE AROUND and around a city that was mostly motels, hotels, and restaurants catering to the tourist trade. When we finally located the campus, we noticed a convenience store near one of the entrances to the college. The store was at the end of a small strip mall.

"This has to be the one." Sammy pulled his truck into the lot and parked at the other end of the line of stores.

"You stay here. I'll go and see if the guy is there." I got out and started for the store. I heard the driver's side door open. Sammy was right behind me.

"You won't know what to ask," he said.

"We agreed on this. I'll call on you if I need scary muscle. Until then, stay out of sight." I waited until he got back into the truck. Huh. Like I'd never interrogated anyone before. Like I'd never been involved in sleuthing out a killer.

There was only one guy behind the counter in the store. No customers. He was the right age for a college kid—late teens, early twenties—and he was reading what college kids might read. A comic book. Several textbooks lay on the counter to one side.

"Hi. You Oscar?" I asked.

"Who are you?" His tone was light, not suspicious, perhaps just curious at being accosted by a stranger knowing his name.

"I'm Eve." I held out my hand. He took it, and we shook. He gave me one of those damp, limp handshakes and a slight smile.

"Maybe you can help me." I put on my friendliest face. "You're Bernard's roommate, right?"

His smile disappeared, replaced now by a cautious look, but he nodded.

"Do you know where he is?"

"Went home, I guess."

"I just talked with his parents, and they haven't seen him. And his car was found abandoned near the casino."

Sweat glistened on his top lip. He swallowed. "I don't know anything about that."

"Did you know he was missing?"

"No."

"Do you think he went off with his gambling buddies?"

"I wouldn't know anything about that."

"But you were the one who introduced him to those guys, right?"

He was about to open his mouth when I interrupted him. "So far I don't think you've outright lied to me, but now I'd guess you're about to. I think it would be better if you told me the truth. See that truck out there?" I pointed to Sammy's vehicle. Oscar leaned over the counter to get a better look outside; then his gaze fastened back on me. I waved at Sammy. He got out of the truck.

"And see that big guy?"

Oscar gulped and nodded. Now sweat began to trickle down the sides of his face.

"If you don't lie to me, we can have this chat, just the two of us. Otherwise, you'll be talking to that guy. He's Bernard's uncle, and he's kind of perturbed at white folks right now, especially those who are in any way responsible for his nephew's disappearance. Like you, Oscar."

"But I don't know…"

I waved at Sammy again, and he began walking toward the store.

"Okay, okay. Bernard and I went to the casino, and he won a lot of money, then next time he lost. Some guys I knew from back home were there. They approached me and said they could help out Bernard. They knew of a high stakes private game, and with Bernard's skill, he could be a winner."

Sammy continued to walk toward the store.

"And you believed them? I suppose you believe in Santa and the tooth fairy too."

Oscar wiped the sweat off his face with the back of his hand. "Listen, these guys are bad dudes. I didn't have any choice. They would have messed me up good if I didn't say what they wanted."

"Then what?"

Sammy now stood at the door.

"They went off together. Bernard came back to the room later, saying he'd won and was back in the game that night. I didn't see much of him after that."

Sammy pushed open the door. The harsh fluorescent lights of the store accentuated the frown lines around his mouth. With his dark skin and long black hair, he looked like a warrior. I wondered if Oscar was thinking what I was. The Florida tribes have never signed a peace treaty, and Sammy looked as if he was about to take up the battle once more.

"When did Bernard's gambling begin?" I asked.

"About a month ago. It wasn't my fault. I didn't know he'd get in so deep with these guys."

"Oscar set him up with some guys," I said to Sammy.

Sammy approached the counter and leaned over, his face inches from Oscar's. "I'd like to meet these guys."

Oscar shook his head. "No you wouldn't. They're bad dudes, into stuff I don't want to know about."

Sammy didn't break his gaze with Oscar. "I'm a bad dude, too. And you don't want to know what I can do if you piss me off. And you're pissing me off."

Oscar's hands began to tremble. He stuffed them in his pockets, but that only drew attention to the shaking of his arms and legs. "Okay, okay. Meet me at the casino tomorrow about nine, and I'll point them out to you. But keep low, would you? I don't want them to know we're together. They'd be suspicious."

Sammy didn't move a muscle, but seemed to be considering Oscar's offer. "The police will be here tomorrow questioning you, and you won't want to tell them you talked to me."

Oscar shook his head. "No sir."

"But you will want to tell them the truth, won't you?"

Oscar nodded.

"And you might want to arrange for them to meet your pals at some time later than nine tomorrow. When I'm through with them."

"Right." Oscar's voice came out thin and squeaky.

Sammy straightened up and gave the store a casual once-over. "Thirsty, Eve? I am. Oscar, how about two of those Slurpees there for me and my lady?"

SAMMY BROKE INTO laughter when we got back into the truck. "I can play a pretty good bad guy, can't I?"

"You had me fooled. I told him you were an Indian

with a grudge against white folks, but I've never seen you so fierce."

He was silent for a moment. "It was necessary. Mr. Nice Guy wasn't going to get me the information I needed."

"We made a pretty good pair. I guess he thought you wouldn't hurt him in front of me."

He seemed to consider this for a while. "There are plenty of white folks I like." He looked over at me. "You're one of them."

"You weren't so sure when we first met, though. What changed your mind?"

"Your friends."

"You like me not because of my personality but for the folks I hang with?"

"Grandfather Egret would say they're the same thing. Think about it. You are adored by a mob boss, a PI, a whole crowd of cowboys, rich women from West Palm, my grandfather, and Madeleine Boudreau, the kindest and most naïve woman in all of rural Florida. That's quite a set of credentials."

"I'm a diversity magnet."

We left the lights of Orlando and headed down the turnpike toward home. The next thing I remembered, we were entering the city limits of Sabal Bay. I could just see the tip of the sun kiss one of the palms in the field east of the highway.

"What time is it?" It wasn't light enough for me to read my watch.

"About five in the morning."

"How do you Indians do that?"

"Do what?"

"Know what time it is?"

Sammy held up his arm. On it was a watch with a luminous dial.

"What do you intend to do with those guys who introduced your nephew to that high stakes poker game?"

"Have a chat with them before they can lawyer up after the cops get them. From what Oscar said, these guys did more than just introduce Bernard to poker. They know something about what happened to him."

"I mean after you've talked with them."

"After I learn what I need to know? Then I turn them over to Frida and Linc. What did you think I was going to do? Torture them?"

"No. I thought you'd lose them out in the swamp."

Sammy's gaze met mine. In it I could see I'd hit on the truth. I'd only been wrong about the sequence of events.

"I'll leave them in the swamps a while, then retrieve them. They'll be ready to talk after a night listening to gators sing to one another."

I rolled down the window to let in the cool morning air.

"What's that smell?" I don't know why I asked. I knew what it was. A building burning. I remembered the smell from when Sammy and I spent the night in the swamp and wandered out the next morning to find a local airboat business on fire. The memory of that night and the fire sent prickly sensations down my arms.

"Something must be burning, something big." Sammy swung the truck around a corner onto the street leading to our consignment shop and toward my neighborhood. Up ahead we could see the flashing lights of emergency vehicles and fire trucks.

"It looks like it's close to your shop." Sammy

braked. A barricade had been set up to prevent anyone from approaching the fire, which appeared to be contained. Black smoke but no flames poured from the strip mall. At the far end where our shop was located, fire trucks continued to pour water onto the structure.

The sign reading "Eve and Madeleine's Second to None Consignment Boutique" lay in the street in front of our burned-out shop.

TEN

I JUMPED OUT of the truck and tried to run around the barricade toward the shop, but a police officer stopped me.

I struggled to get out of his hold. "No, no, no! We were going to move everything out today or tomorrow. Now it's all gone."

Someone approached me from the side. I didn't recognize who it was until she spoke.

"Too bad. You just lost everything. I guess I won't have any competition after all."

Elvira Reed. I swung around to face her and would have punched her in the nose if Sammy hadn't grabbed my arm.

"What are you doing here?" Then it hit me. She had to be behind this fire. "Arrest this woman. She did this. She set the fire on purpose." I grabbed the police officer by the arm to get his attention.

"Oh, don't be absurd. This woman runs the shop, and she's clearly overwrought with her loss," Elvira said.

Sammy steered me away from her and the officer before I could say or do more.

"Eve, calm down. We don't even know if the fire is arson. You said the air conditioner wasn't working right. Maybe it was faulty wiring."

"Yeah, right. Faulty wiring in that crazy woman's head, maybe."

I spotted curly red hair across the parking lot. Madeleine. One more tragedy she did not need right now.

"Madeleine!" I yelled and waved at her. "Over here."

She saw me and ran over. "Thank God you're here. I was worried about you," she said.

"Worried about me? What about this? All our stuff is gone." Crying is not something I often gave into; I'm more of a "turn your troubles into anger and blame someone else" gal, but I could feel myself close to tears.

Madeleine put her arm around my waist. "Don't, Eve. Everything is fine."

"I don't call barbequed clothes, shoes, and other apparel fine. If only we could have moved before this happened." I shot a venomous look at Elvira, who remained at the edge of the crowd, a smirky smile on her face.

Madeline grabbed me and spun me around so that I was facing the street. "See that?"

Parked on the street and taking up at least three out of four car lengths stood a gigantic motor home.

Nappi stood beside it, smiling and gesturing to me to come over. "It's what I talked to you about," he called out. "A consignment shop on wheels."

"Yeah, right," I said. "An empty consignment shop on wheels."

"Look inside." Nappi gallantly took my arm as I ascended the steps. Inside I took a look around. All our merchandise was there, arranged on racks, clothes rounds, and in display cases.

"I don't understand." I stumbled into one of the bench seats near the front of the rig and plopped down.

"There was a change of plans. Mr. Napolitani called

a few minutes after you left and wondered if we could move then rather than on Friday. I was exhausted, but I thought, why not? Let's get our merchandise out of that place and into the newly designed shop on wheels. It's all here, Eve. It's safe." Madeleine gave me a hug. Nappi beamed in his sophisticated way.

I got up from my seat and rushed down the steps and across the parking lot. "Hey, Elvira!"

She was in the same spot as before and still had the same snarky look on her face. Well, here was something to wipe away that satisfied smirk.

"There was nothing in the store. We hauled it all away earlier tonight." I gave her a one fingered good-bye and ran off to my shop on wheels.

"You think that horrid woman set the fire, don't you, Eve?" Madeleine came up behind me and linked her arm through mine. We paused for a moment to look at the charred timbers of what had once been our business, then turned toward our new shop. Would this work? I hoped so…at least for a time.

"Let's move this buggy away from here. The smell is unpleasant." Nappi pulled a white handkerchief out of his pocket and held it to his nose.

"Can I drive?" Tired as I was from getting no sleep last night, the excitement of running this new shop on wheels had swept away most of my fatigue. Besides, I wanted to drive past Elvira and honk the horn, make her jump like a jack-in-the-box.

"Take her away." Nappi handed me the keys.

I started up the coach, listening to the engine as it caught then purred.

I shifted into drive and circled the block, just to get

a feel for the behemoth motor home, aka consignment shop. As I took the turn that would bring us back past the strip mall, I saw Elvira step from the curb and head across the street.

I gunned it.

Madeleine grabbed my arm. "You're not thinking of running over her, are you?"

I kept my attention on the woman ahead and steered in her direction. At the last minute, Elvira heard the bus and turned her head in our direction, a look of terror on her face.

At the very last minute, I whipped the wheel to the right and missed her by one of those ugly brown hairs on her head. I honked the horn, which as I expected, sounded like the air horn on a big rig. Elvira jumped at the sudden loud noise, stumbled and fell into the gutter at the side of the street.

"That was taking quite a chance. You could have hit her." Although Madeleine's voice held a note of disapproval, I caught her face reflected in the rearview mirror. She was grinning like a kid.

"I knew I'd miss her. This thing drives like a sports car. I love it."

"Where do we park it for the night?" Madeleine asked.

Nappi replied, "You have a permit to park it in the flea market lot anytime you want. And here's your license to sell from it at the market on the weekends." He flipped through the papers. "I also was able to obtain a temporary permit for you to open for business at any location in the state, as long as you pay sales tax, of course."

"How did you do that so fast?" I asked. "It had to be

expensive." I pulled into the flea market parking area and drove around to the back.

Nappi wouldn't look me in the eye as he said, "Uh, I had some coupons I used for a reduced rate on the permitting."

"Coupons?" I knew he wasn't using the term in the usual way—as in coupons from the Sunday paper.

"I know some people who know some people in this state." He still avoided my eyes.

"This better be legal. I don't want the West Palm Beach cops surrounding our motor coach and arresting Madeleine, me, and our wealthy patrons when we're trying to sell a few cocktail dresses or feather boas."

"Won't happen," Nappi assured me. This time he looked me straight in the eye and winked.

I would have winked back, but all I could manage was a yawn. Madeleine covered her mouth in an attempt to stifle her own.

"We need a few hours of sleep," I said.

"I'll ferry you gals home." Nappi waved to the car that had followed us, and it pulled alongside the coach. Behind it was Sammy in his truck.

"You give Madeleine a ride. Sammy will take me home. We have a few things to discuss."

Madeleine gave me a warning look.

"We need to talk about Sammy's nephew. That's all."

"It's not your problem," Madeleine said.

"It's a friend's problem, honey." I gave her a reassuring hug and jumped into Sammy's truck.

"So what's the next move?" I asked Sammy as we rolled toward my house.

"I heard what Madeleine said. She's right, you know.

This is my problem, not yours." Sammy pulled into my drive. "I appreciate your help. Thanks."

"That's it? Thanks, but get out of here? Well, let me give you some advice then. Let the cops handle this. Don't stick your nose into something that might not help your nephew but could get you into trouble. This could be dangerous, Sammy."

The sun was fully over the horizon. It filled the cab of the truck, shining its yellow morning light on Sammy's face. Unfortunately, that light was not kind. It showed all the lines surrounding his handsome features. His face was still appealing, but haggard and worn, as if his nephew's disappearance had stamped the cares of an older man there.

"Oscar will introduce me to the guys who led Bernard into those private poker games. I'll find out what I need to know, what they know."

I tried to interrupt, but he held up his hand to stop me. "You are not invited to join me. I'll take the risks because this is my family."

I'd been cut out. Sammy couldn't have made it any clearer. I got out of the truck tired and angry. Sammy waited until I went in, then drove off.

I mentally shrugged. *Oh, well.* Things could be worse. Madeleine and I had our shop on wheels. And I knew when and where Sammy was meeting Bernard's gambling buddies just in case I wanted to intrude.

IT SEEMED ONLY minutes after I'd beaten my pillow into a comfortable sleeping shape that I awoke with a start. Someone was in my room. My back was turned toward the doorway so the intruder couldn't tell I was awake with my eyes wide open. I moved my hand carefully under the comforter, reaching for the brass lamp on my bed table. That lamp had proved handy for beating off another intruder. It would be just as useful now. I was just about to grasp the base…

"Leave it."

I recognized the voice. Alex.

"I used my key," he said.

I turned over and eyed him.

"You gave me one. Remember?"

No, I didn't remember.

"I did no such thing."

"Well, you kind of did. You told me where you hid the extra key."

"That's not giving you a key."

"It's close."

"I should just bean you with this lamp anyway."

"How about I make coffee and we have breakfast together."

"What the hell time is it?"

"It's after ten. Why are you still in bed?"

"I got to sleep at seven. It's a long story. Wake me at two." I rolled over and tried to get back to sleep.

"And I woke up early this morning just to get up here from Miami so I could help you move tonight. Aren't I nice?"

"Mr. Napolitani is nicer. He took care of all that last night."

The silence that followed my announcement was loud enough to wake Madeleine across town.

I pulled back the covers. "Oh, get in here, you big lug. I'll explain everything."

I've never seen a man undress so fast. Hot diggity and sleep be damned. But before we could get to the hot or the diggity part, my phone rang. I looked at the caller ID. It was Frida.

"Something has come up with Sammy's nephew," she said.

"Why are you calling me? Why not call Bernard's family?"

"I did, but this concerns David, and I know he's going to call Madeleine about it. I asked him to call you instead of her. He agreed she might not take it well. I know he's hired Alex to do some work for him, so I told David he could get in touch with Alex at your place."

"How do you know Alex is here?"

"I'm a detective, remember? David should be getting in touch soon." Frida disconnected.

No sleep and no hot diggity this morning. No sooner had I placed the phone back in the cradle when it rang.

It was David, as Frida predicted.

"Put Alex on the other line. I've got something to tell you. I heard about the fire at the shop, and I know Elvira Reed was there. It makes me all the more convinced that the Reeds are trying to frame me for the murder. She's helping him make my life a living hell by creating trouble for you and Madeleine."

"I think she set the fire, but until we find out the cause, I won't kick her in her perfect size six butt," I said.

"Did Frida call you?"

"Just now. She said this was about Bernard Egret's disappearance. I don't get the connection."

"I don't either," Alex chimed in from the phone in the living room.

"It's crazy is what it is. The detectives had me back in the interrogation room early this morning and asked me all kinds of questions about that missing kid whose car they found near the casino."

"Bernard Egret," I said. "He's Sammy's nephew. How does this involve you?"

"They found my business card in his glove box with my private cell number written on the back."

ELEVEN

"WHAT OF IT? Did you ever give him one of your cards?" Alex wandered back into my bedroom, the phone to his ear.

"No," David said. "I don't even know the guy."

"Is the handwriting yours?"

"I don't think so, although the seven in my number has an extra horizontal mark through it. I write my sevens that way."

"So do a lot of people." Alex waved his hand in a dismissive gesture. "It sounds like they're on a fishing expedition. You did have your lawyer with you when they questioned you, right?"

"Yeah, but—"

"David, is there something you're not saying here?" I asked.

"The ink used to write down my cell…"

We waited.

"It was the bright turquoise color, like in Madeleine's favorite pen. It sure makes it look as if I borrowed her pen and wrote the number on the card."

"And you didn't do that for anybody that you remember? Wait a minute. Isn't your cell on your card?" Alex said.

"My business cell, but this was my personal number. I've been racking my brain. I don't give out my personal cell number to very many people."

"First, you'd better make a list of those you have given your personal number to. I'll need it. I'm just back from Miami this morning. I'm going to pay a visit to the family whose son invaded your home."

"The one I killed."

"The one you shot to defend your daughter." Alex's voice was firm, but sympathetic. "Do the police know the significance of the ink? Does your lawyer?"

"Cops, no. Lawyer, yes. He told me to keep it that way."

We ended the call and looked at each other with concern.

"It sure looks like someone is trying to frame David and isn't content to leave it at the murder of his client. Now Sammy's missing nephew is being pulled into the picture. What's the connection?" Alex walked out of the room.

"Do you want coffee before you leave?" I called to him.

"Yep. That's what I'm going to do now. Make a pot. You go on back to sleep for a few hours."

Sleep? Was he crazy? How could any self-respecting gal sleuth sleep when there were leads to be chased down?

"I'm coming with you," I said.

AN HOUR LATER, wired on two cups of Alex's strong coffee, I sat in the passenger seat of his car as we rolled down the highway leading west around the Big Lake and into the small community of Deer Mound. It took me most of that hour to convince Alex I would, number one, not be a problem, number two, not get in his way, number three, keep quiet unless asked to participate, and number four, be useful to him in his interrogation. I don't think he bought any of my reasoning, but I wore him down, and finally wouldn't let go of his shirt when he got into the car. He was stuck with me. The best he was able to accomplish on the way was to get me to promise to stay in the car while he talked to the Warren family. As with my other promises, I had no intention of keeping it, but he didn't need to know that.

The house where the family lived was in a neighborhood of concrete block homes lining dusty unpaved streets that were cut through by canals. The streets were laid out in a grid pattern, but the canals meandered in many directions. The streets dead ended where a canal crossed them and continued on the other side, making it necessary to backtrack to find a bridge that crossed the canal. After several tries, we found a bridge but then were stopped by yet another canal. By the time we finally threaded our way through the maze of streets, bridges and cattail-clogged waterways, my coffee had worn off and lack of sleep was making me groggy.

Finally Alex pulled up in front of a gray house, correct number, correct street. The building was almost identical to its neighbors'. Paint and landscaping were not activities high on these homeowners' lists. There was no grass in the yard and a swing set with a broken slide sat rusted and abandoned in the front patch of dirt. Under each of the two swings you could still see the depressions made by children's feet as they pushed off to gain height. A chain-link fence surrounded the yard. Two ponytail palms, their fronds yellow from lack of water, sat on either side of the driveway. An old pickup truck, one fender duct-taped onto the body, had been pulled into the drive just beyond the gate. I saw a mixed-breed dog, as buff-colored as the dust in the yard, get up when we pulled into the drive and parked beyond the fence. The dog looked as disconsolate as the palms. Opening its mouth as if to bark, it decided not to bother—just eyed us as Alex got out of the car.

"Careful of the dog," I said. "I always worry about dogs that don't make a sound."

The dog again opened its mouth. This time the move ended in a yawn.

Alex approached the gate.

The sun-weathered door of the house opened, and a woman stuck her head out. "Go away or I'll sic the dog on you."

Her words were hostile, but her tone of voice was quiet, depressed, as if she had no hope that anyone would come to her door seeking anything but payment for back bills. She just wanted us gone so she wouldn't have to be bothered. Both she and the dog looked as if they'd seen the world at its worst and now wanted to be left alone. She began to close the door.

I hopped out of the car. Eve to the rescue. "Ma'am. We're sorry to bother you but we need your help. I know this is painful, but it's about your son's death. Is your husband at home? We'd like to talk with both of you."

"Get back in the car, Eve," Alex said through clenched teeth.

Something about the dynamic between Alex and me, his ordering me to the car, my placating tone with her, seemed to get her interest.

"You cops?" she asked.

"He's a detective. I'm kind of a consultant."

She looked at her neighbors' houses. "People are nosy around here. You'd better come in."

"You lied to her about our being police," Alex said under his breath as he opened the gate. As we walked past the dog, it flopped over onto its side, moaned, and closed its eyes.

I expected the inside of the house to be as disheveled as the yard, but I was surprised to see that it was neat and organized. The furniture was old, but in good condition, and the house smelled like pine cleaner. Like her home, Mrs. Warren looked worn out, but her hair was a bubble of salt and pepper curls and her clothing neat and pressed. She even wore a light lip gloss and a pair of tear-drop earrings that caught the light from the window. It was as if she was expecting company.

She gestured toward a slip-covered couch, its tropical colors of blue and pink faded but spot free. We settled in on the couch. A small table was positioned at my end of the sofa. On it was a collection of pictures, most of them featuring an infant, then toddler, and finally male child, his blue eyes twinkling with happiness, his freckles becoming more prominent as he grew older. A candle stood to the right of the photos. The tableau had the appearance of a shrine. Mrs. Warren caught me looking at the photos.

"My son." Her face saddened as she looked at them.

Alex tried on his version of my friendly approach, adding his own element of cop-like firmness. "Mrs. Warren, we're sorry to disturb you, but we have some questions. Your husband not home yet?"

Up until this point, she'd seemed tense, wary, her arms across her chest. At Alex's words, she relaxed and grabbed a cigarette off the coffee table but didn't light it. From the clean smell of the place, I had a feeling no one smoked inside the house. Maybe on the front steps. She smiled at Alex as if she knew something he did not, something that gave her an edge. "Not home yet? Nope, and I don't expect him in this lifetime or any other. He's dead. In Afghanistan. Now, what's this about my son? He's dead too. Killed by some rich man over in Sabal City. I'm all alone."

WE BOWED OUT of Mrs. Warren's house and her sorrow-filled life as gracefully as we could. Alex told her we were just tying up loose ends from the case in which her son was killed.

"What a sad woman," I said, watching her move the curtain to one side as we drove away from the house. "I guess that was a dead end." I caught myself and gave a nervous laugh. "I mean, it's certainly not her husband who's trying to set up David. *If* someone is setting him up, that is."

"You don't think that's true?" Alex said. "You don't believe David killed his client or that he had anything to do with Bernard Egret's disappearance, do you?"

I shrugged. "I guess not. What can be going on then?"

"First I think we need to find out more about Bernard's situation; then I have to follow up on Mr. Warren."

"Is she lying?"

"I don't know. I'm going to track down Mr. Warren and find out if he really was killed in Afghanistan. On my own, Eve. This time I don't need your help."

I really didn't hear much of what he said beyond that. I knew, of course, that I was being chastised for not following his orders to stay in the truck, but I was

glad I'd met Mrs. Warren and I wondered about the
pipe I'd seen on the dash of the truck when we walked
past. She didn't seem like the type of woman who liked
a good bowlful. Aside from my own thoughts about
the Warren family, I also was trying on Alex's idea
of finding out more about Bernard Egret's situation.

I settled into the corner of the front seat. I needed
to get some shuteye before I had to check out our shop
on wheels this afternoon and follow up tonight on the
casino rendezvous with the gambling punks who'd set
up Bernard. Sammy wouldn't know—I'd be in hiding—but four ears are better than two, especially if
no one knows about the second set. Mmm. Sleep now,
spy later.

WHEN WE PULLED up to my house, Sammy's truck sat
out front. He jumped out and ran up to the car, bang-
ing on the driver's side window.

"I just found out from Frida that David Wilson's
card was in my nephew's glove box and that you're
doing some private work for him. I think you'd better
tell me how all of this is related. If David were where
I could get my hands on him, I'd get the truth out of
him about why Bernard had his card. I suggest you tell
me what's going on."

Alex got out of the car and confronted a side of
Sammy I'd never experienced before. The man was
steamed and looked as if he wanted to take on Alex
in a fight. Before I could say something Eve-like that
would only ratchet up the anger, Alex stepped in with
the diplomacy of a Madeleine.

"Sammy, we could use your help here. We know
someone planted that card in Bernard's car. We just

can't figure out who is trying to frame David and connect the two crimes. Maybe you have some insight into
this. You hear things we don't."

Sammy's long black hair was not in its customary
braids. He removed his hat and ran his hands through
the straight, dark mane.

"Sorry. The family is going crazy with worry. No
word from Bernard and then the cops find David's
card. That seems to be all they've been able to manage since they discovered the car last night. I'm sure
Eve told you she and I went to Orlando and spoke with
Bernard's roommate. He's going to introduce me to the
guys who took Bernard to the poker game."

"Really?" Alex directed his gaze to me. Oops. Eve
forgot to tell Alex of her trip to Orlando last night. I
let him believe my lack of sleep was all because of the
fire. My bad. My face felt hot. Could I be blushing? Or
was that a hot flash? Early menopause, maybe.

Sammy must have caught something in Alex's voice;
his own sounded wary as he said, "I'm not taking Eve
with me tonight though."

"You could use back-up, couldn't you?"

They agreed to go together. I would be their back-
up, though they didn't know it.

I'D CONVINCED MADELEINE that Alex and I needed some
time together alone to "reconnect." I did not tell her we
would be doing it by chasing down the lead with Mrs.
Warren. There's nothing like chasing clues to bring a
couple closer. There was no sense in getting Madeleine's hopes up, only to have to tell her the contact was
a dead end. I wanted Madeleine to focus on getting our
new shop together rather than obsessing about David.

"So guess what I did while you and Alex were doing whatever?" she asked me when Alex dropped me off at the motor coach.

I could tell she'd been rearranging the merchandise to make the displays work better. The inside looked more posh than our store had.

"Other than turning this into the fanciest store in Sabal Bay? It looks wonderful."

"Thanks. I'm glad you approve. I was worried you wouldn't like it. I don't really have your fashion sense."

"It's perfect." I gave her a hug. "So what else did you do?"

"I spent about an hour driving it down the roads around here and out onto the highway too. You can't be the only one who drives this bus."

Well, that must have been quite a sight. Tiny Madeleine Boudreau piloting a giant motor home down the street, only the top of her flaming red curls showing through the driver side window.

"How did you see over the dash?" I asked.

"Pillows." She pointed to the three pillows stacked on the driver's seat. "I moved the seat all the way up so I could reach the pedals. I even drove it over to the county jail and visited David today."

I held my breath. Would he have told her what Alex and I were doing?

"He told me Alex was going to follow up on the family of the kid he shot. Is that where Alex is going now?"

"Uh, I don't really know."

"Well, we have the late afternoon left. Let's take this buggy down the road to the flea market on the coast. I think they're open tonight, too."

No, no, no. I had to be at the casino tonight, but if I

didn't want Madeleine to worry about anything related to David's case, I couldn't tell her my plans. I didn't want anybody to know.

"I've got a better idea. Tonight is that Texas hold 'em tournament at the casino. Let's take her over there. We can tap into some sales before the tournament gets going. It's closer than the coast and we have a permit to sell there, don't we?"

"Nappi got us permits to sell almost any place in this state. We could probably pull into the state capital parking lot and set up there." She clapped her hands together. "Let's go."

Now all I had to do was find an excuse to be absent from the rig for a while. If there was anything I'd learned over the past year or so of chasing bad guys, it was how to tell inventive lies. I'd come up with something.

I LET MADELEINE DRIVE. That was a mistake.

"This thing is so big, I feel like I own the road." Madeleine hugged the center line as the headlights approached us.

"I think you should get over a bit," I said.

She held a steady line. The other car swerved off the road onto the shoulder.

"See. People get out of our way."

"You still have to obey the basic rules of the road..." Another set of headlights approached us. This pair was connected to a pickup truck, a dualie—one of those big boys with dual wheels in the back. This one wasn't giving way. A game of chicken had begun.

Madeleine leaned forward over the wheel and

gripped it so tight I thought her knuckles would crack. The pickup driver continued to come straight at us.

"Move over, you putz!" she yelled.

At the last moment, he did.

She shot me a self-satisfied grin. "That's how it's done."

I was just beginning to realize that it was dangerous business to give an undersized woman an oversized vehicle then place her on one of Florida's narrower roads with little in the way of shoulders.

Several more near misses, and we were at the casino. Madeleine pulled up to the entrance, and I jumped out to confer with one of the casino's employees about where we could park for maximum exposure. I showed him our permit. He contacted someone on his walkie-talkie, and for a moment, I worried we would be tossed out of the place, but after several minutes of back and forth between the guy, his walkie-talkie, and a man in a suit who seemed to have the final say over our request, we were directed down the sidewalk to an area just beyond the entrance. I got out our free-standing sign and placed it in front of the bus.

"This is great. The light is wonderful here. Everyone can see us." Madeleine eyes danced around in their sockets as if they were doing the bossa nova.

I wanted everyone to see the business, but I wasn't sure I wanted everyone to see me. Too late. Alex and Sammy strode up to the bus.

"Whose idea was it to come here?" asked Alex.

"Eve's. Isn't she smart?" Madeleine said.

Smart, that's me. Snoopy, that's me too.

Alex grabbed my arm and led me to the other side of the bus, away from Sammy and Madeleine.

"I know what you're up to."

I gazed up into his azure eyes and tried for the most innocent look I could muster. "Whatever do you mean?"

"Sammy. Bernard's roommate. Poker slugs. You know."

"Oh, that. Well, that's up to you and Sammy, isn't it?" I continued to look up at him. If I didn't blink soon, my eyes would become permanently locked in a wide-eyed stare.

"Okay. Fine then. Stay out of this," he said.

When we returned to the front of the bus, Sammy was gone. And so was Madeleine.

She popped her head out of the door as several women stepped down off the bus.

"Which way did he go, Madeleine?" Alex scanned the crowds of people entering the casino.

"I don't know. I was busy with customers. Say, what are the two of you doing here anyway? I never knew you to be gamblers." Madeleine placed her fists on her hips and tapped her foot indignantly.

"Sammy wanted me to meet some of the folks he knows who run this place, that's all." Alex was getting as good at lying as I was.

I caught sight of a tall man with a head of inky black hair turning the corner toward the other end of the entrance. I dashed after him, trying not to lose him in the dim lights around the side of the building. By the time I turned the corner, he'd disappeared. I heard screeching tires and saw taillights head for the back exit. Sammy? Had someone taken Sammy?

TWELVE

ALEX CAUGHT UP with me, and the two of us watched the taillights of the retreating car dim and then disappear as it turned out of the parking lot onto the road.

"I'm sure I saw Sammy come this way, then nothing except for that car." I clenched my fists in frustration.

"This doesn't look good. He told me he was supposed to meet Bernard's roommate and get an introduction to the poker guys. Someone should follow that car and—"

"I only have the bus. You follow it. I know what the roommate looks like. I'll see if I can spot him inside."

Before Alex could say no, I ran off toward the casino, waving at Madeleine as I sped by. "Be back in a jiffy. Sell, girl, sell!"

This casino was not far from Sabal Bay, but almost an hour from the coast. It was smaller than the huge Miccosukee Casino farther south, just off US 41. It certainly wasn't grand, either, no fancy bars and restaurants—only worn and tired carpeting and gray and dingy walls—but it served rural Floridians' need to toss away their money and drink without having to travel too far. That was my take on gambling.

Because of the poker tournament, the place was packed with customers. And smoky. Only one small area had been designated nonsmoking. Bright lights, the noise of coins hitting metal trays, and smoke assaulted me as I walked up and down next to the lines of people at the slots. No Oscar. I've always found casinos exciting for the first few minutes or so, then all the game sounds and people shouting and talking give me a headache. I'm no gambler. I play the slots until I lose my twenty dollars. That usually happens fast, then I'm out the door or sipping a Cosmo at the bar. I doubt I've been inside any casino for longer than twenty minutes.

I checked the other games. Still no sight of him. Maybe he'd gone into the room where the tournament was being played. I'd try that. Sure enough, back in the corner surrounded by several guys his own age, stood Oscar. He wasn't watching the game. His eyes traveled the room, looking for someone. When they came to rest on me, they looked startled, then full of fear. I saw him start to leave, but I was too quick for him.

"Oscar. Don't you want to introduce me to your pals? Didn't you say you had some friends you wanted me to meet?"

One of the young men gave me a once over. "This your mom, Oscar?"

In my four-inch stilettos—and you can be sure I was wearing my four-inch stilettos, I tower at least six feet two inches. This guy was a pimply faced five nine. I walked up to him, stopped an inch away from his face, and looked down into his jumpy pale eyes.

"I'm a friend. That's all you need to know, boy."

He gulped and moved backward an inch or so. I looked at the others, letting my gaze slide from one set of eyes to the next, slowly giving them my best in-your-face-Eve-the-bitch look.

"Uh, sure." Oscar gave names and introduced me as Ms. Appel. I saw one of the guys about to laugh, but I held up a finger as if to silence him. He looked at his feet and said nothing.

I produced what I hoped was a wicked, cold smile and grabbed Oscar's arm.

"Those idiots aren't the ones Bernard met, are they?"

He shook his head.

"I told them I had another guy for them to meet, but they haven't showed yet."

"And you also stupidly described Sammy to them, right?"

"Well, yeah. I had to, in case I couldn't make it to-night."

"You might not have made it tonight? You were told to make it. No excuses." I grabbed him by his shirt collar and began to shake him.

"But stuff can come up." Or at least I think that's what he said. His teeth were clacking together so hard from my shaking, I really couldn't say for certain. One of the employees came over and asked us if anything was wrong.

I let go of Oscar's collar but kept my hand on his arm. "Nothing, nothing, except my nephew was dumb enough to lose all his money at the dollar slots. In the first hour we were here. Dumb kid." Oscar hung off my hand like an overcooked beet top.

"Kids!" the employee said. "They'll learn. Don't be too hard on him."

Not too hard? Oscar might have gotten Sammy killed along with Bernard.

"Can I go now?" Oscar asked.

"Sure." I shoved him away from me and into the arms of Alex, who had just come up behind Oscar.

"Now you can talk to my friend here and then maybe to the cops."

"He already talked to us," said Frida, who'd just joined us, accompanied by Linc. "I think he may have given us the same story he gave you and Sammy last night. Maybe you can provide a more accurate story down at the station."

Alex obliged her by turning terrified Oscar over to Linc, who led him away.

"I want to thank the two of you and Sammy, wherever he is, for screwing up my case. Oscar was going to lead us to the guys Eddie met and gambled with."

"I don't think so. I think he set all of us up, but he really did a job on Sammy." I told her and Alex about Oscar's describing Sammy to the gambling guys.

"Dumb, damn kid," Frida said.

We nodded our heads in agreement.

Alex told Frida about trying to chase down the car we thought Sammy might have been thrown into and being unable to catch it. "I never got close enough to catch a plate number."

"Did you see a fight? Are you certain Sammy was taken?" asked Frida.

"Not certain. Neither of us saw what happened, but there must have been some kind of scuffle. I found his hat on the ground." Alex held up Sammy's hat, the one with the silver hatband.

Frida reached out and took the hat. "Let's not jump to conclusions. I'll take a look outside if you show me where you found the hat. Then you'd better wait back at your car, Alex. In case he returns. I'll take a walk through the casino. He could still be around here someplace."

"What about me?" I said. I wanted an assignment too.

"You get back to the bus," Alex said. "You're supposed to be helping Madeleine sell clothes to take her mind off David. Be her best friend, would you?"

He was right. I should be a better friend to her instead of running all over, trying to play tough little sleuth.

I nodded and headed for the bus.

"You abandoned me to gamble." Madeleine sounded both hurt and furious. I couldn't blame her. I'd left her with the whole responsibility for our business.

"Sorry."

"Do I need to send you to Gamblers Anonymous tomorrow?"

"I'll be fine. I think I've had my fill of gambling for a while."

She looked at me for a long time, and I wondered if she suspected I was keeping something from her. I didn't have a good lie made up for this occasion.

"I'll do better," I said. "No more casinos."

"Good. Then we'll go to the flea market on the coast tomorrow like I suggested originally. We didn't do too much business here. These ladies are into collecting quarters in cups, not making fashion statements with their apparel. Did you see how most of them dressed?"

I shook my head. I hadn't noticed.

"See that woman leaving? The one with that tall, skinny guy? That's what I mean. White blouse, mauve slacks with an elastic waist, no pizzazz at all. Maybe we should give fashion makeovers. What to wear for... you know."

Madeleine had a good idea but I wasn't listening

because I was concentrating on the woman and man she'd pointed out. In the dim light it was hard to see the woman's face, but the salt and pepper curls certainly belonged to Mrs. Warren, the mother of the boy David had shot. And the man whose hand she was holding? Maybe he was her pipe smoker.

LATER THAT NIGHT, after Madeleine and I had parked the motor coach in our slot at the local flea market and I'd denied Alex a sleepover because I was too knackered to be friendly, the phone rang. It was Grandy, and I immediately felt guilty. I hadn't talked to her in several days. I started to apologize, but she interrupted me.

"I know you're busy, love. And it's okay. You don't have to check in with me, unless you've been up to something I might like to know about, something like a murder, maybe." She laughed. "How many killings can one sassy gal stumble into?"

How many indeed. So far I counted three over the year since I'd moved to Sabal Bay.

Her tone turned serious. "You *have* been keeping something from me, haven't you?"

I gulped. There were so many things. Where did I start?

She kept on, "Do I have to hear about your business becoming fodder for a local barbeque from Mr. Napolitani? I like the man, don't get me wrong, and I can even ignore his, uh, choice of professions, but you are my granddaughter."

I began apologizing again, and again she stopped me.

"I know most of it. The rest can wait. I'm coming up there tomorrow to help you out. Max is doing an overhaul of our cantankerous engine again, and I'm no help to him, so I've got free time. See you around eight."

She hung up.

That was my Grandy. Always on top of things, even when I didn't want her to be. She'd heard the story about the fire from Nappi? How close were those two, anyway? It sounded like they talked more often than she and I did.

I set my alarm for seven, enough time for me to shower, make coffee, and choose an appropriate wardrobe for the first day of selling on the coast. I hoped the flea market there was a bit more sophisticated than our local casino. We were losing money and needed to regain lost ground fast. I made a mental note to check our inventory. One of us should visit our ladies in West Palm to see if they had any goodies for our shop. Maybe I'd drive the bus down there on Monday evening after I made a few calls. It couldn't hurt to show off our traveling shop to the wealthy matrons of the coast. But I couldn't turn off my brain. The image of Sammy lying somewhere, hurt or dead, kept me awake until the early hours of the morning.

THE ALARM MUST have gone off and I ignored it, because the next thing I knew Grandy was hovering over my bed. Lucky for me she was hovering with a cup of hot coffee in her hand.

"Eve, wake up. Madeleine's here with the bus. We need to hit the road. It'll take us a good forty-five minutes to get to Stuart and then a few more to set up."

I scrambled out of bed, gave Grandy a hug, and jumped into the shower.

When we walked out of the house, I saw Madeleine

sitting in the driver's seat. I visualized the narrow road that led to Stuart and groaned. I could see the headlines now: "Local Business Women Found Dead in Wrecked Motor Home. Cause of Death Thought to Be Designer Clothes Obstructing Driver's Vision."

"I'll drive." I grabbed Madeleine's arm and pulled her out of the seat. "You drove home last night."

"And we made it home safely, didn't we?" she said.

I adjusted the seat and the mirrors while Madeleine stood there, giving me her Madeleine-isn't-happy look. I ignored her and backed out of the drive.

"She's a bully…a tall bully." Madeleine did that flouncing away thing that short girls are so good at, and she curled her bottom lip like a six-year-old.

"It's no good pouting, my dear," Grandy said. "Eve is immune to the needs of others when she wants her way."

Was Grandy taking my side or criticizing me? Ah, well. I was driving.

The flea market in Stuart had been in operation for so many years that folks in the area treated it like any other mall, only with limited hours. Many of the stores were housed in permanent booths in several long buildings on the property. Most of these sold merchandise that was new, while those with used items were set up in less permanent structures, open on either side with only a roof overhead. Behind all these vendors were others featuring used merchandise sold from the backs of utility trailers, vans, cars, trailers, or from under canopies erected for the day. We found our assigned slot in the back, near the parking area. I pulled in between two occupied spaces; one held a canopy, the other a minivan.

"I'm glad you're the one navigating this narrow space," said Madeleine. I interpreted that as an apology for her earlier mulish behavior.

Grandy whispered in my ear, "Maybe you should apologize to Madeleine now."

"For what?" But I did direct a smile in Madeleine's direction. Grandy just shook her head at me.

By nine thirty we were doing a brisk business, which continued until two in the afternoon, when our trade dropped off to nothing. The market stayed open until three, but we closed an hour early. The three of us talked about the fire.

Madeleine brought up the murder. "Eve thinks the murder and the fire are connected."

Grandy looked curious.

"I think the Reeds set up David for the murder, and I think Elvira Reed is harassing us as another means of making David's life miserable." I was about to tell Grandy about Sammy's nephew and Sammy's disappearance, but I decided Madeleine had enough to worry about and shouldn't know about Sammy right now.

"What's their motive?" asked Grandy.

"To put David out of the hunting business so Reed won't have any competition," Madeleine replied.

"And Elvira just wanted to join in on the fun," I added.

Grandy thought this over for a minute, then nodded. "The Reeds make a poisonous pair, don't they?"

My opportunity to talk about Bernard and Sammy came when Madeleine wandered off to see what the petite shop in Building G had to offer. I could tell Grandy wanted to go with her, but I turned my back on Madeleine and mouthed a "no" for Grandy's eyes only.

Once Madeleine was out of sight, I told Grandy about Bernard and Sammy, and David's business card in Bernard's abandoned car.

"I think there's some kind of a connection, or why else would someone want to implicate David in Bernard's disappearance?" I said.

Grandy nodded in agreement.

"There's something else," I said. "Alex and I thought perhaps the father of the boy David shot in the home invasion might have a motive to set up David."

"That happened, what, over two years ago. Isn't that revenge served up icy cold?"

"Losing a child. That has to set hard for a parent. But we found out the father is dead. Or so his wife says. Killed in Afghanistan."

"Something tells me you don't believe that story."

"Alex is checking it out, but I saw her last night with some guy. She'd told us she was alone."

"It could have been just a date."

"They looked too comfortable and too fond of each other. He's in her life. I don't get why she would lie to us about him."

"It seems to me you should keep your eye on what concerns you most." Grandy always got right to the nitty-gritty.

"Like what?"

"Let Alex find out more about Mrs. Warren and the cops follow up on Bernard and Sammy. This Reed couple…the murder and the fire in your store are both too close to them to be a coincidence. I'd sure like to know more about them. And their ranch."

I was worried about Sammy, but there wasn't much I

could do to find him. I'd leave that to Frida. Grandy was right. We needed more information about the Reeds.

"Someone needs to snoop around their ranch," Grandy said, "and I don't mean in the dead of night. I mean *legitimate* snooping." Then she laughed. I did too. We were thinking the same thing. Mr. Napolitani might like to spend the day hunting.

"He's done so much for us already. I hate to ask him for another favor," I said.

But I didn't have to ask. Out of the crowd of people milling around the aisle in front of our bus emerged a man in dove gray slacks and a light yellow knit shirt. His black hair was smoothed back except for a solitary lock that the afternoon breeze lifted and flipped onto his broad forehead, giving him a rakish look. His dark good looks caught the attention of several women, who turned to look as he passed by. He stopped in front of our rig, kissed Grandy's hand and then mine.

"What a beautiful day for the market." He gestured at the cloudless blue sky. "I trust the day has been profitable? Is there anything I can do to make it even better for you?"

Yes, there was.

THIRTEEN

GRANDY AND I were excited that we had a plan to scope out the Reed's ranch. Madeleine, less so. It wasn't that she didn't like Mr. Napolitani, but she, like our detective friend Frida, worried about ethics and legality, issues that Nappi rarely thought about except in his own terms, meaning Family terms. And I do mean capital F, as in Mob. I knew Alex wouldn't be happy about Nappi's involvement either, but Grandy was right. We needed to go to the source of all this—Blake Reed and his nasty wife, Elvira.

As we locked up the bus for the night in our flea market parking slot in Sabal Bay, I noticed someone in the shadows near the last building. Nappi had followed us back in his black SUV.

I tapped his shoulder as he drove us out of the parking lot. "I saw someone back there."

He smiled. "One of my men. Like you, I assume the fire in your former store was arson, and the intention of the fire bug was to destroy your inventory. Now that it's safely in its new home, I don't want anyone trying again. My man has been here since Thursday and will remain in place."

A funny tingle ran up my spine. "It isn't Jerry, is it? I hate to be negative, but he'll just fall asleep and let an arsonist rob us blind before he makes toast of both Jerry and our rig."

Nappi sighed and gave me a parental look. "You really must get beyond this negativity about Jerry. It's not good for your sense of well-being, my dear."

"Jerry isn't good for anyone's sense of well-being." I realized I was being ungrateful. "I'll try to be more Zen about him. Sorry."

"I like that." Nappi reached over and patted my hand.

AROUND MY KITCHEN TABLE, the four of us—Madeleine, Grandy, Nappi and I—planned our strategy.

"I wish I could be in on this visit." I hated inactivity. Thinking was good, but action was more rewarding—well, most times, anyway. Maybe I could have some fun of my own, though. My earlier thoughts of Jerry reminded me of what he'd said about the grandmas who ran a private poker game, the one in which he'd lost his car by underestimating the power of postmenopausal savvy. Maybe they knew of other games run off the casino grounds.

I began to hum under my breath. I felt a whole lot better today than I had last night. Things were moving ahead.

Grandy turned a skeptical eye on me. "Why are you making that sound, Eve? You sound like the cat that swallowed a canary then tried to purr with it halfway down. You've got something up your sleeve."

"Sorry. Nope, just thinking that having Nappi check out the Reed ranch is such a good beginning."

"I don't like it," Madeleine said.

"Why not?" I asked.

"Something always goes wrong with plans that you

have a hand in, that's why." Madeleine got up from the table and poured herself another cup of coffee.

"I am wounded to the core that you should feel that way," I said.

Nappi walked over to her. "Nothing will go wrong. I'm not pretending to be anyone I'm not. I'm just a mob boss who needs some recreational hunting. No lies. No chance of anyone finding out about my ties to you or Eve or David. Don't worry, little one."

Madeleine still looked doubtful, so I thought I'd joke her out of her worries.

"Now, if you were in on this caper, then we'd worry. With your clumsiness, who knows who might get hurt?"

Madeleine turned on me, eyes snapping with anger. It was the wrong thing to say—a case of mouth engagement without brain involvement, typical Eve thoughtlessness.

"I am wounded to the core that you should feel that way." She'd used my exact words.

"Okay, now we're even." I waited for her anger to pass. It did. It always did between us. Nothing, but nothing could sever our bond. Unless it was something like keeping information from her—the detail about David's card in Bernard's car, for instance. I'd have to tell her sometime. Soon. After Nappi visited the Reed place.

"When are you going?" I asked Nappi.

"Tomorrow or the next day."

I looked at my watch. It was after eight. I still had the entire evening ahead to do what I needed to do. But first I had to get rid of the three musketeers. A knock on my door was followed by the appearance of

Alex, bearing a pizza and a six pack of beer. Now I not only had to get rid of the three musketeers, but also D'Artagnan. And there were so many secrets spinning around in my head that I was getting dizzy trying to keep them all straight with respect to who knew what and who couldn't be told more.

"I'm really not in the mood for pizza. I'm going out to get some fried fowl. Back in a jiff." Grabbing my purse and jacket, I fled before anyone could ask me any questions, like why I suddenly had a taste for a food I'd always hated.

I had just enough time to get back to the motor coach to ask Jerry about the ladies who'd taken his car off him, but not enough to go to the casino to locate them tonight. Unless I snuck out of the house later. Could I lie to Alex yet another night and tell him I didn't want him to stay over when I really did want him in my bed but only if he could wait until I in-terrogated some white-haired con artists? I certainly couldn't take him with me. He wanted me to stay out of this murder investigation/possible abduction more than he wanted me naked between the sheets. Well, he couldn't have it both ways. Frida had enough work to do, enough clues to pursue in Bernard and Sammy's disappearances. Certainly, as a friend, I should help her where I could. And Alex was working on the case for David. Everyone was so busy. Superhero Eve to the rescue. Besides, it was only a talk with some little old ladies. What harm would that do?

I drove past our old shop. It was silly, I know, but I wanted to see it again. There wasn't much to see, only rubble where a strip mall once stood. It looked as if all the charred timbers and twisted debris had been cleared. It wasn't ours any longer, but it also wasn't Elvira Reed's, and that gave me a moment's satisfaction…until I noticed a sign that had been erected in front of the leveled strip mall.

It read, "Reed Construction Company. Coming Soon, Elvira's Nostalgia Closet: The Finest in Vintage and Secondhand Designer Wear."

Oh crap.

What else could go wrong?

I found out when I got to the flea market. There was no Jerry, but worse, there was no bus.

"WHAT DO YOU MEAN, 'The bus is gone'? Where did Jerry put it, I wonder." Nappi's voice on the other end of phone sounded calm enough. It was optimistic of Nappi to put such a positive spin on its disappearance. It was possible Jerry had driven it to a safer place. I hoped. Did Jerry even know how to drive one of those giant things?

"Wait there." Nappi disconnected.

My cell rang. Caller ID said it was Alex, and he didn't sound nearly as sanguine as Nappi. "Where the hell are you, and what have you done now, Eve?"

"The bus is gone, and I didn't take it. This is all Jerry's fault. He's driven off with our store. I knew this would happen." I remembered my earlier vow to be more Zen about Jerry, but then traded serenity for the more satisfying promise that I'd kill Jerry when I found him.

I should have guessed that Nappi would arrive with everyone in tow—Madeleine, Grandy, and Alex. We searched the flea market grounds, but found no bus, no Jerry. As we stood talking, my attention was caught by a lone figure walking toward us from the other side of the parking lot.

"Jerry, what have you done with our shop?" I strode toward him, fists clenched at my sides.

"Don't hit me."

"I have no intention of hitting you. Nappi, hand me your gun. I want to shoot him."

I held out my hand.

"No, I think since he's my employee, I should shoot him." Nappi reached into his jacket as if pulling a gun from a shoulder holster.

Jerry began to shake and his face turned some color I could only describe as a mauvy, pukey green.

"Let me at him first," Alex said.

"My pal." Jerry held out his hand to Alex.

Alex grabbed him by his collar and pulled him into his chest. "If you've permanently misplaced my girl-friend and her best friend's means of making a living, I'll turn you into a eunuch."

Jerry gulped. Madeleine and Grandy shot death ray looks at him.

"Listen, guys. Calm down. We can get it back, I'm sure." Jerry's certainty was offset by the squeak in his voice.

"Get it back from where?" I asked.

"It's really simple. I noticed one of the tires was going flat, and since I knew you'd need it tomorrow early, I decided to take it to that all night gas station at the corner of Highways 98 and 441 and air it up. Well, I did that, but I was worried it might have a nail in it, so I drove it down the road to see if it held."

The whole ugly evening began to unfold in my

mind. "So you took it down the road, as in down the road to the casino. Right?"

Jerry nodded. "And when I got there, who should I run into but those ladies I told you about, the ones who won the car off me. They were driving the car, and I thought, this is perfect, I can get the car back off them because I know how they play now and I'm wise to their 'tells' when they're betting. So I invited them into the motor home and we had a little game, right there."

"Let me guess. You bet the motor home and lost it too. You idiot." I didn't want to believe Jerry was that dumb, but he was.

"Yeah, but here's the good part. They dropped me off and said they'd be interested in another round of poker if I could find someone to stake me. And here you guys are. I really know how they play now. I can win. I'm certain."

Nappi appeared calm. His only "tell" was a muscle in his temple that seemed to twitch in bursts of three, followed by moments of no movement. "So where are you supposed to meet them?"

"They should be by here in a few minutes. You'll stake me for more Texas hold 'em, then?"

I wanted to stake him to a post and then build a fire under him, but I could tell Nappi had a plan that necessitated keeping Jerry alive. That Nappi. What a generous guy.

"Introduce me as your uncle and tell them I want in on the action." If anyone could gamble his way to motor home repossession, it was Nappi, but he looked too smooth, too sophisticated. No Sabal Bay grannies would want him in on the game.

Grandy seemed to be thinking as I was. "That won't

work. Tell them *I* want in on the game. They won't be able to turn down one of their own."

"You a good player?" asked Nappi.

"Watch me." Grandy's grin was reassuring. I racked my brain to remember if I'd ever heard of her playing poker. Ah, well. My Grandy didn't lie about what she could do. I wasn't worried. Maybe a little worried.

"Okay, here they come. Pull your car around back, Eve. Everybody but Grandy hide." Jerry waved us behind the buildings.

The rig pulled up next to the black SUV. I was impressed. Whoever was driving had maneuvered it well. They stopped and opened the door on the passenger's side.

Jerry introduced Grandy as his grandmother.

"Get in," said one of the women.

"I thought we'd play here," Jerry said.

"Nope. We'll go to my place. Too tight in this buggy with all these clothes and things. You can leave your car, lady. We'll bring you back here after the game."

Another voice could be heard from the back of the rig. "I hope your grandma here can offer us more of a challenge than you, sonny. I'm beginning to feel guilty about taking all these vehicles off you. Soon we'll have to set up a used car lot."

"Poker's a lot like gin rummy, right?" I heard Grandy say. Suddenly I wondered what we'd set her up for. Did she really know nothing about poker?

Laugher erupted from the women inside.

Grandy and Jerry entered the bus, the door closed, and they rumbled down the gravel road and turned south onto the highway.

Everyone looked nervous except for Nappi, who

seemed amused by the thought of my Grandy taking on the geriatric gamblers of Sabal Bay.

WE WAITED FOR over two hours. The others had it over me. They had eaten the pizza while I had nothing. My stomach growled.

"You didn't get your chicken, did you? And now nothing is open in this town." Madeleine strode around the parking lot, her arms tucked into her waistband to keep warm.

"The chicken run was a lie, wasn't it?" Alex said. "You were up to something, going to see someone. Who?" He took my arm and turned me to face him. Nappi leaned on his car and watched us.

I wanted to look up at Alex with innocence written across my face, but I knew that was no good. I was bad at that pose and he knew it. I might as well tell him the truth…or something like it.

"I thought I might run out to Sammy's and talk with Grandfather Egret, see if he heard anything from Sammy. Or maybe Bernard." Well, that was close to the truth. The airboat business was on the way to the casino. I could have stopped there if I wanted to.

"And you couldn't do that by calling him to see how he was?"

"Friends don't just use the most convenient means to let others know how they feel. Friends go out of their way for friends."

"We could have come with you. We like the Egret family. We were concerned too, you know."

"You may like Grandfather Egret, but you have no use for Sammy." I had him on the defensive now. Just where I wanted him.

"I like Sammy fine. I just don't trust the two of you together."

"Oh, like we'd get it on out in the swamp that night we were dumped there. Is that what you mean?"

"What he means is, he wonders what you and Sammy were doing together in Orlando the night the store burned." Madeleine had walked up and overheard our conversation.

"So you told him about that? You couldn't just keep your mouth shut? Madeleine Boudreau, you are a poor excuse for a friend."

"And you, Eve Appel, are just as bad. Why didn't you tell me about David's business card in Bernard's car?"

"Because I was trying to spare you. You had enough on your mind." I stood toe to toe with Madeleine. Alex was at her side, facing me. "How did you find out?"

"David told me. Obviously he thinks I'm adult enough to handle these things. And I know that Sammy's missing too." She and I continued to stare at each other, neither of us blinking.

Finally, Alex broke the silence, cutting through the tension. "Let's put this all behind us. Eve has confessed to what she was up to tonight. Let's just drop everything else. For now."

Madeleine reached out to touch me. "I know you were just trying to do the right thing for me."

Alex gave me an awkward pat on the shoulder. "And I know you and Sammy are only friends."

I let out my breath in a loud whoosh, unaware until now that I had been holding it. We all continued walking around the parking area, waiting for the rig to return, or for my cell to ring, letting us know the rig was lost.

As I walked past Nappi, he grinned at me.

"What's so funny?"

"Your friends think you're finally telling the truth. They both love you so much they can't see what's right in front of them."

"And that is?"

"You are a prisoner of your own snoopy nature. I don't know what you were up to tonight, but I know it had something to do with either the murder or Bernard and Sammy's disappearances. You hate seeing others in action while you sit on the sidelines. That's going to get you seriously hurt or worse one day."

He was right, of course. "There must be some way I could come with you to the ranch. I could wear a disguise and—"

"And if you were discovered, what do you think would happen?"

"If the Reeds aren't involved, we'd get thrown off the ranch."

"And if they are as bad as you think?"

"We'd be killed?"

My cell rang.

"Jerry?"

"No, it's Frida. I hope I'm not calling too late, but I thought you'd like to know that we got the report on the store back from the fire marshals. It was arson."

"I'm not surprised. Are you going to arrest Elvira Reed?"

"I've got as much reason to view you as a suspect as I do her."

"Me? Why would I set the store on fire?"

"Elvira was competition. You got your merchandise out of the shop then you torched it so she couldn't move in."

"I was with Sammy in Orlando."

"So you say, but he isn't around to serve as your alibi, is he?"

In the favorite words of Eve Appel: oh, crap.

"And another thing…while I have you on the line. What are you, Madeleine, Alex, and your mob friend doing wandering around the flea market at this time of night?"

Double oh crap.

FOURTEEN

"How do you know where we are?" I asked.

I heard the sound of a horn near the street. Frida's cruiser sat near the entrance to the flea market. The headlights came on, and the car pulled down the road and stopped near us.

"To answer your question, Eve, one of our cruisers came by here a few minutes ago on his nightly rounds." Frida got out of her car and looked around the area. "Say, shouldn't your motor home be parked here?"

"Nice detective work, Detective." My tone might have been flip, but inwardly I groaned in despair. Now we'd have to explain to Frida about Jerry and the gambling grannies.

Before I could open my mouth and put forth my version of the night, the motor home pulled into the flea market entrance and started up the road, then stopped with a screech of the brakes. Through the windshield I could see the white-haired woman at the wheel turn her head to talk to someone in the back of the rig.

"I'll bet the grannies aren't too happy to see the cop car," I said.

"Who?" asked Frida.

The rig started up again and maneuvered into its parking slot. The door opened, and Jerry got out, followed by Grandy. I expected to see the rig back out in a hurry and speed away. It didn't.

"Where is everybody?" I asked.

"That's the first thing you say. Not 'Thanks for winning back our shop'? Where are your manners, girl?" Grandy may have sounded angry, but I caught the twinkle in her eye, and knew she was just ribbing me.

Madeleine clapped her hands together. "You got it back. Hooray!"

Nappi and Alex each gave Grandy a hug.

"What were you doing while she was saving your bacon, ya dumbass?" I said to Jerry.

"Now, don't bother the boy, Eve. He makes a mean Cosmo and a tasty platter of nachos." Grandy rubbed her stomach and licked her lips.

Nachos. I could just drool.

"Everybody hop in, and I'll chauffeur you where you need to go." Nappi gestured toward his SUV.

"Wait just a damn minute." Frida rarely swore. I knew she was steamed at getting no explanation for what had transpired tonight.

"Oh, for heaven's sake, Frida. Lighten up. Grandy and Jerry were taking the rig out for a spin with some friends, followed by an evening of cards." *I am so quick on my feet with the lies*. Nappi lifted his eyebrows in surprise.

"And everyone else thought it would be fun to stand around the deserted flea market?" Frida tapped her foot and looked skeptical.

"We were meeting them here. Now we're off for coffee. Care to join us?" Madeleine asked.

Frida merely shook her head, got back in her car, and drove off without a word.

What a team we were—the three musketeers, D'Artagnan, and me. Oh, and dumbass too.

Madeleine sat in the front seat between Nappi and Alex while Jerry sat in the back between Grandy and me. I whispered in Jerry's ear, "Do you remember how to get to the house where the grannies played poker tonight?"

"Oh, sure. What do you need?"

"I need to talk to them. They seem to know their way around the off-casino gambling games, and I'd like to pick their brains."

"They won't tell an outsider about those games." Jerry sounded skeptical, and the expression on his face indicated he was smug about knowing something I needed to know.

"They will if I threaten to sic Frida on them," I said.

"What are the two of you whispering about back there?" Alex turned around in his seat and shot me a cautionary look.

"Nothing much. I was just asking him for his recipe for nachos. I'm starved, and I think I have all the ingredients at home to make some." I gave him an innocent grin.

The headlights in the car approaching us lit up Grandy's face. *Grandy knows you're lying*, it said.

"What do I get out of this if I help you?" Jerry asked, leaning into me and waggling his eyebrows suggestively.

"Not what you think. Now shove over, will you?" I jabbed him with my elbow.

"What then?" he insisted.

"Money to gamble with. How's that?" I hated myself. I was going to pay for information by giving a gambler money to feed his addiction.

"Eve." Alex turned in his seat again.

"Garlic, you say? In nachos? You gotta be kidding me." I slugged Jerry in the arm so hard, he slid into Grandy, knocking her into the door.

"Stay out of my space, will you?" she warned him.

BACK AT MY PLACE, I found that garlic in nachos is quite good, but seems to discourage late night romance. Alex slept in my bed but didn't seem very interested in kissing me good night. Or in any follow-up either. I drifted into garlic-infused salsa and chips dreamland.

THE NEXT DAY Nappi called me on his way to the Reed ranch. "I'm turning into the drive now. I'll be in touch later."

"Come to the house. We'll be back from the flea market on the coast by five. Better yet, you've got my cell so you can give us updates." Again, I wished I could be with Nappi. Maybe Madeleine was right. I did find chasing down killers more exciting than selling fashionable used clothing.

"I'll call you later." Nappi disconnected with a chuckle. He knew what I was thinking.

I'd been driving the motor home down the 714 highway. When I got off the phone, I checked my rearview mirror and caught sight of Madeleine and Grandy in the seats behind me. Both of them had similar expressions on their faces, happy that I wasn't with Nappi on the caper at the Reed's ranch and scared that I might be cooking up some other equally dangerous adventure for myself.

"You can wipe those looks off your faces. I'm here and will be the entire day. What trouble can I get into selling clothes?"

They had to know how I struggled with being left behind when there was some exciting sleuthing to do. I had my own plan to set in motion once we got back from the coast, but they didn't need to know about it. Besides, I told myself, talking to a bunch of gambling grannies about what they knew of poker games privately held was hardly the stuff of danger. Was it? I shook my head no in answer to my own question and took another sneaky peek in the rearview mirror. Madeleine was out of her seat and looking through our merchandise, but Grandy was still giving me that I-don't-trust-you look. Or maybe it was her I-want-to-be-in-on-whatever-you're-doing look. I mean, I got my nosiness from someone, didn't I?

"What?" I said.

I slipped the motor home in between our two neighbors at the flea market, and we set up shop for the day. Trade was brisk because it was the perfect day for shopping outside. A cool on-shore breeze blew in from the ocean, lifting the heat and humidity and making it a perfect seventy-two degrees—just the right temperature for trying on cocktail dresses, slacks, and shirts without breaking a sweat.

"Maybe we don't really need a permanent location," I said to Madeleine. "This is working out really well."

As if to deny the truth of my words, the breeze quickened, blowing in some dark and ominous looking clouds from off shore. By noon, the skies threatened rain. Lightning flashed between the clouds, and the wind whipped the palm trees around, fronds flying to the ground. The flea market patrons headed to their cars, abandoning their Sunday shopping and heading for the safety and sheltered interiors of the local mall. So much for our sales today.

We buttoned up the rig and headed back to Sabal Bay.

"Half a day of sales won't keep us in business," Madeleine said as she added up our receipts while I drove the canopy road home. In good weather the oaks and palms hung over the road, making a tunnel of shadows broken by shafts of sunlight. I usually loved this stretch of highway more than any other in Southern Florida, but today I gripped the wheel with white-knuckled hands to keep the big rig on the narrow road. There was no shoulder, and if the wind blew us off, we'd collide with a tree or plunge into the watery ditch on the side. I made it to the Beeline Highway and turned right toward Sabal Bay, breathing a sigh of relief that if pushed off this stretch of road, I at least had a broad shoulder before the motor home headed off into the weeds.

With my attention less focused on the road, I had time to consider Madeleine's remark about our low sales.

"There's the annual ranchers' rodeo coming up next weekend. We ought to consider some kind of a special sale for that," I said.

"Here's an idea," said Grandy. "You get as many items of Western wear as you can and have a round-up sale of rodeo duds."

"Hey, great idea. Our clients from West Palm will be sure to come to the rodeo. We can offer them outfits to fit right in." I signaled left and turned into our local flea market parking slot.

"It means we'll have to make a trip to the coast again

to see if we can collect some Western shirts, jeans, and boots," Madeleine said. "I can do that tomorrow, Eve, if you've got something else you want to do."

I whipped my head around to look at her. Was she reading my mind? And condoning whatever plan I was hatching to snoop into the grannies' gambling information? But she returned my look of suspicion with one of innocence.

"It will take my mind off David. You can come along too, if you want, Eve."

"Do you need me to drive?" I asked.

"I'll take my car. No sense in using all the gas the motor home requires. We haven't developed a schedule for the week, yet. Maybe we should sell here on Mondays and take a few other weekdays to visit West Palm, then do Friday and the weekend in Stuart."

"The only reason we didn't do well today was because of the weather, but I think the flea market in Stuart will prove to be a great place to sell." I turned off the engine.

Grandy left her seat and came forward. "I wouldn't mind helping out here tomorrow. I can sell. You have something you need to do, Eve?"

"Uh…"

I was saved from answering the question by my cell ringing. I looked at the caller ID. "It's Nappi."

"I'm back and I have very little to report. Except for a visit to the Reeds by the county sheriff."

"Where are you?" I asked.

"I'm just turning into your drive."

"We'll be there in five minutes."

Nappi made himself comfortable on my couch, and as he relaxed and sipped a Scotch, recounted his day at the Reeds' ranch. "Reed and his foreman took me around the ranch and showed me some of their hunting area. I shot a few quail, but indicated I found the birds boring game. 'How about something more challenging?' I asked. He offered wild boar. I yawned and said I could get that at any game ranch, 'even next door at the Wilson place.' That got him going, and he indicated he was getting some exotics in a few days, hinted at Cape Buffalo."

"Did you bite?" I asked. Alex and Jerry had joined Madeleine, Grandy, and me to listen to Nappi's story.

"You're not going to have much chance to snoop around," Alex said.

"This may take more than a few visits, but I think the man did some checking on me and knows my line of work. If he's doing something illegal at his ranch, I'm just the kind of client he'd be interested in sharing it with. I'm going back there when he calls. I promised to bring some friends." Nappi finished his Scotch, and I jumped up and poured him another.

"You said something about the sheriff paying a visit." I handed him the glass.

"Sheriff Leopold, I believe his name was. He showed up with a few of his deputies, and your friend Frida and her partner Linc Tooney accompanied them. Leopold was inquiring after some Guatemalan workers who had disappeared recently. They were working at one of the dairies around here, but told their families they were leaving to work on one of the hunting ranches. They'd not been heard from since then. I guess Leopold thought questioning Reed was a waste of time, but Frida didn't. Leopold and Reed both told her that the Guatemalans often left jobs and then dropped out of sight, but Frida seemed to think these guys were different because they had families here. Reed indicated that he hadn't hired any Indians lately, and his foreman backed him on that. Frida seemed skeptical of his story. Why was that, do you think?" Nappi crunched on a bit of ice.

"Frida says the Guatemalans who have worked there weren't happy with the work conditions. Not that they complained, according to her, but the grapevine reported that Reed was a horrible boss." I got up and checked the salmon fillet baking in the oven.

"Did the sheriff do any kind of search?" asked Alex.

"Nope. In fact, he and Reed went off a ways and seemed to be having a good laugh about everything." Nappi's smile was twisted. "Then Leopold came back and told Frida she should let it go. He called her 'little lady.'"

Grandy lifted her eyebrows in surprise. "That didn't go over well with Frida, did it?"

Nappi laughed. "No, it did not."

"Did Frida indicate she knew you?"

"She did not. When Leopold called her a 'little lady,' I gave her a wink. She knew what side I was on, so even if she's not one of my fans, she wasn't about to blow my cover."

"I assume we'll hear from her this evening at some point. She'll want to know what you were doing at the ranch." Frida is a good detective, and she was right to pursue the rumor about those missing Guatemalans being employed by Reed.

Hearing a car pull up in front of my house, I smiled. Sure enough, it was Frida. I went to the front door.

"You're just in time. I'm making a baked salmon fillet. Join us."

She looked unhappy and bone weary. "I've got some bad news, I'm afraid."

"You off duty?" I asked.

"For the night, but I've got to go back in early tomorrow."

I grabbed a glass, plopped in a few ice cubes and a splash of Scotch. I looked at her with a question. "Unless you want iced tea or a coke?"

"Are you kidding? After the day I've had? Keep pouring." She reached out and took the glass.

I gestured to the couch, and she slid into the seat beside Mr. Napolitani and nodded a greeting.

"You said you had some news?" asked Nappi.

"I just came from Sammy Egret's half-brother's place. This won't be something you'll want to hear either, Madeleine." She took another long draft of the Scotch and sighed.

"Bernard Egret's body was found on David Wilson's ranch. He'd been shot in the back."

FIFTEEN

AT FRIDA'S NEWS, Madeleine swayed and her knees buckled. "I think I need to sit down."

Grandy and I ran to her and gathered her into our arms. Alex got out of my big easy chair and helped her into it.

"Water," said Grandy.

"Scotch," said Alex and Nappi.

I ran to my liquor cabinet and poured her a snifter of brandy.

"Thanks, Eve," she said and slugged the contents of the glass down.

The color returned to her face.

"When did he die?" I asked.

"We know David has nothing to do directly with his death. He was in jail when Bernard was shot. The medical examiner said he had an alcohol level of .10, indicating he was pretty drunk, but his blood also held traces of other drugs. We're finding out what they were now. He'd been severely beaten, and he had scratches all over his body. He was dehydrated and hadn't eaten in a while. The bullet came from a high-powered rifle. We confiscated all the rifles at David's ranch and those at Reed's place too."

"Thank God David was in jail when Bernard was killed." I knew it was a horrible thing to say, but Madeleine glanced over at me with a look of gratitude.

Frida finished her Scotch and sat forward on the couch. "Yeah, but you're not going to like what else I have to say."

I sat on the arm of the easy chair and took Madeleine's hand in mine. "Say it."

"One of the rifles at David's ranch had been recently fired. It belonged to Dudley Thomas, his foreman. He claimed there had been no hunting going on at the ranch since David was arrested, but Dudley has a long history of getting into fights in the bars around here. His favorite targets seem to be Indians. I guess he doesn't like them much. We took him into custody and he's being questioned now."

I was surprised Frida wasn't the one doing the questioning.

"Isn't this your case?" I asked.

"It is, but the captain told me to take some time off and let Linc handle the interrogation."

There was something else Frida wasn't telling us, but Alex broke in before I had a chance to ask.

He slapped his hand against the top of the coffee table. "Don't you see what's going on, Frida? This is all too convenient. David's rifle kills his client, but David had stopped hunting because of his hatred of guns. David's card is found in Bernard's car, but he never met Bernard. Now it appears Dudley's rifle might be the weapon used to kill Bernard Egret and on David's ranch. Someone wants David Wilson responsible for all of this and is willing to frame even his foreman for Bernard's murder. Who benefits if his ranch goes under because no one is running it? Blake Reed, that's who." He ran his hands through his thick hair in a gesture of frustration. "I know you can't arrest Reed. You've got no evidence. I also know he's just too smart to get his own hands dirty. Maybe he's using someone else."

"I think you should let me in on what you intend to do, because you've got the look of a man who's about to take action," Frida said.

She shouldn't have worried that Alex would do anything outside the law. The man was careful about that—more careful than I was. He had to be. He could lose his PI license.

"I have to begin somewhere. I'm going back to talk with Mrs. Warren, the mother of the boy David shot breaking into his house several years ago."

"And I'm going with him," I said. "I've got a few questions to ask her. Like is your husband really dead? Who was the guy you were with at the casino? And why did you lie to us about being alone?"

Frida shook her head. "Mr. Warren is dead. I already checked on that. He was working for a utilities contractor in Afghanistan. The Taliban wiped out the unit when they went in to replace an electrical power station north of Kabul. It's a dead end, Alex. She told me you already talked with her. What can another visit do?"

"He's dead, but she's not," I said.

"You think a woman did this?" Frida asked.

"Why not? Her only son was killed. You think she likes the man who's responsible? And maybe she had help." I remembered the tall thin man she held onto the night Sammy disappeared from the casino. "Maybe she had a lot of help. Maybe Reed helped her by paying her. The woman looks like she could use the money."

"You really don't like that man, do you, Eve?" asked Frida.

"You don't either," I said.

Her cell rang. She held up her finger to signal she had to take it. "It's my boss." Frida got off the couch and went into the kitchen. I couldn't hear much of her conversation except for several yeses and nos and then an exclamation of "That's not fair, sir." When she rejoined us in the living room, her face was drawn and white. She held her glass out to me.

"Pour me another of these."

"You'll have a doozy of a hangover tomorrow when you go in," I said.

"I won't be going in tomorrow. I might as well tell you. It's now official. I've been taken off the case. There have been complaints about the way I've been handling the murder investigation on David's ranch and Bernard's disappearance and murder."

"Who complained?" I asked. "I'll bet it was Reed. What right does he have to interfere in police business?"

"No, actually it was Sheriff Leopold. He told the captain I led him on a wild goose chase at Reed's ranch earlier today. He questions my professionalism. I think the captain would like to leave me in place, but we need the cooperation of all the law enforcement agencies on this murder. Since it's clear Leopold doesn't want to work with me, he thought it was better to remove me for now."

"You knew this was brewing when you stopped by, didn't you?" I reached out and gave her arm a pat.

"I suspected it was coming. I know what my captain is doing, and I can't blame him. Leopold doesn't think women belong in law enforcement. I've had difficulty working cases with him before." Frida gave a heavy sigh and straightened her shoulders. "My feel-

ings are not important. What's important is solving
these murders."

Frida was such a dedicated cop. I hoped her boss
knew that about her. Now I had two reasons for wanting these murders to be solved. One was clearing David's name—for Madeleine's sake but also because
David was innocent—and the other was to put Frida
back into her rightful place as the best detective on the
force. Sitting this case out would be hard on her. She,
like me, was an action kind of gal. Of course she had a
legitimate reason to be. She carried a badge, while all
I carried was a half-off Prada bag. There was more. I
worried about Sammy. Where was he? And did anyone from the police care? Frida did. She was the only
one on the force I could trust. How things had changed
since that day only a week ago when David, Madeleine,
Alex, and I were relaxing on board David's boat. Then
Blake Reed came into our lives and spoiled everything.

"I know you want to help, but I don't think having a
cop along when I talk to Mrs. Warren again will make
any difference." It was the next morning, and Alex was
speaking on his cell to Frida as he and I headed back
out to the Deer Mound area to revisit the Warren house.
I had told him about the pipe in the truck parked next
to the Warren house and also about the man I'd seen
with Mrs. Warren—her date or friend or boyfriend or
accomplice—the night Sammy disappeared at the casino. I surprised even myself with how forthcoming I
was being about my suspicions. Usually I kept everything to myself and ran off to follow clues alone like a
hound on the hunt. I did keep to myself my intention
to follow up with the grannies about the off-site poker

games. Somehow Bernard got from gambling to David's ranch and dead, but how and why?

I thought about Sammy often and asked Frida what she had found out from Oscar about his disappearance. She told me Oscar had been released and the Bernard Egret case had been sidelined until he was found murdered. As for Sammy, she said the department saw him as just another Indian off drinking and doing whatever it was Indians do. Sammy was right when he told me no one cared about an Indian disappearing. The authorities had been wrong about Bernard. He was dead. The police seemed to be taking the same nonchalant attitude toward Sammy. Would it take Sammy's death to make them take action?

Although it had been only two days since the night Sammy disappeared, I knew something terrible had happened to him. Sammy wasn't an irresponsible Indian, drunk out of his mind and holing up somewhere until he got sober. I knew better.

We'd lost our most important advocate in Frida. She knew Sammy. And she knew he'd never leave his grandfather with no one to run the business. I had told Nappi about Sammy on Saturday night, and he did the most generous thing: he sent Jerry out to the airboat business to help out Grandfather Egret. Jerry had pitched in before, so he knew how to operate the boat. It was only a temporary measure. It meant Jerry had to guard the motor home at night and work for Grandfather Egret during the day. I managed to hide my smug expression when I heard this. Working both places should keep Jerry out of trouble. It also reminded me that I had to talk with the grannies to see what they knew about other Texas hold 'em games going on in the area.

Today I wanted to help Alex with Mrs. Warren. And then there was my business to run. Yikes, but I had a lot on my mind. Maybe there was help at hand.

I knew Frida wouldn't want to spend her time pushing paper around a desk even though her boss told her explicitly not to follow up on any leads in Bernard's murder. Now how could she help herself? She'd be off doing something she shouldn't. Like me. Maybe the two of us could put our heads together and...

"Eve. I know you're plotting something." Alex gave me his best I'm-a-PI look.

"I am. I mean, I am?"

"Let me be clear about your being here. I think Mrs. Warren found you, um, nonthreatening. I think she might be willing to talk to you rather than me, a man."

"Sure and—"

"And that's the end of it. You chat her up and find out what you can. Then you're out of this. Understood?"

"Sure and—"

"The end of it, hear me?"

"Yup." I smiled my best trusting-girlfriend-Eve smile at him. He scowled back at me.

We parked in front of the Warren house. There was no truck in the drive this time.

"Maybe she's not home today," Alex said.

I saw the curtain in the kitchen window move. "Someone's there."

We knocked and heard footsteps inside. Mrs. Warren opened the door and said, "I've got nothing more to say to you folks. I've had my fill of folks snooping around here, digging up my son's death again. And what for? You never even tried that guy who shot him. Said it was justifiable. He was only a thirteen-year-old kid."

Alex opened his mouth, and I knew he'd want to soft pedal what he had to say, to turn on his PI charm—and he had plenty of it—trying to wheedle information out of her by playing sympathetic. I had a lot of work to do, plans to lay, people to see, sneaky stuff to accomplish before day's end. I couldn't spend my time holding the hand of some woman who might simply be nothing more than a killer and a schemer. *Enough*, I thought and cut to the chase.

"Mrs. Warren, don't waste our time. You know damn well your son was in the wrong. He was carrying a gun himself and threatening a child in her bedroom. What did you expect would happen? The man was protecting his daughter."

At first I thought she was going to slam the door in our faces.

Alex grabbed my arm and pulled me toward him. "Eve."

"I know you've had a hard time of it, losing your son and then your husband, but you can't just let other people lose their lives too."

She hesitated a moment, then opened the door wider. "What can I do to help?"

Gosh, I was even better at this interrogation business than I thought. Who knew my tough love approach would work? I think I was more surprised than Alex. Maybe she just appreciated honesty for once. Her willingness to talk with us either meant she was the best actress and criminal I'd ever met or she wasn't responsible for those two deaths. I chose to believe the latter. I could be wrong, but what did we have to lose? At least we were in and had the opportunity to talk to her. We entered her living room and sat in two straight-backed chairs while she sat on the couch.

Shocking her had worked so far, so I continued in the same vein.

"Do you know Blake Reed?"

Again Alex laid a restraining hand on my arm as if it would prevent me from continuing. I shook it off.

"He's the guy who runs the hunting ranch outside of Sabal Bay," she said.

I nodded. The next question was a real shot in the dark. "You know him. How?"

She looked startled at my question and seemed about to deny any knowledge of Reed, but she sank back into the couch and sighed.

"I worked as his housekeeper for a while."

"When? For how long? And what happened?" Now it was Alex who was asking the questions.

"I was with him for several years. I, uh, left shortly before I got the news that my husband had been killed."

The hesitation in her voice told me she wasn't telling us the whole truth. "Why did you leave? It seems to me you could have used the money then. I mean, with your husband's death and all."

"I couldn't stand working for Mrs. Reed."

Still not quite the truth. I pushed more. "You gave notice then?"

She nodded.

"Don't you mean she fired you?" Another wild guess, but I was on a roll.

Her head came up and she looked at me with fear in her eyes.

"She told you?"

"No, she didn't, but I imagine she threatened you somehow. It seems to be her style. What did she say?"

"She said she'd tell the police I stole money from her."

"And did you steal?" I asked.

"No. I didn't care if she fired me. I would have quit anyway. The woman was impossible. She treated everyone there like dirt. She even shortchanged me on my salary—twenty or thirty dollars every week—and I was getting sick of it."

"So you're not working now?" Alex asked.

She twisted her hands around in her lap and wouldn't make eye contact with him.

"Mrs. Warren?" I said.

"Not officially," she said.

"What's that supposed to mean?" Alex asked.

I guessed the answer. "Under-the-table work."

She nodded. "I do house cleaning and pet sitting for some of the folks out on the highway, folks who live in that over fifty-five retirement community. They pay cash, and word of mouth around the community is enough for them to trust my work."

"Why do you think Mrs. Reed fired you?" I asked.

"I don't really know. She never gave a real reason. Just said my work wasn't good enough."

"But it was fine for almost two years. Doesn't that seem off to you?" It seemed off to me.

"The ranch was growing—lots more business and more livestock trucks coming in with species I'd never seen before. I was curious so I asked about those animals. She told me it was none of my business. She let me go soon after that."

"Did your husband know you worked there?" Alex asked.

She nodded. "I wrote him several times each week and told him about my work and about how the ranch was expanding. Then I had to tell him I was fired. I think that was the last letter he received before being killed." She wiped a tear off her cheek with the back of her hand. "His company settled a small death benefit on me. I invested the money. Really, I work because I have nothing else to do. No husband and no son. I get lonely. I got too much time on my hands and too many bad memories."

I heard a truck pull up and the front gate open. When I looked out the window I saw a man drive the truck through and then get out to close the gate. He was the tall, skinny dude from the casino. He walked toward the house, a pipe stuck in his mouth. Just before he got to the front door, he stuck it in his pocket.

Mrs. Warren greeted him with kiss a on his cheek. "Some people here talking about the Reeds."

"Those no good bums!" he said. "I told her she was better off not being around them. I think they're up to some funny business."

"My name's Alex Montgomery and this is my assistant, Eve Appel. And you are?" Alex arose from his seat and crossed the room to shake hands.

"Moses Ermlich. Mrs. Warren, Maimie, is my friend."

"And you know of the Reeds, how?" asked Alex.

"I was his ranch foreman until he tossed me out because he hired another guy, the one who's still there now."

"Where do you work? Another hunting reserve?"

"Nope. Reed gave me a lousy recommendation. And for no reason. I'm just as glad of it because I got a job as a janitor at the casino. I'm treated better there, and I got benefits too. I'm through with hunting reserves. Working for Reed left a bad taste in my mouth. The man treated his workers like slaves, especially the Indians and Guatemalans."

"Did you ever report him?" asked Alex.

He gave a bitter laugh. "After I left, one of the workers who was a friend of mine said he was going to the cops because of the beating the foreman gave one of the workers. Poor guy could hardly continue his work. This was after I had left the ranch. The next day my friend called me and warned me not to say a thing about Reed. He had his foreman pay my friend a visit. The foreman gave him a beating worse than that the poor Indian suffered. But you didn't hear it from me."

WHEN ALEX AND I left, it was with the promise not to reveal either Mrs. Warren or Mr. Ermlich as sources of information about the Reed ranch. They were not people who were easily frightened, I thought, but the threat of a beating or worse was enough to make them cautious about what they said and to whom.

"Frida was right about that place," Alex said.

"But she's got no real evidence against him, and she's riding a desk right now. And how does any of this figure into the killing of the client and Bernard? I wish I could tap into the Miccosukee rumor mill, but Sammy was my source, and he's gone." I pounded my fist against the car door in anger.

"It's going to take Nappi some time to get Reed to trust him enough to let him in on anything illegal that might be going on at the ranch. And he might discover absolutely nothing. Too bad the cops don't have enough to get a search warrant." Alex paused, then added, "Snooping there would be dangerous. And illegal." He gave me a meaningful look. "There's probably enough firepower in that place to start a small war."

Well, there were warrants, and then there were warrants. As for all the weapons in there, I wasn't foolish enough to try the job myself. Now who did I know who might be willing to do a bit of snooping? I missed Sammy and couldn't stop worrying about him.

SIXTEEN

GOSH, IT WAS great having Alex do detective work here in Sabal Bay instead of someplace where he had to spend the night or entire days away. On the other hand, it was hard to get time to myself, especially when I wanted to do my own detecting. It seemed to me that everyone had a job to do except me.

Today Madeleine was keeping her mind off David's stay in the county jail by contacting our clients for clothes for our rodeo sale. Nappi was busy doing whatever a mob don did as well as awaiting the phone call from the Reed ranch inviting him back there for a unique hunting experience and hopefully some snooping. Grandy had opened the motor home consignment and intended to sell at the Sabal Bay flea market for the day, and Alex said he'd been working on David's case later in the afternoon. He didn't supply details, so he was intentionally keeping me in the dark. He thought that would keep me out of his business and out of danger. Did he really know so little about me?

I wanted to contact Jerry and visit the gambling grannies, but first I had to come up with some kind of cover. I was bored, jobless, and at a loss for a good story to justify my absence. The only other person who could have sympathized with my dilemma was Frida, who had to be going out of her mind sitting at a desk and shuffling papers.

Frida. *Hmmm*.... I thought to myself. It was Monday afternoon. Alex and I had just talked with Moses Ermlich and Mrs. Warren, and he'd dropped me at my house with a warning to stay out of trouble. I was sitting around, stewing over my inactivity. I should have gone to the consignment rig to help Grandy, but she could handle that by herself. She really didn't need me getting in her way. Of course, I could have asked her for directions to the grannies' poker games, but she'd either say I was looking for trouble or she'd want to come with me to find that trouble.

After an hour of mulling over my alternatives, I picked up my cell. I should reassure Alex I wasn't doing something sneaky and keep him from worrying. Or from trying to stop me.

"Alex? It's me. I just called Frida and asked her if she had time to drop by the motor home and take a look at some new items we got in. I knew she'd welcome any excuse to get out of the station for a few minutes."

"Fine. Thanks for staying in touch. I'm following up on the stories Ermlich and Mrs. Warren gave us about the Reed ranch. Somebody around here has to be willing to talk about the Reeds. Why don't you see if Frida can stop by the house this evening? I'd like to share with her what we found out and compare stories about the treatment of the workers at the ranch. Do you think she'd be willing to do that?"

"Oh, sure. I mean, I can only ask, but I'll bet she's as interested as we are in those stories."

I ended the call. It was decision time. Did I really call Frida and ask her to the motor home as I'd told Alex I'd already done, or did I leave that for later, after I talked to Jerry at the Egret's airboat business and paid a visit to the geriatric gamblers? I'd call Frida later, I decided.

I had to wait at least a half hour until Jerry came in with a boat of customers he had taken out into the swamps. I spent the time talking with Grandfather Egret, something I always enjoyed, but this time our conversation was tinged with his grief over Bernard's death and his concern for Sammy, who had been missing since Friday night. As worried as he was about Sammy, he seemed positive about the outcome. That surprised me.

"I worry that Sammy found the men Bernard gambled with and got himself into something he won't be able to get out of," I said.

Grandfather tapped his pipe against the side of the tall stool at the airboat business's counter.

"You don't have much confidence in Sammy's ability to get out of tight situations, do you?" He sounded disappointed in me. "He got you out of the swamp in a big storm, and that's no little thing."

He was right, of course. How could I doubt Sammy's skills, intelligence, and cunning? I'd never seen the men who led Bernard astray. Maybe they were just a bunch of college kids who set him up. Or they could have been career criminals.

Grandfather Egret did his usual melding minds maneuver with me. "Even if those men are the baddest of the bad, I've been doing chants for days, and I feel the gods favor us over them."

"Us is who? And them would be...?"

"Us would be our tribe, and them would be whoever Sammy met up with."

"I wish I could be as certain as you."

Grandfather shook his head. "It's such a shame you've learned so little in the time we've been friends. Sammy got you out of the swamp, and I helped you capture a couple of killers. And you still have so little faith in us? Take that sad look off your face. You should try a few chants. It can't hurt. And when he gets back, I'll tell him how you helped. It might be better to sing than what you have planned. Safer, maybe."

"Grandfather, sometimes I wish you couldn't read my mind."

He raised his eyebrows in surprise. "Do I know what you've got planned? No, but you want to talk to Jerry and that means you're desperate enough to do something foolish." He paused. "So are you going to do this thing alone?"

I nodded.

"Then you'd better take this with you." Grandfather took something from his pocket and handed it to me. It was a leather pouch about half the size of a man's wallet. There was a strap attached to it.

"An amulet for protection?" I hung the pouch around my neck with the strap and tucked it into my blouse.

"Is that what you white folks call it? Anyway, here's the airboat and Jerry."

I gave Grandfather a hug, then headed down the path to the airboat landing.

Jerry helped the customers to the dock. Most of them were women dressed expensively enough for me to think they must be matrons from the coast who had heard about the Indian airboat ride. The problem was Jerry was no Indian. I heard several women grumbling that they had been expecting a handsome warrior but got only an old man selling tickets and an airboat pilot who drove the boat erratically and knew little about the swamp.

Jerry looked as if he could use some sleep. He had dark circles under his eyes and a weary expression on his face.

"These women are driving me nuts, Eve. All they do is ask where the Indian is. What do I tell them?"

"Maybe you could darken your skin and wear more Indian-like clothing. Seems to me you used to be pretty good at disguising yourself." I was referring to the time Jerry dressed as a woman to fool the cops. He'd fooled all of us.

"Forget it, Eve. I can't go on like this. It's only been a few days but I can't spend my nights guarding the motor home and my days helping Grandfather Egret in this business. I'm gonna fall asleep at the helm and crash these women into the swamp somewhere."

Oh great, I thought to myself. I gave a sigh deep enough to rupture my appendix. Eve to Jerry's rescue. Again. "I'll give you a hand tonight if you tell me where the grannies' gambling den is."

"I think I could find my way back there, but I don't think I can give you directions."

What choice did I have but to wait until the last airboat ride of the day? My plans were almost trashed by a call from Grandy.

"Eve, dear, I just heard from Max. The boat engine is purring away again so he took on a fishing charter early tomorrow morning. I've got to get back to Key Largo to help."

"I guess I could take over…" I know I sounded reluctant.

"Don't bother, dear. There's been no business all

day, so I can't believe anyone will be wandering in now. And I'm sure you have other things to do."

What did she mean by that?

"Grandy."

I heard her chuckle. "Just stay out of trouble, would you?"

"Thanks for all your help. I'll stay in touch."

"Right. If I don't hear from you by tomorrow afternoon, I'm coming back up here." She disconnected.

Grandfather looked at me and asked, "You need something?"

He knew me almost as well as my Grandy.

I think he was a little disappointed that I only wanted him to guard the shop and not sell anything. He'd pitched in once before and did amazingly well pushing designer fashions to West Palm matrons. If Madeleine and I had the money, we'd give him a permanent position as a sales associate.

When we drove up to the rig, Grandy was just leaving. We hugged goodbye and she drove off.

Grandfather continued to look morose, so I gave in. "Sure, go ahead. Open up again, but I'm telling you there will be no business. Grandy said she got only one or two customers all day."

Grandfather said something in Miccosukee, which I assumed translated into "hot diggity." He opened the door, pulled out a chair and set himself up on the pavement.

"If you don't mind, I'd like to continue with my chanting," he said.

Why would I mind?

Now I could pick up Jerry and drive us toward the casino and the grannies' house. It seemed like a lot of

trouble to me, especially when I had no reason to believe they would know about other games. Or maybe
they did know and wouldn't tell me. Or better yet,
maybe I could promise them another run at Jerry. He
was just enough of an idiot when it came to gambling
that he'd want to try his luck with them yet again. Of
course, he had no money, meaning I'd have to keep my
promise to back him.

"Nope, nope. This isn't right. Wrong way again. Turn
around." Jerry sank back in the passenger's seat of my
car and leaned his head on the headrest.

I reached over and shook him. "Stay awake."

We had been driving around the area adjacent to
Deer Mound, dead ending when the street was cut off
by a canal, then turning around and trying again, only
to find we'd hit another street ending at a small lake
or a patch of swamp.

I peeked at my watch. I was running out of time.
Alex expected me home and would want to know about
the talk I hadn't had with Frida. As usual my plan was
unraveling.

"Okay, let's try this," I said. "I'll go out to the casino and you can try to route your way to their place
from there. That's what you did the first night you
met them."

"Might work." Jerry yawned.

"Grab a short nap. I'll wake you when we get to the
casino. It's about ten minutes from here."

I shouldn't have bothered talking. Jerry was already
asleep, breathing heavily through his nose. The breathing turned into a snore.

As it turned out, I didn't need Jerry. Pulling up behind me as I turned into the casino parking lot was a car filled with four white-haired ladies. I was pretty certain I recognized them from the evening Jerry gambled our motor home away. I got out of my car and rapped on the driver's side car window.

The woman took one look at me and gulped. "Honey, it was a fair game. You got your motor home back and your husband too. That grandmother of yours was a ringer. We should be furious at you."

"First of all, that guy is not my husband, not anymore. And second, Grandy is not a ringer. She was really just lucky and smart. She learns rules really fast—not that she obeys many of them. I'd like to chat with you for a minute. You might have some information I could use."

The driver conferred with her three passengers.

"You buy us all a drink, and we'll be happy to answer any of your questions," she said.

They all piled out of the car. When I saw them the other night in the dim lights of the flea market, I could have sworn they were clones, but in the afternoon light, they were quite distinctive. The driver, whose name was Sara, reminded me of Grandy. She was short, plump, favored the color combination of purple and red, and had short, bouncy white curls. Madeleine would look like that when she was sixty, I thought.

The granny in the passenger's seat was tall and angular, with long white hair pulled back into a bun at the nape of her neck, but she wasn't dowdy looking at all. Her makeup was expertly applied and her warm-up suit was designer quality. Her name was Gilda. She appeared to be the quiet one in the group.

Sissy, whose hair shone a bluish-silver, wore a Western shirt, jeans and cowboy boots. She and the last woman, May Belle, had distinctive Southern accents. May Belle was a blonde with leathery tan skin. She smiled a lot, making it difficult to say whether the wrinkles in her face came from sun exposure or simply happiness.

I left Jerry asleep in the car while all of us trooped into the bar area.

"I'm surprised you're at the casino this early in the day. From what Jerry said, you like hanging out here at night."

"Well, he's right, sugar," said May Belle, "but tonight is spaghetti night. Five dollars for pasta with sauce and two meatballs, small salad, and garlic bread. We like to come early, get in a game or two, then go off to dinner at six. The line forms at around five thirty. It's popular with everyone so the food goes fast. They're usually out of meatballs by seven."

After we ordered our drinks—I stuck to coke, but the ladies each ordered a Cosmo—I got right to my questions. Time was a-wastin', and I would soon be in trouble, my cover blown.

"Tell me about the games that people run off site, like the four of you," I said.

The ladies exchanged looks with one another. I could tell by the way their butts shifted around on the seats that the abruptness of my question made them uneasy.

"Look, I couldn't care less about what you're doing. I'm interested in some other games, and I thought you might know something about them."

Gilda took a sip of her Cosmo, smacked her lips, and said, "We usually play at my house and bring in some of our friends from around here who like a more casual setting. Jerry was somewhat of a fluke. We were glad we asked him to play with us. He wouldn't have had a shred of clothing left on his back if some of these guys got a hold of him. Oh, by the way, we returned the rental car we won off him. We wouldn't keep it. And we kind of suspected that motor home wasn't his to gamble away. Sometimes we get bored and then we like to play jokes on people—fun jokes, not mean stuff. Your husband, or whatever he is, is such a patsy."

"Yeah, I know."

Sissy held up her drink to the light then took a tiny sip. "We know there are guys around here who take their private games very seriously. They would eat your Jerry alive."

"It may be that they ate some friends of mine alive," I said.

The grannies told me about two other games they knew were operating at private locations, but neither of them was run by guys who sounded dangerous— like the types Oscar had mentioned, the ones who'd helped Bernard win and then lose.

"We'll keep our feelers out to see if anything else turns up," said Sissy. "The guys we know who set up games are like us, people looking for another person or two who wants to play some serious poker. They'd never let someone like Jerry into a game and then allow him to bet someone else's property. But Jerry was kind of a fun guy, and he was someone we knew we could beat. The four of us play together so much, it gets to be dull. We know one another's 'tells' and styles. Jerry was a breath of fresh air." She paused, then added, "Say, wasn't he in the car with you just now? He wouldn't be interested in a game later, would he?"

I explained that he would be interested in a game, but that he had no money.

Three young men came into the bar, took a look around and then headed back out. I watched them move toward the room where the Texas hold 'em tournament had been held. One of them turned his head and looked back at me. He said something to his buddies when he caught up with them. They changed their minds again and backtracked toward the entrance.

"Excuse me a minute," I said to the ladies. "I'll be right back."

I started to follow them to the door. They picked up their pace until they were almost running. They were the young men who'd been with Oscar the night Sammy was taken. I knew they weren't the ones who'd grabbed Sammy, and Oscar had told us they weren't the ones who got Bernard into those poker games, but I thought they might know something they hadn't told Frida, and I was anxious to talk with them. She told me Oscar had told the cops nothing. Maybe he didn't know any more than he'd told Sammy and me. He could have at least described the men who ran the poker games in which Bernard lost money, but Frida said he clammed up and acted frightened. I couldn't pass up the opportunity to talk with Oscar's friends. Maybe these guys would give me more than they and Oscar had given the police. It was worth a try.

The three men were through the doors and outside. I was right behind them, but was blocked by a crowd of people who were jammed into the doorway. My quarry managed to thread their way through the crowd, and I lost sight of them.

An ambulance and a sheriff's car had pulled up at the entrance, but curious onlookers blocked my view of what was going on.

"Hey, I thought you were going to back me in a game." Jerry had sidled up behind me. "You owe me, Eve."

I swatted him away like a pesky insect, intent upon seeing what was happening.

He grabbed a hold of my arm and clung to me. "I helped you find the grannies."

"You helped me do nothing. I found them myself." I pried his fingers from my arm and worked my way forward, losing Jerry in the crush of people behind me.

"I think he's dead," said a woman in the crowd.

"Did you see what happened?" asked a sheriff's deputy of one of the casino employees.

The employee held up a finger for the deputy to wait a moment, then he spoke into his walkie-talkie, his words lost in the rumble of people's voices.

The employee turned his attention back to the deputy sheriff. "Here's what I saw. A car drove up to the entrance, going really fast, screeched to a halt and someone opened the rear door and threw out this guy. Whoever did it had to be strong. Look at the size of the guy. He must have been dead weight."

I got a funny feeling in my stomach, and I pushed a woman standing in front of me to one side.

Lying on the sidewalk with two EMTs kneeling over him was Sammy Egret.

SEVENTEEN

"SAMMY, SAMMY, CAN you hear me?" I leaned over the hospital bed and held Sammy's hand. Grandfather Egret stood beside me.

Sammy was alive, and I wanted to lend my voice to the chant of thankfulness Grandfather sang softly as we drove together to the hospital.

"I don't think he can hear you," said the doctor who had entered the room after us. "He's sustained serious injuries, some broken ribs, lacerations, a bullet in his shoulder and a blow to the head. He's lucky to be alive. And he's dehydrated—probably had no food or water for several days. It looks to me as if he's been outside for forty-eight hours or so. If he does awake, don't tire him. I'll give you five minutes, no more." I saw Frida enter while he was speaking. The doctor gave us all a serious look and a cautioning wag of his finger, then left the room.

My heart leaped with joy. "Are you back on the case?" I asked.

She shook her head. "I'm here as a friend only." She came over to Grandfather and me and gave each of us a hug. "Does he know about Bernard yet?"

I shook my head. Grandfather continued with his quiet chanting.

"Have the police had time to check on the bullet they removed from his shoulder?" I asked.

Frida looked away for a moment, then fixed a sorrowful look on me. "I'm sorry, Eve, but the police charged Dudley with Bernard's murder and the attempted murder of Sammy. The sheriff seems to think Dudley was simply following orders—David's."

"Oh, isn't that great. So the authorities finally think Sammy wasn't just some Indian who wandered off to get drunk." Frida started as if I'd slapped her. "Not you, Frida. I know you don't think that. The sheriff has conveniently removed you from the case and wrapped the two murders plus Sammy's attack into one tidy package. I can't help but wonder how much Reed had to do with that."

A groan from the patient in the bed drew our attention. Sammy's eyes fluttered open. "I feel like I wrestled a gator and lost," he said.

"You're here and alive, so I'd say it was a draw." I touched his unbandaged shoulder lightly.

"The police want to talk with you," said Frida.

Sammy looked puzzled. "You are the police."

Frida's brow furrowed in irritation. "I've been taken off this case for now, so you'll have to talk to Linc or someone else from the station. I think they're waiting in the hall."

"They can just wait a little longer. Can you help me up so I can use the bathroom, Eve?"

"I don't think you should be getting out of bed. Here, use this." I extracted the bedpan from where it sat on a shelf on the bedside stand.

He shook his head.

"We'll turn our backs." I tried to suppress a laugh at Sammy's shyness.

Something passed between Sammy and Grandfather. The communication lasted only a second. Maybe I imagined it.

"I think the ladies should leave the room," said Grandfather, breaking off his chanting.

Frida and I joined Detective Tooney in the hallway.

"Did he say anything?" asked Linc. "Did he tell you what happened, where he was, who kidnapped him?"

Frida gave Linc an annoyed look. "No, no, no, no to answer your questions, but he did say something significant."

"What?" Linc leaned forward eagerly.

"He said he had to pee." Frida turned on her heel and stormed toward the elevator.

"I guess she's still a little peeved that the captain took her off the case, huh?" Linc said to me.

"Yeah, it's not you she's mad at. It's Sheriff Leopold. How could he not see her for the great cop she is? The guy must have swamp cabbage for brains."

That got a chuckle out of Linc. "The sheriff can't get beyond her makeup and body. The guy's a piece of work. A holdover from when the dinosaurs roamed the earth."

"Maybe an asteroid will hit—one exactly the right size to wipe just him out. We can only hope."

Linc looked around to see who might be listening and suppressed a smile. "I shouldn't say any more," he said.

We waited a few more minutes, thinking Grandfather Egret would summon both of us back into the room. When that didn't happen, I reentered to see what was going on. The room was empty. No Egret of any generation. The bathroom door was closed, and when I tried to turn the knob, I found it was locked.

"Okay, both of you come out of there. Sammy, you've got to talk to the police sometime." I pressed my ear against the door, trying to hear any sound from the other side. Nothing. I knocked again.

Still no answer.

"I'll get the duty nurse," said Linc.

The nurse arrived quickly and pounded on the door, but she was no more successful than I had been. She extracted a key from her pocket and opened the door. The bathroom was empty, but the door on the other side, the one leading to the next room, was open.

"How far can a six-foot-five Indian wearing a hospital gown and toting an IV stand get?" asked Linc.

"As far as he needs to," I said. "Besides, he's got help. Grandfather Egret is with him."

LINC AND SEVERAL uniformed officers searched the building and questioned anyone who might have seen the duo escape, but no one inside or outside had seen anything. The pair had evaporated like the fog rising off the lake in the early morning.

"I'm gonna get it from the captain," said Linc. "I should have pushed my way into the room sooner, insisted he talk with me."

"What good would that have done? He'd only just regained consciousness."

"So you say." Linc shot me a doubtful look, then raised his eyebrows helplessly. "Don't mind me. It's just that I get my first case without Frida, and I blow it. I'd better get back to the station and tell the captain."

Where had our escapees gone? Not far, not in Sammy's condition, but far enough. They'd be headed back to a world they found more hospitable than a, er, hospital.

My cell rang. It was Alex. Again I had forgotten all about him when I should have kept him in the loop. I hit my forehead with the palm of my hand. I was such a dummy.

When I told him, he was not happy with what he called "your version" of the afternoon and evening.

"What do you mean, you found Sammy and then lost him again?" Alex asked.

"*I* didn't find him, and *I* certainly was not responsible for losing him."

"What then?" His tone was accusatory.

"You know, Alex, not everything that happens to my friends is my doing. I'm not God. I do not control the universe."

"I know that, rationally, but sometimes I wonder."

I heard a deep sigh from the other end of the phone. "Okay, let's try this. Do you know where he's gone?" asked Alex.

"I think so."

"Where?"

"Well, I can't be certain, but where would you go if you were hurting and wanted to heal?" I asked.

"Your place?"

"Don't be dense. Sammy would not go to my place. He would go home."

Sometimes Alex can be so literal. It's probably what makes him such a good detective, not taking anything for granted, spelling out the alternatives in a clear and rational way, but sometime the concreteness of his thinking infuriates me.

"I'll meet you there," he said.

"His home, not mine," I said in case he did not get it, but I was talking to dead space.

When I got to my car in the hospital parking lot, Jerry was standing beside it. Whoops. I'd left him at the casino when they'd loaded Sammy into the ambulance.

"How did you…?" I began.

"How did I get here, Eve? Well, luckily some gambling grannies took pity on me and drove me. How's Sammy?"

I could tell he was peeved at being left behind, but not peeved enough to make an issue of it. He didn't like needles, people in white gave him the creeps, and blood made him faint. This hospital phobia increased as a result of a concussion he'd suffered several months ago when a pair of robbers accosted us and hit him with the butt of his own gun. Jerry might have been angry at my insensitivity at leaving him behind, but he seemed happy not to visit Sammy.

"Get in. You might as well ride along." I unlocked the car door.

"Where to?" Jerry buckled up, eager to accompany me wherever I was going.

"To find Sammy."

"I thought we'd already found him."

"We lost him again. And Grandfather too."

"Was he bleeding a lot? Were there broken bones? Does he smell like hospital antiseptic?" Now Jerry looked worried.

"We're going to the airboat business. You can wait in the car or play around with the boat. I don't care."

I wasn't in the mood for Jerry's neurotic ramblings about the healing professions and wounded people. I was worried about Sammy.

"You think I'm being childish about this blood and needles thing, don't you?"

I pulled into the airboat business parking lot and slammed on my brakes.

"Okay, Jerry. Here's what I think. First, I think it's kind of crazy to be so phobic about doctors and medical people, especially considering the business you're in. Mob folks get hurt a lot. Second, this is not all about you. Why do you try to make everything your issue? In fact, get your ass out of my car, come with me to the house, and tell Sammy how sorry you are about his condition. Man up, Jerry." I spit out the last sentence. I knew I was being hard on him, but I'd put up with his adolescent behavior for too long. Time for him to grow a set of gumptions.

"Uh, okay." He slowly got out of the car. "But I've got a question."

"What now?"

"What if they're not there?"

"Then you just got lucky." I pushed him ahead of me up the grassy path to the house.

GRANDFATHER EGRET SAT on the porch in his rocking chair looking as if he'd been there all day or all his life.

"He's inside." Grandfather nodded toward the house.

"Did you tell him about Bernard?" I asked.

"Yes." Grandfather's voice was hoarse with sadness.

I left Jerry on the porch to practice his apologies for not visiting at the hospital. As I opened the door I heard Grandfather say, "I know. I hate hospitals too. Too white. No character."

Sammy sat at the kitchen table. Someone had removed his IV. The pole holding the drip had been shoved against the far wall.

"You're going to have to talk to the authorities

sooner or later." I pulled out the chair across from his and sat.

"Later will do just fine." He sipped a cup of coffee and gestured toward the pot. "Have some?"

"No thanks." I waited, thinking if I could demonstrate patience for once in my life he might talk to me. No such luck. Sammy continued drinking his coffee, looking up now and then to meet my gaze, then shifting his eyes to the wall behind me. I finally caved.

"What happened? Or won't you talk to me either?"

"You don't understand, do you?"

I sighed. "Maybe I do. It was a shock to learn of your nephew's death, especially since you think it could have been prevented if the authorities had taken his disappearance seriously. And you need a little time to yourself to grieve. And you also think that the authorities will just shove your abduction to the back burner because they will assume you went on a toot like they think all Indians do and then got in a fight."

Sammy looked surprised for a minute, then nodded.

"You know Frida doesn't think that, don't you?"

"Sure, but the Indian telegraph says she's off both the murder cases, so I can't see what difference it makes what she believes." Sammy picked up the pot and filled his cup again.

"I think Linc might be open to hearing your story."

Sammy made a dismissive harrumphing sound. "Linc Tooney, you mean Looney Tunes?"

"What?"

"Linc and I went to high school together. He was kind of the class clown. All the kids called him 'Looney Tunes' after the cartoons."

"So that makes him a bad guy?"

"No. Being a cop may, however."

"Frida told me the authorities are taking your abduction seriously." I was about to spell out for him how the sheriff thought all these crimes were linked. I knew he'd find that theory as absurd as I did, and we'd be back to square one—the place where Sammy saw the authorities as worse than idiots.

We were getting nowhere. I didn't want to be cruel, but I sidestepped his grief at his nephew's death and the pain of his own injuries and plunged ahead in true Eve Appel fashion—damn the consequences or people's feelings.

"Are you going to tell me what happened to you or not, Sammy? Or is our friendship worth nothing?"

"Would you prefer Scotch rather than coffee?" he said. "I don't think there's any here."

"I'd prefer the truth. Maybe you have a reason to be feeling so sorry for yourself, but it won't help us find Bernard's killer."

The candor in my words registered in his eyes. "Okay, but let's get more comfortable."

"Fine." I got out of my chair and started toward the couch.

"No, the bedroom." He smiled and winked at me, then grimaced as he tried to rise from the chair.

"See, this is why you should be in the hospital." I slipped my shoulder under his arm and helped him into the back bedroom.

"Don't lecture me," he said.

If he hadn't been in such pain, I could have told him that lecturing was not on my mind, not when I was tucking a tall, muscular man with mahogany skin into bed.

A clothes bureau sat at the foot of the bed. A rickety chair with books and a lamp on it served as a bedside table. The space was so tiny there was hardly room for one person to stand between the bed and the door. And here we were once more, alone with our uneasiness at being forced into physical closeness.

I plumped his pillow and sat on the edge of the bed.

"Better?" I asked.

"Much."

His gaze locked with mine. There was more than friendship in it, more than warmth. I felt as if we'd set the room on fire.

"Hi, Sammy. How's it going?" Jerry's head appeared in the doorway. I hadn't heard him turn the knob to open the door. Cursed by Jerry's timing! Or had he saved me from doing or saying something I'd later regret?

"C'mon in," said Sammy.

When I looked at Sammy's face, I wondered if I'd imagined the whole burning exchange of looks thing. He seemed to be genuinely happy to see Jerry. He held out his good hand, and they shook. Jerry sat down on the bed beside me. I was wedged in between two men, kind of a turkey breast sandwich made with one slice of whole wheat, one slice of white bread.

"I really want to apologize to you. I should have visited you in the hospital. Eve told me I'm an insensitive SOB."

"No, you're not," Sammy said at the same time I said, "You really are, Jerry."

Jerry acted as if he intended to settle in for a chat, and I knew that was just the excuse Sammy needed

not to talk about his abduction. I had to find a way to
get Jerry out of the room.

"Get out of here, Jerry. Sammy and I need to talk."

Sammy shook his head. "We could do it later."

"No we couldn't. Jerry, go ask Grandfather Egret
about gambling. He knows a lot about poker and craps."
Of course, I had no idea if he did or not, but Jerry took
the bait.

"Right. Take care of yourself." Jerry backed out of
the room and closed the door behind him.

"Now, where were we?" I asked, then reconsidered
my question. "I mean, you were about to tell me what
happened to you."

Sammy paused a moment, then sighed in resigna-
tion. "You know the guys that set up Bernard for gambling grabbed me outside the casino."

"And you got a good look at them?"

"No. It happened fast and they were pros. They
drove the car up beside me. Two of them grabbed me—
they were big guys—one hit me over the head, and
that's all I remember until I woke up some time later."

"Where?"

"I don't know, some kind of a shack or house, I
think. I was tied up, blindfolded, gagged, and my back
was up against a wooden wall. I think I was there only
one night. They took me out of there and dragged me
into the woods, then shoved me into a cage. I could
feel the bars on my legs, back, and side when I tried
to move around. I don't know how long I was there,
but I had no food and no water. I decided I needed to
make a break when an opportunity presented itself.
They took me out of the cage—I'm pretty sure it was
night by the temperature and the animal sounds—and

I knocked one of them off balance and started to run. I couldn't see where I was going, but I figured being blind in the woods was preferable to being starved in a cage or whatever else they might have planned for me."

"And that's when they shot you?"

Sammy nodded. "Then they loaded me into the back of a pickup. After about an hour of traveling on unpaved roads, we stopped. They got out, dropped the tailgate, and I heard someone approach the truck and stand there for several minutes, as if he was examining me. I had the sense they were shining a light on me. I was being displayed as some kind of specimen. But I'm not clear about that, because my shoulder was hurting so bad by that time that I was in and out of consciousness. I heard the tailgate slammed back into place and voices. It sounded like an argument."

"Could you hear what they were saying?"

Sammy closed his eyes for a moment as if concentrating on the images in his head. "One guy said, 'you fools' and another said, 'so you don't want him' and then a 'get rid of him,' from the first man. I heard an engine and the sound of a vehicle leaving. I must have lost consciousness for a while. When I awoke, I was back in that cage, and I could hear men talking. This time I tried to listen carefully. All I got was one man saying, 'I'm not doing his dirty work for him. Dump the Indian.'"

"Would you recognize the voices if you heard them again?"

"I might be able to pick them out of others, but I'm not about to do that."

"What do you mean?"

"One of the voices I did recognize."

My heart jumped in anticipation. "Who was it?"

"Sheriff Leopold."

Now I understood why Sammy didn't want to talk to the authorities.

EIGHTEEN

I KNEW THE SABAL BAY POLICE and the county sheriff's office would catch up with Sammy and force him to talk with them, but I didn't know how much he'd be willing to say. I hoped they would stay away from the service for Bernard and not try to seize that opportunity to ask Sammy or other family members questions about his disappearance. I was sure Linc wouldn't be so crude, but what about the sheriff's department?

I was visiting Sammy with Alex the evening before Bernard's funeral when a county deputy and Linc showed up. I was relieved they were showing some sensitivity in choosing the privacy of Sammy's home to question him. He tried to avoid taking their questions by saying he was too beaten up to discuss his abduction.

"But you managed to sneak out of your hospital bed yesterday," Linc said.

"Look, I think it was all a misunderstanding. The guys who nabbed me mistook me for someone else. They let me go, so what's the big deal?"

"The deal is that you got shot and we're comparing the bullet found in your shoulder with the one that killed your nephew. Even if they nabbed the wrong guy, which I doubt, they still committed a criminal act. We want them," Linc said.

"Just find out who shot Bernard." Sammy shrugged his shoulders and turned to face the wall.

Linc and the deputy left the bedroom. I heard the deputy say, "Damn Indians. First they want us to take the disappearance of one of them seriously; then they want us to dismiss it. He probably was drunk or high on something."

I would have been out the door to tell him what I thought of his prejudice, but Alex restrained me. Sammy gave me one of his shy grins. Through the open door I saw Grandfather get up from his porch rocker and step in front of the deputy.

"No one invited you here, but I am inviting you to leave and take your mean mouth with you. We're grieving the loss of a good boy, and I think the family and the tribe are due a little respect."

"Sorry, Mr. Egret," said Linc. "I'm sure he didn't mean what he said. He's just overzealous and wants to wrap up this case. Two men have been killed, a hunting client and Bernard, then Sammy is taken and shot. We're concerned."

"No, you're not, not really," said Grandfather. "You're worried leaving the murders unsolved will make you look bad, and the sheriff is coming up for reelection, isn't he?"

"We're out of here." The deputy headed to his car, then turned and walked back to the porch. "You think about this. Next time you need us, we may not be there for you."

I heard the county cruiser and Linc's SUV pull out of the drive and turned my attention back to Sammy.

"How are you, really?" I asked.

"Well enough to go to the service for Bernard to-morrow."

"We'll be there too—Madeleine, Alex, and I."

"Don't. I know you mean well, Eve, but leave the tribe members to ourselves. I don't think white faces would go over big just now."

The next morning, Madeleine and I drove south on the Turnpike to sell at the largest flea market in southeast Florida.

Since we travelled on the turnpike with three wide lanes in either direction, I let Madeleine drive. She needed the practice, something I wasn't keen on her doing on the narrow country roads around the lake. Besides, I felt safe. I was wearing Grandfather's amulet. I patted it for reassurance.

"Alex told me he hasn't been very successful getting workers at the Reed ranch to talk about their poor treatment, even after they've been let go," she said. Another large motor home blasted past us, creating a side wind that threatened to push us onto the right shoulder. Gripping the wheel with her tiny hands, Madeleine kept the rig in the lane.

"Nice work holding her steady."

Madeleine took her eyes off the road for a moment, and the motor home drifted toward the left lane.

"Hey, watch it!" I saw the angry, white face of a dump-truck driver who swerved left to avoid us. He shook his fist as he breezed past.

"Alex is trying his best to discover how Reed is involved in the client's death," I said, "and I suspect we'll also find he had something to do with Bernard's murder."

"I know you hate the guy, and I do too, but wishing

he was the guilty party doesn't make it so. How is he connected with an Indian college student who was becoming addicted to gambling?" Once again Madeleine started to turn her head to look at me.

"Don't do that!" I said. "Eyes ahead, or we won't be able to help David because we'll be splattered all over the turnpike."

She gritted her teeth and concentrated on the road.

"The authorities have arrested David's foreman, Dudley, for Bernard's murder and for shooting Sammy. And that's absurd." I crossed my arms over my chest and sat back in my seat.

"Sammy must know something the authorities can use to catch Bernard's killer or killers. Doesn't he have any idea who nabbed him?"

I thought of what Sammy said about Sheriff Leopold being at the scene when he was thrown into the bed of the pickup. "He knows too much, I think."

Madeleine turned her head to look at me and her mouth dropped open in surprise.

"Madeleine!"

"Yeah, I know. Eyes on the road, but when you say something like that, what do you expect me to do?"

She was right. "I'll tell you all about it when we get to the market." I added, "We need Frida back on this case."

As with the market in Stuart, we had been given a spot for our motor home near the other vendors selling used merchandise. We were enough south of West Palm that we attracted an entirely new clientele, not from the Stuart or West Palm area, but nearer to Ft. Lauderdale. Our customers turned out to be mostly snowbirds and not full-time Florida residents. This market was even busier than the one in Stuart, and trade was heavy from the moment we set out the sign and opened the motor home door. We seemed to have found a new lucrative locale for sales. Maybe a shop on wheels wasn't so bad.

When we arrived back in Sabal Bay, Alex waited at my house with good news. He'd located someone who worked for Reed around the time Mrs. Warren had left there and when Reed took on his new foreman.

"The guy wasn't eager to talk to me, but he finally caved when I told him about the murder of David's client. He said he knew David and respected him. He couldn't believe he could be responsible for killing anyone. Anyway, the guy's name is Luis Mendoza now and he works at one of the produce stands in the local flea market here. Nice fellow, but wary of police. He came here from Guatemala after armed troops came in and massacred hundreds of the Indians there. He was one of the lucky ones, getting out with his life and his family." Alex sat on my couch and sipped a beer. I could tell from the expression on his face that he wished he had a better lead, but he wanted to make as much of this one as he could. "Luis is a guy who keeps his head down. He wants no trouble with the local law enforcement people."

Madeleine perched on the arm of the couch nearest Alex. She leaned forward, expression open and eager, and said, "And?" She wanted him to get on with his story.

"And Luis told me Reed was bad enough, punishing his men by hitting them or taking a whip to them, but things got worse when the new foreman showed up. That guy he called *El Diablo*, the devil. He took the men into the woods and sometimes tied them to trees overnight, left them there until the next day, no food, no water."

"And he looks like the innocent one with his blue eyes, freckled face, and blond hair," Madeleine said.

"The perfect cover for a psychopath," I said. "Did Luis say anything about Sheriff Leopold? Did you ask him about the sheriff?"

"I did, and that's when he said he couldn't talk to me anymore. He turned his back and busied himself with other customers."

"Which creep do you favor for the killer?" I asked, "Reed, his foreman, or the sheriff? Or all three, a deadly mix of depraved men?"

"Don't forget Elvira Reed, the perfect wife for any creep." Madeleine got up from her seat. "I talked to David today on the phone, just for a minute."

"How's he doing?" I asked.

She shook her head, didn't answer and headed for the kitchen.

"This is knocking the stuffing out of our usually re-silient Madeleine," I said to Alex. I whispered because I didn't want her to hear my concerns.

"I know. I'm worried about her, too. I don't think I'll get anything more out of Luis, but maybe Mrs. War-ren can remember the names of other men who worked at Reed's ranch. It can't hurt to pay her another visit."

"Tonight?" I asked.

Alex nodded. "I think you should come along. The woman's touch, you know."

How about that. He needed me. I was his partner in— "Eve, I can hear you thinking. This is a one-time deal, so get any ideas of helping me in the future out of your head."

"Oh, sure, of course. Why would you think otherwise?" I batted my eyes at him.

Madeleine came back from the kitchen, wiping away tears. She'd obviously had a bit of a cry, then recovered her composure. For a time, anyway.

"Why are you doing that eye batting thing?" she asked. "Whenever you do that, it's a sign you're trying to hide something."

"Me?" I batted a bit more, then caught myself. "Sorry about that."

She gave Alex a questioning look, but he pretended not to see her or understand what she wanted.

Madeleine picked up her purse from the table by the door. "Okay, you two. I'm going home to leave you to yourselves. You deserve some alone time."

"Hey, don't go. We can order out something." Alex got off the couch and held out his hand to her.

"Not hungry." Madeleine shrugged into her sweater. She hesitated with her hand on the front doorknob. "We sold well today, and the inventory is down. One of us should go to the coast and rustle up some items. Rodeo days are this weekend."

I could hear the fatigue and lack of enthusiasm in her voice. I mentally whacked myself on the head. I'd let her carry more than her share of responsibility for the shop since David had been arrested. Under other circumstances she'd be fine, but she needed someone to lift the load off her, and that someone should have been me.

"I wouldn't mind a road trip tomorrow. You can set up the rig on Main Street downtown while I visit our clients and grab some clothes for the weekend rodeo event."

"Will you really do that or are you just saying you will? I know you; you'll just go off and do some nosing around, get yourself into trouble." Madeleine held up a finger. "And don't start that batting stuff again."

I tried to hold my eyes perfectly still. "Of course I'll pick up merchandise. Why would you think otherwise?"

Alex choked on his beer and began coughing.

Of course I'd get consignment items tomorrow. I was somewhat miffed that Madeleine didn't trust me. After all, I was going to accompany Alex tonight to visit Mrs. Warren. That should satisfy my snooping needs, shouldn't it?

MRS. WARREN AGAIN welcomed us into her tidy home and offered coffee. "I don't have anything stronger, I'm afraid. I'm not a drinker and neither is Moses." She gave a nervous laugh. "We like to gamble a little. I guess that's our addiction. My husband was a heavy drinker, but I never joined him."

I watched her twist her hands around in her lap as she mentioned her husband. The thought that he might have gotten violent when drinking crossed my mind, and I wondered if she kept things under control by remaining sober and calm, placating him whenever possible. Of course, with his work abroad, he wouldn't have been home much. I also wondered if she'd preferred his absences to his presence.

"I hate to bother you again, Mrs. Warren, but—"

"It's fine. I know you're trying to get David out of jail."

"You don't sound too angry about having the man who shot your son out on bail."

She looked down at her hands, twisting them still, then glancing up and quieting her movements. "My son was like my husband. An angry boy. I'm devastated to have lost him, but I understand what happened. I also heard that David hasn't picked up a gun since then." She raised her eyes and met mine. "So what can I do for you?"

"Can you remember the names of any workers at the Reed ranch when you were employed there? Or maybe you ran into one of them somewhere around town and might know where the person works now?" Alex leaned forward on the couch in a posture of friendliness.

Mrs. Warren leaned her head into the chair back, her hands now lying still in her lap. She appeared to be thinking back to her work for the Reeds. Alex and I remained silent, giving her space to review the past.

The sound of a vehicle entering the drive interrupted her thoughts. Moses Ermlich entered the front door and stopped when he saw Alex and me. His down-turned mouth and the anger in his eyes indicated he assumed we were again bothering Mrs. Warren.

"What are you doing here?" he demanded.

Mrs. Warren seemed eager to defuse the tension. "I'm thinking back on my time at the Reed ranch to see if I remember anyone who worked there. Maybe you recall the name of that guy who did the landscaping around the place. Wasn't it Pepe something?"

"No, I don't," Moses growled.

"He did landscaping?" Alex asked. "That might help. There are only a handful of guys who do that around here. Maybe some of my contacts would know of him."

"Maybe." Moses clearly wanted us to leave.

Alex decided to bring Moses in on the conversation. "I don't suppose you know much about the foreman who replaced you, do you? We've heard he's spelled trouble for the men at the ranch."

"Don't know him. I was gone by the time he was hired." Moses headed toward the kitchen, opened a cupboard and removed a cup.

"Have you heard stories about him? Maybe you've run into him someplace." Alex appeared desperate to extract any bit of information from him.

"Wouldn't know him if I stepped on him." Moses poured coffee into his cup and took a sip, then moved to Mrs. Warren's chair, put his hand on her shoulder and squeezed gently. A gesture of comfort and affection. His gruffness was all for us. He only wanted to protect her.

"Oh, you wouldn't step on him. He's a huge guy, sandy reddish hair, blue eyes. Looks like an overgrown boy, but we hear he's a brute," Alex said.

Mrs. Warren and Moses exchanged looks. They had communicated something important, made some decision.

"I think you should leave now," Moses said. "We need our privacy."

"What do you think?" I asked Alex when we were back in the car.

"The same as you. Once we described the foreman at Reed's ranch, they both reacted. They know him."

"How? And what do they know?" I asked.

Alex ignored my question. "I need to keep an eye on Mrs. Warren and Moses."

"A stakeout, right?"

"Yes, and not something you can join me on. It's boring and a long shot that anything will come of this."

"But we upset them somehow, and I think they're going to take action, maybe tonight." I was excited that our questions had stirred up something.

"That's why I need to offload you right now." Alex pulled over at a convenience store at the corner of Mrs. Warren's road and the state highway.

"You expect me to walk back home?" I looked down at my feet. Of course I was wearing my lizard skin sandals with four-inch heels. Alex gave them a glance too.

"Hardly. I'm calling Jerry to come get you."

"But he's guarding the motor home, and I don't even know if he has a car. Please, please, anybody but Jerry." I put my hands together in a gesture of prayer.

"Damn. You're right. Plan B then. It'll be better than having Jerry drive you. The two of you could get into trouble, but Plan B will prevent that from happening."

Plan B was Frida.

I WAS STANDING outside the convenience store eating an ice cream bar when Frida pulled up.

"Is that your dinner?" She rolled down her window and called out to me.

"You think Alex was too cheap to feed me before he dumped me in this, uh, dump?"

"Get in. My mother has the kids tonight, and I could use a rib fix. We can go to the Biscuit. How about we pick up Madeleine and have her join us?"

"I don't think she's doing much eating lately."

Frida smiled. "There's more at the Biscuit than eating and drinking, dancing, and cowboys."

"There is?" I was puzzled.

"Yep, there's karaoke tonight. You, me, and Madeleine. The Lennon sisters, or the Supremes, whatever girl group you like."

"I can't warble a note." I finished off my ice cream and tossed the wrapper in the overflowing trash can. "But it might be just the thing to take Madeleine's mind off David."

I got into the car and fastened my seatbelt. "Oh, boy, ribs."

Frida was about to pull onto the road when Moses Ermlich's truck shot past the store. Behind it, at a discreet distance, came Alex. He gave us a wave as he passed.

"Follow them. That's Mrs. Warren and Moses. That's who Alex is staking out. We think they know something about the Reed foreman."

"You got it." Frida punched the accelerator, and we became the third car in this three car convoy.

Oh boy, I thought. We're hot on the trail of something big.

My stomach growled.

NINETEEN

AT THE INTERSECTION with the highway, Ermlich turned his truck east.

"Well, it's for certain they're not going to the casino. It's that way." I pointed down the road in the opposite direction.

"Maybe they're just headed to town to pick up a few groceries." Frida kept a good distance from Alex's car so as not to alert him that he wasn't the only one doing the following.

"I have a crazy hunch."

Frida gave me a look. "Most of your hunches are crazy."

I ignored her sarcasm. "I think they're headed to the Reed ranch."

"Why? Neither of them works there now. And why at this time of night?"

"I'm not sure, but I'm certain they don't want anyone to know what they're up to."

Sure enough, after heading north out of Sabal Bay, the truck and Alex's car took the right turn onto the county route heading toward David's place and the Reed ranch. I expected them to turn into the Reed driveway, but instead, the truck made a left onto a poorly marked dirt road just beyond the entrance to the Reed ranch. Alex followed.

"The back way in, I'll bet," I said.

Frida slowed and waited a minute before she negotiated the turn. She looked at me as we bounced down the rutted road. "You just love all this, don't you? Did you ever think you're in the wrong business?"

I leaned forward, peering through the darkness at Alex's taillights ahead.

"Huh? Oh, yeah. This is great. I'm just a natural born snoop, right. That's what you meant. I should be a private detective? Or maybe a cop, like you?"

"No, I meant you should be a cat. You know, curiosity and the cat thing."

"What a cruel thing to say, Frida. That cat lost its life to a curious nature, you know. I mean, really." I huffed and crossed my arms over my chest. Just then Alex's brake lights came on, his car stopped, and he got out.

"We'll hang back," Frida said. "Maybe you should stay in the car, Eve. Better yet, maybe we should get out of here. I'm not even sure this is legal."

"Don't be such a wuss. We're just driving down a country lane at night, then stopping for a walk." I opened my car door and jumped out.

"Eve," Frida hissed at my retreating back.

I walked past Alex's empty car, certain that the footsteps I heard behind me belonged to Frida. Wuss or not, I knew her own curiosity wouldn't let her back out now.

Suddenly a hand grabbed my arm.

"Let go of me, Frida. We need to find out what's going on."

"It's me, Eve." It was Alex's voice. "I saw your headlights behind me. Now will you gals be quiet? I'd like to find out what's going on without scaring off my prey."

"We may be trespassing," Frida said in a whisper. "I don't remember this road on any map."

"This road is actually on David's land, and I'm sure he wouldn't mind our using it." Alex put his finger to his lips to signal silence then moved ahead.

"But what are Mrs. Warren and Moses doing? I was certain they were headed for the Reed place, not David's," I said.

"We can cut west at the end of this road and get into the Reed property the back way, which is what I'll bet Warren and Ermlich are doing. Pretty smart of them, I'd say." Alex led the way, careful to stay on the road and not wander onto the side that bordered a swampy area. I could see the moonlight reflected off the water. Cattails and bulrushes undulated in the night breeze. I stopped my imagination from providing me pictures of the animals that might be enjoying a late night swim out there.

"So if we turn west, we will be trespassing," Frida said. "And onto property owned by a person who makes his living by shooting things. The guy is into guns. Think about it. If he catches us, he has a perfect right to defend his land." Frida was right, of course. And she had more to lose than we did. She was law enforcement, a detective who had been removed from the murder cases. She could lose her job if she got caught sneaking around Reed's ranch.

"On the other hand," she continued, "I feel kind of silly saying I'll wait here for you."

"Listen." Alex held up his hand for us to stop walking or talking.

We all stood still for several moments and heard… nothing.

Alex broke the silence. "Damn. We've lost them. I was sure they'd drive in the back way. Unless they left the truck and went in on foot. Either way we'd hear the truck or see their taillights or hear them. If they're on foot, where did they leave the truck?"

"Why would they go in on foot? Unless they don't want anyone at the ranch to know they're coming. Why would that be?" An idea was forming in my head, and it was in direct opposition to Alex's theory—that Mrs. Warren and Moses Ermlich were confederates of Reed or the foreman.

"We need to find out if they're at Reed's," Alex said.

"We can keep going and maybe come up behind them. I just think it's odd they'd want to sneak in as if they didn't want anyone there to know…" I didn't finish my sentence. A twig snapped behind us. We all whirled around, expecting to see that Mrs. Warren and Moses had spotted us and circled around to take us by surprise. Instead the figure of a huge man materialized from behind a live oak. A rifle rested in the crook of his arm. When he stepped toward us, a shaft of weak, milky moonlight fell across his face.

"Sammy! What the hell are you doing here? You're supposed to be home in bed recovering," I said.

He gave us his crooked smile. "I guess you don't know. David arranged for me to keep an eye on his place while he and his foreman are in jail."

"When did all this happen?" asked Alex.

"Today, after you and Eve left my place."

Frida stepped forward. "I'm not saying I don't believe you, but it's more than convenient that you're right on top of the Reed place, given your suspicions about the man."

I thought Sammy might take offense, but instead he gave a little chuckle of laughter. "Isn't it just as convenient that here you are in the middle of the night at the edge of his property when you're equally suspicious of Reed and his treatment of his workers? And you're not even supposed to be investigating this case."

Frida seemed taken aback by his accusation, but only for a moment; then she grinned and said, "You got me there."

Alex waved his hand in a dismissive manner. "Yeah, yeah, we all think Reed is a shithead, but I seem to be the only one hot on a lead that might shed some light on this murder. Could we move on? I need to find the people I'm following. They're up to something."

"You think they're somehow involved in the murders?" asked Frida.

"Yep, and they're covering their tracks, trying to make contact with Reed," Alex said.

"Uh, could be. On the other hand, it's just as likely—"

I was interrupted by Alex before I could get out my own take on the situation. "Let's confront them." Alex turned back toward his vehicle. "You interested in accompanying us, Sammy?"

"My job is guarding David's place now that it's not occupied. I've no interest in tangling with Reed or his men. I'll stay here. If you miss Warren and Ermlich, they'll come back this way. If someone lends me a cellphone, I'll let you know."

I tossed my cell to Sammy. He grabbed it and faded back into the shadows.

"I'll go in the front way, like a law-abiding citizen. But just in case there's trouble, maybe you and Frida should wait on the main road." Alex hurried toward his car.

"You got that, buddy," said Frida. "I'm in enough trouble with my boss. I don't need to create more by showing up in the dead of night at the Reed place asking about some people I don't even know. C'mon, Eve. We're out of here."

"No, no, no. I want to go with Alex. It's either that or I march in there on foot."

I was bluffing. I didn't know how to get to the Reed complex through the woods, and the road leading there was two miles long. By the time I showed up, I would have missed anything interesting.

Alex stopped short ahead of me, and I ran into him. In the darkness I couldn't see the expression on his face, but his tone of voice indicated he was at the end of his tether.

"Fine then. But you stay in the car."

"Are you sure you want her along?" asked Frida.

"Hey. Don't talk about me as if I'm a liability who isn't here." I trotted along behind Alex.

"I can keep an eye on her this way." Alex stopped and grabbed me, pulling me into him.

"Oh, goodie." I looked up into his eyes, hoping to see respect there, but the sliver of moonlight revealed nothing more than an arched eyebrow of skepticism.

"Okay. I'll meet you on the road." Frida jogged off toward her car.

"Here's the deal, Eve. I want to see if there's any evidence that Mrs. Warren and Ermlich have been there, and I want to have a civilized talk with Reed. Let him know we're aware of his history of poor treatment of his employees, and that we think it's connected to the recent murders."

Alex shoved me into the car, then got into the driver's seat.

"We do? I mean how is all this connected?" I was confused by Alex's approach.

"Well, I don't know, do I? It's just a bluff."

"It seems very—"

"What?" He slammed the car door and started the engine.

"I don't know. Very vague."

I watched Alex's jaw work back and forth, a sure sign he was about to explode.

He put the car into gear and backed up, then turned toward me. "It *is* vague. This is a situation where you play it by ear. Improvise. It's a detective technique. I don't have the foggiest notion why Mrs. Warren and Moses Ermlich are sneaking in to visit Reed, but it can't be good. Can it?"

"No, but I—"

"Leave it at that." Alex put the car into drive and followed the dirt road back to the highway. He drove past Frida's car on the shoulder and skidded into the Reeds' driveway.

I worried that Alex and I were on different pages when it came to the Mrs. Warren's and Ermlich's visit tonight. I thought I should tell him what I thought was happening, but he was not receptive right now. I knew he was close to tossing me out of the car to make my way down a darkened road back to Frida. I wasn't crazy about the idea of walking a country lane in rural Florida, a place where gators crossed roadways to get to water, food, and mates during the night. And then there were all those feral pigs running around. Nasty tempers, I'd heard.

I kept silent as we pulled up to the Reed house. I'd tell him after. I could play good girl. Alex went to the door while I sat in mock obedience in the car.

Blake Reed appeared, and the two men talked for a few moments, then he let Alex into the house. Less than five minutes later, Alex came back out.

"So?" I spoke the word tentatively in case he was still in a mood.

"I don't think he bit. He acted interested, but not particularly worried. And there was no sign of Mrs. Warren or Moses." Alex backed the car around, and we headed out the drive.

"Exactly what did you tell him?"

"I kept it vague. Just said I'd talked to some people who were former employees, and I'd followed them here tonight."

"And he said 'so what.' Right?"

"I told him he was foolish to believe these people would keep their mouths shut about his operation or his role in the two murders—David's client, and the young Indian."

"And he gave you another 'so what' when you said the people you'd followed here might consider informing on him?"

"Not even the twitch of an eye. His foreman walked in at that point, and Reed told me to get out or he'd have the foreman throw me out."

"You didn't tell him it was Mrs. Warren and Moses Ermlich who you'd followed, did you?"

"No."

I breathed a sigh of relief, which Alex caught.

"I know you kind of like Mrs. Warren, but that's no reason to give her a pass on what she and Ermlich were up to tonight."

"You don't really know what they were doing."

Alex's jaw was working again. I should have left it at that, but I couldn't.

"Just because you didn't find Mrs. Warren and Ermlich and your detective technique of vague bluffing didn't pay off with Reed doesn't mean you should take it out on me, you know."

Alex opened his mouth to say something, then snapped it shut.

Oops. I'd gone too far.

WE TURNED ONTO the county road and drove the quarter of a mile until we got to Frida's car.

She rolled down her window when we pulled up alongside. "Anything?"

"Maybe I shook him up. He's a cagey one. I couldn't tell." Alex didn't look happy.

"Any word from Sammy? Have Mrs. Warren and Ermlich come back down that road?" I asked.

Frida shook her head. "Did Sammy call Alex?"

Before Alex could say no, his cell rang. It was Sammy.

"I walked back up the road to the end right after you left. I thought I might spot Ermlich's truck. It was parked at the end of the road, so they hadn't gone on to Reed's place after all. The truck just sat there with its engine idling. After a few minutes, I saw headlights coming down the road fast from Reed's place. Before Ermlich could leave, the other vehicle pulled up beside him and Reed's foreman jumped out, ran up to the truck, and yelled for Ermlich to 'get the hell off the property.' Ermlich pulled out, wheels spinning, and took off back down the road. If Frida didn't spot the truck coming by her, I guess it must have headed east when it hit the county road."

An uneasy feeling crept up my spine. I grabbed Alex's phone and said, "Did he see who was in the truck, do you think?"

"How could he miss? His headlights lit up the cab of that truck like it was daylight."

"Oh, crap," I said.

"You okay?" asked Sammy.

"Not really."

"Listen, I've worked my way to the road and I can see your cars. You want your cell back?"

"We'll grab it before we leave here." I disconnected.

Alex gave me a questioning look, as did Frida.

"I've got a really bad feeling. Now the foreman knows who was sneaking around the ranch tonight. And we don't know if Mrs. Warren and Ermlich met with Reed tonight. I mean, did they go in the back way so no one—like us—would see them or was it so that no one at the ranch would see them?"

"And it matters for what reason?" asked Frida.

Alex started to answer her, but I beat him to it. "If they were trying to hide from anyone following them, then it means they're somehow involved with the murders. That's what you think, right Alex?"

He nodded, but didn't look so certain of his suspicion now.

"And if they went there to spy on Reed and the crew, then they may be in trouble now," I said.

"Because the foreman saw who they were?" Frida was quick, but did she get what I meant?

"I don't quite get why that's an issue, Eve," said Alex. "Who cares if Reed and his foreman know they were trying to spy on the ranch?"

"I don't think Reed likes anybody down his back," Frida said.

We could all agree on that. Reed wanted privacy when it came to what he chose to do on his land. But that's not what worried me.

"Did you see any pictures at the Warren house of Mr. Warren?" I asked Alex.

TWENTY

"I DON'T REMEMBER any photos," Alex said.

"Well, I do. She had a kind of altar set up at the end of the couch. There were pictures of her son, most of them as a baby or from childhood, but none of her husband. I should have been more observant. That boy had bright blue eyes and freckles."

"Lots of kids have those features. I don't understand where you're going with this, Eve." Not only did Alex look confused, but his face was beginning to take on that look of aggravation I seemed to inspire in him so often.

"I think I know what Eve's saying." Frida's eyes shone with understanding. "Maybe the next time you visit Mrs. Warren, you might ask to see a picture of her husband. Meantime, I should be tracking down the specifics of his death."

Alex shook his head. "I already did that."

"Frida," I said, "if you do that, you should make sure there's someone in the office you trust to help you. Your captain will have your ass if he finds out you've been poking around a case you're no longer on." I chuckled to see Alex's expression remain so confused.

I took pity on him. "You remember the circumstances surrounding our getting tossed out of the Warren house this afternoon?" I asked.

"We both do. I was talking about Reed's foreman

and his treatment of the employees being worse than Reed's and then—"

"Then you described the guy, and we got thrown out. We both thought something changed between Mrs. Warren and Moses at that point. It made us suspicious, and it led to you following them," I said.

"I figured they were feeling pushed by my questions about Reed. I stirred up something. What do you think is going on, Eve? Frida? So Mrs. Warren doesn't want pictures to remind her of her dead husband. Why is that so odd? Maybe it's just too hard for her to remember how he died."

"She had photos of her son all over the place, and the memory of how he died can't be pleasant," I said. "Either Mrs. Warren doesn't want anyone to know what her husband looks like or she'd rather forget the guy. I saw how she reacted to talking about Mr. Warren. I got the feeling she was afraid of him."

"So she put away the photos of a violent husband. Now he's out of sight, out of mind," Alex said.

"That's what I think too, but when you described the foreman, she and Moses exchanged looks that I think meant they both recognized the guy. I think they sneaked into the ranch to see if they could get a look at him without Reed, Elvira, or the foreman knowing. They weren't trying to make contact with anyone there at all."

Frida interrupted the discussion. "If Warren is the foreman at Reed's then he's no ghost. And Mrs. Warren and Moses Ermlich may be in danger."

"Warren is dead," Alex insisted. "I checked with the company he was contracted to do work for. He was killed by a car bomb."

Frida shook her head. "The army would find DNA to link the body with that of a dead soldier, but do you think a private company would be willing to go to those lengths for one of their employees? Maybe Warren wanted everyone to think he was dead."

Alex looked puzzled. "Why? Unless there's something fishy about the guy."

"Well, there's something fishy about this whole night, don't you think? Why would Mrs. Warren and Moses rush off to spy on the Reed place? Let's do what Sherlock Holmes suggested," I said.

"And that would be what?" asked Frida.

"We've ruled out all the possibilities. Now let's assume the impossible. Let's assume Mr. Warren is not dead." I smiled at my cleverness.

"You read too many mysteries, Eve." Alex kicked a clod of dried mud at the side of the road.

"We've got nothing to lose with Eve's plan, and if we don't make that assumption and we're wrong, Mrs. Warren and Moses Ermlich could end up in trouble or worse." Frida grabbed her cell. "I'm calling Linc now. At home. I can trust him to do some digging on Reed's foreman. And then we'll see if we have a ghost or not." Frida punched a number into her cell.

The truth of what I'd said finally hit Alex. "He saw them in the headlights of his truck." Alex shifted into gear. "We'll be in touch, Frida."

We sped down the road, screeched to a stop when we saw Sammy to grab my phone and then did a U-turn back toward the Warren house, hoping we'd find Mrs. Warren and Moses there, watching television and drinking coffee.

Alex slid to a stop and shut off his lights. The Warren house was dark. The truck was not in the drive and the gate was open. The only one at home was the dog, who got up, turned once, and settled back down with hardly a look at us.

"It looks the same as when I left to follow them."

I ran to the door and banged on it. No answer. Mrs. Warren and Moses Ermlich were in the wind. If the impossible was possible, Reed's foreman would be after them. I hoped they had a good hiding place.

I AWOKE ONLY an hour after Alex and I rolled into bed at my house, not so much exhausted by the physical activity involved in chasing down Mrs. Warren and Moses as emotionally drained by the worry that they were now in danger from Reed's foreman.

Alex must have heard me jerk to consciousness. "What's up, babe?"

"If Mr. Warren is alive, and he wants us to think he's dead, why would that be?"

It was a question I knew was on Alex's mind and on Frida's as well. And all night long each of us would be wrestling with the answer.

Alex got out of bed and headed toward the kitchen. "I'm making coffee, because neither of us is going to sleep."

I dragged myself from the bed and followed him. I perched on one of the kitchen stools and leaned on the counter. "We go back to the beginning. Who had the motive and the opportunity to make it appear David was the killer of his client?"

"Reed or someone at his ranch." Alex stopped filling the coffee pot and looked at me. "Mr. Warren blames

David for his son's death. What better revenge than to have David accused of killing the client."

"And of Dudley being the killer of Sammy's nephew. With no one to run the ranch, David would be forced to sell, which is what he wants, but he'd have to practically give away the place. Who would want to buy a place from a convicted murderer, a man who killed one of his clients and on that property? Creepy. But Reed would be standing right there, eager to take it away from him."

"That's good work, wrapping Reed into this suspicion." Alex poured us each a cup of coffee. "You think Reed knows anything about what Warren is doing?"

I set down my cup. "I don't know, but I think he's dirty too. I'll bet it has to do with Bernard's death, and I think that's tied to the treatment of his workers."

"How?"

"Damned if I know." I yawned. "This caffeine isn't helping me think, and it's not even waking me up. I'm going back to bed."

We had settled back into the bed and were snuggling ourselves into either sleep or romance—neither one of us seemed to care which—when another thought occurred to me. I untangled from Alex's arms, turned on the light and sat up.

"What now?" he asked.

"Mrs. Warren has a reason for wanting David in jail too, you know. I should have thought of this before."

"Go on." He propped himself on his elbow.

"The same reason as Warren's. David killed her son."

"You think that poor, sad woman positioned herself at David's ranch, got a hold of his rifle and shot that client. And then she grabbed Bernard, planted David's card on him and killed him also. I find that hard to believe, Eve. Forget it." He turned off the light. "Now where were we?"

I turned the light on again. "She has Moses to help her."

Alex sighed and stared at the ceiling. "Maybe."

We both lay there pondering this newest possibility. Neither of us was much in the mood for romance now. I turned off the light and rolled over.

A few moments later, I turned the light back on. "Boy, are we stupid."

"Okay. I'll bite. How are we stupid?"

"Because Mrs. Warren could be protecting her husband. She and Moses may have known all along that he was alive, and the three of them are working together to make David look like a killer."

Alex was silent for a moment. I thought he'd fallen asleep, so I jabbed him in the side. "Hey."

"It's possible, I guess, but honey, I'm too tired to think this out right now. And anyway, we don't know if Warren is alive."

"We know Mrs. Warren is alive," I insisted, "but here's something we haven't considered—"

My phone rang.

It was Nappi. "I know it's late, but I just got a call from Mr. Reed, saying he had a special hunting treat for me this coming Sunday. He wouldn't be specific, but he indicated it was something challenging, and he termed it just the kind of adventure for a man like me, 'someone who would be comfortable taking his street game into the woods.'"

"What does that mean, do you think?" I asked. My

bedside clock said it was nearer to one in the morning than midnight. "He sure does business at odd hours, doesn't he?"

"I don't like this, Eve. This man is without principles. And his foreman appears to be worse than he is." Nappi sounded worried, not what I expected from a man so used to dealing with criminals.

I shared with him our suspicions about Reed's foreman.

"Hmmm. What was the name of the company he worked for in Afghanistan?"

I put Alex on the phone to tell Nappi what he had learned about Warren's supposed death.

Alex ended the call. "He said he'd get back to us. And he also said we should get together and talk, maybe over drinks tomorrow night."

"You mean tonight." I pointed at the clock. "Maybe we can go to the Biscuit. I didn't get my rib fix, and the peanut butter and jelly sandwich I had when we got home just isn't doing it."

I rolled over toward Alex, and he wrapped his arms around me.

"Sleep or…?" he asked.

I was still wide awake and the "or" part of his question sounded appealing.

As we were getting well into the "or" thing, the phone rang. Caller ID said it was Nappi.

"That was quick," I said. "Just a sec." I covered the receiver.

Alex hopped out of bed and said, "The man must have spies planted in the house. When he's around we never get any time to ourselves. I'm going to make myself a Scotch while the two of you talk, or plan something, or hatch a not-so-legal plot." He stalked out of the bedroom.

"I contacted my associates," Nappi began. I never questioned him about his associates. He seemed to have a great many in many places of significance. He probably wouldn't have been willing to tell me much if I had asked, and to tell the truth, I really didn't want to know about them—names or positions or titles. For all I knew the President of the United States was one of them.

"Mr. Warren was not a favorite employee of the company he was with in Afghanistan. He'd been deployed there previously on three tours of duty with the U.S. Army, and they found him equally—what can I say—*irresponsible* when it came to dealing with the Afghanis. The military was glad when he decided not to re-up. He was an arms expert, oversaw training of Afghan police and military. He continued in that role with the private company, which hired him to train security people. My associates tell me they were not pleased with his work. He treated the Afghanis like primitives. When he lost his life in the car bombing, it was suspected he might have been targeted by some of the men he was supposed to be working with, but the company never pursued that theory, simply sent the notification and his effects home to his wife and let it go."

"No attempt to identify who was killed?" I asked.

"No. For nonmilitary personnel, it's a real mess over there. And his company couldn't have cared less. They were glad to pay the small survivor benefits and wash their hands of him. I did find out that one of the men he was training went missing about the same time he was blown to bits."

That gave me pause. "So he could have set up that

guy to take the hit in the car bombing, then walked away from it and into another identity."

"More than likely. It occurred soon after his son was killed. He sent several threatening letters to David. Did you know about them?"

"Yes, Frida told me. The authorities knew about them too."

"Another of my associates claimed to have known him in high school in Illinois," Nappi said. "The guy has since moved down here and works in a Western wear store over on the west coast."

"You have associates in retail? What's that about?" I shouldn't have asked.

There was a pause at the other end of the line. "Some of my contacts are just like you and me, Eve."

Well, maybe like him, but like me? Or did he, when talking with others, claim he had associates in the consignment shop business?

He continued with his story, "My retail friend said a guy looking like Warren came in the store about a year ago. When my friend approached him, he said his name was Wallace. Is that the name of Reed's foreman?"

"No. It's Mike Hunter."

"Hmm. Well, isn't that fascinating. And you'll find this even more interesting. Sheriff Leopold and Blake Reed were in the army over in Afghanistan together. And they could have run into Warren there."

Well, I'll be gobsmacked.

"How did you find out so much at this hour?" I asked.

I could almost feel him giving me that Cheshire cat smile over the phone. "I hope I've been useful to you, my dear."

When was he not?

"Drinks and ribs at the Biscuit tonight?" I asked.

"Of course." He disconnected.

Alex walked back into the room, a Scotch on the rocks in each hand. He handed one to me. I repeated what I'd learned from Nappi.

Alex's face clouded up like the storms gathering over the Big Lake. "That guy knows everything. What's with him? How does he do it? Are you sure this is all true?"

"He knows lots of stuff, but not everything. I'll bet he doesn't know the kind of stuff you do."

Alex looked surprised. "Like what stuff?"

"Stuff there." I pointed to the bed.

He tossed my cell out onto the back deck and disconnected my landline. Some "stuff" shouldn't be interrupted or shared, not even with close friends and important associates.

I WAS CONGRATULATING myself on getting Alex back into doing his "stuff" when he untangled his leg from mine. "Wait a minute. What you said earlier… You said there was something we hadn't considered."

I rewrapped by leg around his. "We can consider it later."

He turned on the light. "Now."

"Alex." I ground my teeth in frustration.

"No, really. I can't sleep or do anything, um, fun because I can't concentrate. What was it?"

I gave in. Alex could be as stubborn as me when he wanted to.

I took a sip of my Scotch. "The break-in at David's house when he killed the Warrens' son happened when…about four years ago, wouldn't you say?"

Alex nodded.

"Why did it take Mr. Warren or Mrs. Warren or Moses Ermlich or whoever might be gunning for David so long to work out a way to get him?"

Now neither of us was in the mood for sleep or that other "stuff."

It was just as well we got up and began to play gin rummy because more interruptions were on the way. A rap on my front door ended my three-hand losing streak. The sight of Jerry standing there made me think, *Oh, crap, I just lost another one*.

"Who's taking care of the shop?" Images of it going up in a fireball ran through my head.

"Oh, no problem. Grandy and Max are here. Well, I mean they're not here, of course. They're at the rig, but—"

"Get on with the story, Jerry." I stood in the doorway, hands on my hips, blocking Jerry from entering.

Alex followed me to the door. "What the hell, Eve? Let him in. Gin rummy with two people is boring. And there's nothing on television at this hour." Alex waved him into the living room.

"Well, why didn't Grandy and Max call me if they were coming?" I followed Jerry as he made his way to the kitchen.

"They tried, but they couldn't get through. Your land line rings busy, and your cell just keeps ringing until it goes to voicemail. Got anything to eat?" Jerry pulled his head out of my fridge and started toward the cupboards.

I remembered Alex tossing the cell into the yard and turning off the unit on my bedside table. *Oops*.

"Is there anything wrong?" I asked Jerry, grabbing

my wall phone in the kitchen and dialing Grandy's cell number.

I couldn't hear Jerry's reply. He was continuing his attempt at grazing by poking around in my freezer. "I thought you might at least have an old frozen pizza here."

My call connected. "Grandy. Are you okay? Why didn't you stop by the house?"

"We're fine, honey. We drove up this way for a boat part and decided to come on over to visit. But I couldn't get in touch with you by phone, and when we drove by the house, we saw Alex's car there, so we figured the two of you needed some time together. We didn't want to impose on Madeleine at this hour, so we stopped by the rig."

"I know you're there. Jerry came by here."

"Oh, dear. He's really hard to get rid of, isn't he?"

Yeah, I thought. Divorcing a man usually creates distance, but Jerry was like a recurrent rash, coming and going, never completely cured.

Grandy continued talking, "I assumed he had a motel room he could go to when he left here. Well, don't worry about us. We're tucked into that little bed in the rear of the motor home. We're as happy as spooning lovebirds."

I tried to imagine birds spooning, but failed.

"But that bed is tiny. We're up, and I have the spare room. Come on over here."

Jerry tossed a loaf of bread onto the kitchen table and grabbed peanut butter out of my cupboard. He heard what I'd said to Grandy, and in that whiney voice of his asked, "But where will I sleep then?"

"Does it look as if I'm running a boarding house?" I asked.

"Of course not, honey, but you know the guy doesn't have any place here in town to stay except for the motor home." Alex always seemed to take Jerry's side. The two had had one male bonding experience some time back. It seemed to have had a lasting effect.

I held the phone receiver in my hand. Grandy must have heard the discussion. "Don't be silly, Eve. We're all tucked in here, and this bed isn't any smaller than the one on our boat. We'll see you in the morning. I'll stop by with donuts."

Jerry leaned in to speak into the receiver as he slipped past me on his way to the table. "I love donuts."

I gave up. I was too tired to think straight. "Sleep where you like. I'm off to bed. We're taking the rig to West Palm tomorrow to visit our longtime clients there. I need some sleep."

I stormed off to the bedroom with Alex's voice calling after me, "Be there soon, babe. I'm just going to have a little snack with Jerry first."

Jerry was still talking to Grandy, ordering a dozen chocolate cream-filled donuts for tomorrow morning, when sleep took over. The next thing I knew I smelled peanut butter and felt Alex's body slide into bed beside mine. My stomach growled. I'd never get to sleep again tonight.

TWENTY-ONE

I<small>T WAS A</small> crazy morning. Neither Alex nor I had gotten much sleep. Grandy and Max arrived with donuts—the only thing that moved Jerry out of bed—and Madeleine called to ask where I'd been last night.

"I called and called, but both your phones kept going to voicemail."

"Uh, sorry, but Alex and I needed a little together time."

"Oh, how insensitive of me. Of course you did. I'm sorry."

And how insensitive of me not to understand how lonely Madeleine must be with David in jail and me out of touch.

"Grandy and Max stopped by with donuts. Why don't you join us?"

"I already had breakfast."

"Donuts aren't really breakfast. They're like a snack," I said.

"For you," Madeleine said, "but for the rest of us they're calories we can't afford. I'll see you when you pick me up. Say hi to everyone for me." She disconnected.

I didn't want to get Madeleine's hopes up, so I intended to keep what I knew about Mr. Warren, aka Mike Hunter, to myself. I did share it with Frida when she called, but she chose to sit on it for the time being.

She said Linc had checked into Mr. Warren's background and gotten the same information as Alex and that's all. When she heard what Nappi had uncovered, she was impressed but skeptical.

"I've got to find a way to verify that through legitimate channels."

"What's not legitimate about Nappi's contacts?" I asked.

She hung up on me.

"Frida still doesn't trust Nappi," I said to Alex.

"And you find that puzzling? No one trusts mobsters." Alex paused. "Except for you, Eve."

I gave him a squinty look, waved goodbye to everyone, and left to pick up the rig.

First I picked up Madeleine, then the motor home. Realizing that we hadn't collected our mail for several days, I drove us to the post office. When I stepped inside I heard the music I'd come to associate with my life in Sabal Bay: the sounds of jangling spurs as cowboys from the area checked their post office boxes before they hit the pastures to ride herd on their cattle. I knew some of these guys from dancing with them at the Biscuit. I greeted their cheery hellos and "see you soon for a little two-step" with my own merry hi and a grin. Others tipped their hats to me, and I gave them a smile in return.

When I pulled the mail out of our box, an envelope of heavy vanilla-colored paper caught my eye among the usual advertisements and bills. It looked like a wedding invitation, but I wasn't aware of any upcoming events for friends or relatives—either Madeleine's or mine. I got back into the rig and showed Madeleine the envelope.

"So open it. Maybe it's from a business acquaintance." Madeleine's tone of voice evidenced little interest, only boredom or maybe fatigue. She tried to hide a yawn behind her hand. I'd only glanced at her this morning when I picked her up. Now I took a longer look. Her freckles stood out in stark contrast to her pale face. The bags under her eyes indicated she hadn't gotten any more sleep last night than I had. She leaned her head against the passenger side window and stared out the windshield.

I ripped open the envelope and read the invitation inside.

"Well, I'll be damned. She's got some nerve." I tossed the contents across the seat to Madeleine.

"What?" she asked.

"Read it."

Madeleine scanned the paper and then burst into laughter. "That's really funny, that is."

"I don't think it's funny at all. Elvira Reed sent us a formal invitation to the special opening of her consignment shop. That's really shoving it in our faces, don't you think?"

"I think we should accept." Madeleine gave me a devilish smile.

"You can't be serious."

"I am. I'm dying to see what she's doing with her shop and curious to find out who comes to this shindig. Will it attract any of our clients?"

Madeleine was right. I was curious too, but I hated to give Elvira the satisfaction of seeing me give in to my curiosity.

Madeleine eyed me. "Oh, get over it, Eve. What happened to your sense of adventure, your snoopy nature, your need for an opportunity to match wits with the Wicked Witch of the Reed Ranch?"

"Well, the invite is for Saturday. We'll do the flea market on the coast then dash back here in the late afternoon. We'll make her think we're not going to show and then, *bang*! There we'll be. Sure, I need a challenge, and matching nasty remarks with Elvira sounds like my kind of fun."

Madeleine gave me a broad grin, the broadest I'd seen since before David was arrested. Elvira had unintentionally provided her with just the lift she needed.

"Big weekend ahead," she said.

I turned on 714 to head down the canopy road to the coast. "What?"

"You know, the invite, and then there's Nappi's hunting at the Reed ranch the following day."

I'd almost forgotten.

WE WERE AS successful at the market at Stuart as we'd been when we'd gone farther south the other day. The designer Western wear was a big hit, and I worried we'd be out of merchandise before we had a chance to take our fashions back to Sabal Bay to sell to our faithful customers there. With the rodeo less than a week away, it looked as if we might have to try another run to West Palm and hope the ladies could dig some more boots, cowboy shirts, and fancy jeans with rhinestone-studded pockets out of their closets. The rub was that we really didn't have the time to make another trip without it cutting into selling time.

We'd had no opportunity to take a break during the morning and by early afternoon both of us were starving. The smell of kettle corn from one of the nearby stands tempted me, so during a lull, I dashed over and grabbed two bags. Madeleine and I sat in our chairs outside the rig and munched on our treat. When I told her my thinking about the upcoming rodeo and our diminishing inventory, she agreed we needed to find more items.

She licked the salt and sugar from her fingers and took a slug of her bottle of water. "We'll have to split up again. One of us sells, and the other picks up merchandise."

I preferred the more flexible schedule of finding items to sell than the selling. I knew Alex wouldn't be very forthcoming about what was happening with Mrs. Warren and Moses. Had they returned home? Was there any sign of them elsewhere? He would not keep me in the loop, so I'd have to do some footwork myself. That meant I'd need time to go visit the Warren home, check it out and then try to wheedle information out of Frida. Maybe Frida didn't know anything either. She'd been shoved to the sidelines. Perhaps she might be interested in joining me in a little snooping. Tomorrow might be a perfect time.

"Eve, are you listening to me?" Madeleine's voice broke into my musings.

"Sorry, but I'm a little distracted this morning."

"I guess that invitation from Elvira really got to you, huh?" she asked.

"Oh, yeah. Right."

"So I'll sell here the rest of the week and Saturday and be back in Sabal Bay in time to get ready for Elvira's opening on Saturday. You hop down to West Palm for more clothes."

"Are you sure you're up to driving this thing on that narrow canopy road?" I asked.

"Sure."

I arched my eyebrow in skepticism. I knew it wasn't nice to doubt her, but I didn't want the rig off the road in the swamp kissing a palm tree and disturbing the local wildlife.

Madeleine returned my look with one of irritation. "I'll show you. When we leave here, I'll drive home."

Oh, oh. What I liked less than the idea of Madeleine in the swamp was me in there with her.

I gave in, knowing I couldn't deny her a chance to prove herself right. "Fine, but don't kill us or wreck this thing. It's not ours, you know. It's only on loan."

Her eyes filled with tears this time.

"Oh, c'mere." I pulled her to me and gave her a big hug. "I'm sorry, honey. I'm sure you'll do fine."

"I MISSED THE TREE, didn't I?" Madeleine asked as she maneuvered the rig into our parking spot in the local flea market. Jerry was there to meet us.

I tried to smile and look reassuring as I noticed her backing the rig too close to the building. "Uh, maybe you should leave a little more space between—" I didn't get the opportunity to finish my sentence. A scraping sound from the rear of the rig interrupted me.

"Damn. Where did that come from?" she asked.

"That's one of the structures that's been there for about twenty or so years. Kind of sneak up on you, don't they?" I said.

Madeleine laid her forehead against the steering wheel and began to sob. "I'll never get the hang of it. Never."

Jerry hopped into the passenger's side and seeing Madeleine's distress as well as the rig's proximity to the building, offered to help. "If you've got some time right now, I could take you out and give you a few pointers."

I decided not to tell him she'd already had several lessons from both me and Nappi. Who knew? Maybe Jerry would excel as a teacher where we had missed the mark.

"Great idea." I was almost convinced that nothing could help her drive the thing, but having her occupied for some of the evening might leave an opening for me to check on Mrs. Warren and Moses. It was probably better to snoop around under cover of darkness than tomorrow in broad daylight.

I waved her and Jerry off to their driving experience, crossing my fingers that the rig would suffer no ill effects and they would return alive, with Madeleine now an accomplished driver. Yeah, like that would happen.

First, I needed to check in with Alex. There was no way I was going to visit the Warren house if Alex was still sitting on it. What would that accomplish, other than making him tell me to butt out as usual?

"Grr-umph?" came a voice from my cell when I connected.

"Hi, Alex."

"Grr-umph? Is that you, Eve?"

"You were expecting another woman?"

"I was asleep."

I wasn't surprised. I was running on empty too and jealous that he'd found time to grab a nap.

"Was anybody at the Warrens' place the last you checked?"

"Nope, and no sign they'd returned since I began tailing them earlier last night. Frida called me and said she had today and tonight off, so she's sitting on the place."

Really? Hmm. That meant she might enjoy company...my company.

"Are you still worried about Mrs. Warren and Moses' safety? Still think they're innocents in all this and not in on something illegal?" Alex clearly thought my speculation about them was absurd.

"Look, it's as good a guess as yours."

"I don't think so. You are so naïve about people, Eve."

I heard a yawn over the phone.

"Get some sleep. Give me a call when you wake up."

"You need sleep too. Are you home yet?"

"Um, yep. Sure am. I'm just about to turn in right now. Sleep tight." I disconnected, uncrossed my fingers and jumped into my car. *Frida, honey, you're about to have help. Here comes Eve to the rescue.*

"DOES ALEX KNOW you're here?" Frida asked.

I didn't reply, only gave her a sheepish look.

Our two cars sat on the road that intersected the one on which the Warren house sat. It was a good spot from which to keep an eye on the house as we'd positioned the cars behind a palm tree and a large century plant.

"They sure grow them big out here, don't they?" I said, admiring the size of the spiny plant in front of us.

We sat in silence for a while. I rubbed the amulet Grandfather had given me. It was itching. I moved my hand to my throat, thinking I would remove it, but I hesitated. Maybe it was trying to tell me something.

"Would you stop that infernal scratching? It's driving me crazy." Frida leaned out of the driver's side window and put her binoculars to her eyes.

"Nothing. It's as if they've gone away on vacation."

"Or they're hiding from someone."

"Maybe. It'll be dark soon, and we won't be able to see much unless we get closer. Wait a minute. There's a truck coming."

"It's them."

Moses pulled his truck up to the open gate and pulled in. Mrs. Warren got out and headed toward the front door. We heard the dog barking from inside the house.

"Poor thing!" I said. "It's probably hungry. And now, time for a little come to meetin' time with Eve." I got out of my car before Frida could react, and I sprinted to the Warren house, catching Moses just as he was about to close the driveway gate.

I heard Frida call my name.

Moses squinted in the dim light of the setting sun. "You! And it looks like you brought the cops this time. Now what do you want?"

"To ask you a few more questions and to tell you I know about Mr. Warren."

The expression on Moses' face became more shuttered than before. "I don't know what you mean, but we're tired of you coming around here, bothering us."

Frida came up behind me. I saw the curtain on the front window move; then Mrs. Warren stepped out on the front stoop. "Let them in, Moses."

He looked as if he was about to refuse, but then he gestured toward the door.

Mrs. Warren had just fed the dog, which was wolfing down his bowl of dry food. I decided to get right to the point. "We followed you last night and know you went out to the Reed ranch. My PI friend thinks you went there to warn Reed and his foreman that the law was getting close."

Mrs. Warren and Moses exchanged worried looks.

"Is that what you think?" asked Moses, his glance taking in Frida and me.

Frida opened her mouth to speak, but I beat her to it. "When we described the foreman to you last night, what I saw in your faces wasn't 'The jig is up, better warn everybody,' but rather 'Better find out if what we suspect is true.' Both of you looked surprised to me and more than a little terrified."

Mrs. Warren's hand went to her throat. "I didn't know he was still alive. I don't understand how that can be. But he is, isn't he? We wanted to see for ourselves, but then we decided it was too dangerous."

"Someone reported a truck coming up on you last night. The person driving it saw both of you clearly in his headlights. If that was your husband, Mrs. Warren, you could be in danger."

Frida finally broke into the conversation. "Eve here thinks Reed and the foreman who calls himself Hunter are a threat to you, but I'm thinking she's wrong. I think it's just as likely that you knew all along your husband was alive and you and he planned a way to make David pay for your son's death. Maybe Moses helped you."

A vehicle slowed to a stop in front of the house. I

peeked out the window and spotted a black pickup. Someone got out. In the weak light from a streetlamp on the far corner, I could see a man who looked like Hunter. He stared at the house then got back into the truck. It started up again and continued down the road.

"I've got a bad feeling," I said. "Reed's foreman who goes by the name of Hunter just cruised by the house, made a quick stop, and now he's turning around. I think it might be smart to get out of here no matter what you think, Frida."

Frida nodded. Mrs. Warren grabbed her purse off the kitchen counter, Moses snatched the dog up in his arms, and we dashed out the back door. The overgrown backyard provided us cover from the road. From behind a clump of palmetto, I had a clear view of the front yard and the truck. Hunter had stopped the vehicle and gotten out again. He walked toward the house carrying something in his hand, some kind of a bottle. Was he having a beer? Maybe he was drunk and wanted to scare his wife and hassle Moses. When he stopped I heard the sound of a click and saw a small flame flicker in his other hand. Was he lighting a cigarette? Maybe I was wrong, and he was visiting his partners in crime. But why had Mrs. Warren and Moses grabbed the dog and so eagerly followed us out of the house? No, they were afraid. I knew it.

He moved the fire toward the bottle. Flames leapt out of the top of it. He drew back his arm and pitched the bottle through the front window. A Molotov cocktail! The room exploded, bright yellow and red tongues of fire shooting out through the window, the smell of gasoline strong in the night air. Now I could see Hunter's face lit by the leaping flames. He was smiling, a devil's grin, and I heard laughter as he got back into his truck and drove off.

TWENTY-TWO

Mrs. Warren collapsed against Moses. "We could have been inside there if the two of you hadn't come along." Their dog barked at the fire, showing some animation for a change.

Frida nodded. "You were right, Eve. They didn't know anything about her husband still being alive, and he's determined no one finds out he's not dead."

"But people do know. We're on to him," I said.

"He doesn't think so. He's certain he's covered his tracks. His only worry was seeing his wife with Moses on Reed's property last night. Now he's sure he's taken care of that problem."

"I think we shouldn't allow him to think otherwise or he'll try again." I watched as Mrs. Warren cried into Moses' shoulder and the dog whimpered, its tail between its legs.

Frida chewed on her thumbnail. "Now I have to decide what to say to my boss. Knowing that Sheriff Leopold was buddies with Reed in the army and that he might also have known Warren makes me uncomfortable. If my boss tells him what we know—"

"Why tell him anything? You said yourself you'd have to check Nappi's information. Until you do, it's not official."

"There's Mrs. Warren and Moses Ermlich to consider. I think you're right, Eve. They need to remain

dead for now or Hunter will take another shot at them."
Frida spun around on her heel and looked back at the
house. "Let's see if we can make Mr. Hunter's life a
little uncomfortable. Eve, do you think you can find
a public phone in town some place? One that still
works?"

I thought for a few minutes. "I think there's one
at the gas station down from the intersection of the
roads leading to the casino and the state park. It's not
far from here."

"Good. We need to call in a tip about the fire from a
phone that doesn't lead back to one of us. Tell the police
you think you saw a man at the fire tonight and give
them Hunter's description and the description of the
truck. And be sure to mention the Reed ranch sticker
on the truck."

"Okay. Will do. That ought to make him squirm a
little when the cops come to pay him a visit."

Frida's lips formed a satisfied smile. "We all saw
what happened tonight, and it's our duty as good citizens to call it in, but it's also my duty to protect us. I'll
have to make up some story about why I was out here."

"You're going to lie?" I was shocked. Frida was a
by-the-book kind of cop.

"Not at all. I was driving out this way, and I saw a
house in flames. I'll just leave out anything else for the
time being. However, the fire department will comb
the house for bodies and—"

"It'll take some time for them to find there are none,
won't it?" I asked.

Frida nodded.

"By then, something will break. Meantime, Mrs.
Warren and Moses can bunk at my house." It was usu-

ally filled with visitors anyway. A few more couldn't make a difference.

Frida gave me a penetrating look. "'Something will break,' you said. Just what were you referring to, Eve? Something's afoot, something that involves your not-so-worried-about-how-legal-the-plan-is friend, Mr. Napolitani."

I gulped. Frida could read me so well.

"He's going to do a little hunting at the Reed ranch on Sunday. That's all. Just to determine the lay of the land. Nothing illegal about that, is there?"

"If you and he hatched it, then there's got to be something funny going on."

The sounds of sirens interrupted our conversation. One of the neighbors must have already called in the fire. Mrs. Warren still clung to Moses, crying softly into his shoulder. The dog just sat staring at the fire—what energy it had, spent. At the sound of the fire trucks, the dog began to howl and Mrs. Warren wiped her eyes and looked back at her burning house. "Maybe it's time for a new beginning. That house held too many bad memories."

"You've lost all those pictures of your son—" I said.

"I've got this one left, taken several months before he died." She pulled a snapshot out of the small purse she'd snatched off the counter. "And copies of his baby pictures and others from his childhood are at his grandmother's house. And of course, if there were any of his father still left in there, I'm glad they're gone."

"I think you should get out of here before someone from the police or fire department spots you. As for me…" Frida gave me a wave and began to walk toward the house. I knew she didn't relish concocting a story about the fire, but I hoped she'd only have to prevaricate for a short time about what she knew. She wouldn't lie; she'd just sidestep the truth until her conscience got to her. I hoped that would be sometime after Nappi came back from the Reed ranch. Maybe we'd know more then.

I hustled Mrs. Warren, Moses, and the dog into my car and headed for the back way out of the neighborhood. I patted my chest where my amulet rested between my breasts. Maybe it had nothing to do with our getting out of the house before it went up in flames, but I'd never be without it again.

Well, I thought to myself as I drove home, I had a bit of explaining to do to Alex. That could wait until tomorrow. I struggled to keep awake. Why did crime fighting always seem to involve lack of sleep? Did criminals lose sleep or were they up nights also? I hoped so. I gritted my teeth and focused on the road ahead.

THIS WAS GOING to be a great day, I said to myself as I drove down the Bee Line Highway toward West Palm and the clients there who would be only too happy to see me and consign their Western duds to our store. I'd visited clients yesterday also, collecting items for the rodeo. I rolled down the window and hummed a little tune as I sped by a pair of Sand Hill Cranes and their gawky young offspring breakfasting by the side of the road.

Everything was coming together, I told myself, although I couldn't say just how Jerry had reported that Madeleine had done well driving with him the other night. No more dings or scrapes on the rig. That meant the trees and wildlife on the canopy road to Stuart were safe for the day. Mrs. Warren and Moses Ermlich were securely ensconced in my guest bedroom, having been warned not to go out or make contact by phone with anyone. The dog was staying with one of Frida's friends who ran a dog boarding business out of her home.

Frida decided her boss didn't need to know they had escaped from the burning house, at least not yet. She rationalized her silence by pointing out that she wasn't involved with the homicides of either David's client or Sammy's nephew Bernard, so why would she know anything of an official nature about anyone connected with the Reed situation? I wondered how long she could continue to tell herself that before she broke down and spilled what she knew to her captain.

I pushed that little worry out of my head and focused on the conversation I'd had with Alex Thursday morning when he dropped by for coffee. Our talk went amazingly well, but then, what was done was done. I had house guests and now he had something important to tell David about the case. Alex and I agreed that Madeleine should be kept in the dark about everything concerning Mrs. Warren, Moses Ermlich, the fire, and Mr. Warren, aka Hunter. No sense in worrying her or giving her what might turn out to be false hope for David's release.

And then there was Elvira Reed's grand opening party on Saturday. I could hardly wait. I had no idea of what I wanted to say to her or what I would do, but I was itching to see her face when Madeleine and I took her up on her invitation. I knew she'd sent it to be bitchy, shoving it in our faces that she had a shop and we didn't. Correction. We *did* have a shop. Ours rolled. Hers didn't. Whatever might happen at her place this afternoon, I'd never buy a thing from her. I was certain of that. Unless she had some shoes I couldn't resist. I mentally slapped that awful thought out of my head and drove into the morning sun.

My first stop at Jeannette Randolph's netted me very little merchandise—only one Western shirt, and it was a small petite, a size that was difficult to sell. Most of the gals in Sabal Bay were womanly in their proportions. True, some of the anorexic matrons from West Palm might be able to fit into it, but it was a horrible blue plaid that I had little hope of pushing on anyone with taste. Further, Jeannette seemed eager to get me out of the house in a hurry.

My next stop, only two blocks away, shed some light on what was going on. Marjorie Sinclair—my client who had told me not to worry about Elvira as competition—answered the door. The warmth of her smile made it clear she was happy to see me. When I told her that I was here to pick up any items she might have for the rodeo, she gestured for me to follow her down the hall to her bedroom.

"I've been meaning to get up to Sabal Bay to drop these off and save you a trip down here, but I've been busy. I heard you wanted items for the rodeo, so here you go." She pulled several large bags out of her closet. "My friends and I got this together knowing you could use the merchandise."

"I'm so grateful to you." I grabbed both bags while Marjorie stepped back into her walk-in and pulled several more bags from the back of the closet.

"No, no. We're grateful to you to be able to sell our

items. Each of the items is tagged with the name of the owner."

"I stopped by Jeanette's just now, but she didn't have much. Too bad! She's such a clothes horse that I was certain she'd load me down."

Marjorie leaned against the closet wall. "I hate to tell you this, but she's been consigning with that Reed woman. So have some of the others."

"Damn."

"Most of us have remained loyal to you."

"And I appreciate it, but I know it's been difficult. Now that we don't have a location, at least one that doesn't move, it's hard to find us unless you hop over in the evening and catch us in our parking slot at the market. Some of you have done that, even though it's inconvenient."

"Don't be silly. It's not a problem. It's an adventure. It works out just fine for those of us who want to take in the sights in Sabal Bay and then do a little dancing at the Biscuit."

"What 'sights' are you talking about?" I asked.

"Well, you know. That airboat tour. I've been on it twice this month." She winked at me.

I laughed. "You devil you. You're not talking about taking in the tour. You're talking about drooling over my friend Sammy."

"Well, yes, and then there's that real cowboy experience at the Careful Ranch. You know, riding, learning to rope, bullwhip cracking."

"Now that's one I've not done yet. I guess I should check it out." I picked up two bags, and Marjorie got the rest. We toted them out to my car.

"I hear Elvira Reed is having a grand opening Saturday," said Marjorie. "I got an invitation, but I'm not going."

I dumped the bags in the trunk. "Why not? It might be fun. If you come in the late afternoon Madeleine and I will be there."

"Now *that* I'd like to see. I'll bring the other girls who'd like to see Mrs. Reed take a tongue lashing from you." Marjorie chuckled and walked into the house.

The rest of my stops yielded many more items, so that by the end of the day my trunk was full.

"YOU KNOW," I SAID to Madeleine as we spent the evening sorting through the clothes I'd collected, "once David is back at the ranch, I think we should set up a day of shooting for our customers on the coast. I think the women would love it."

"What made you think of that?" asked Madeleine.

"Marjorie said her friends like to come over here to take in the sights. That's one they've not yet done."

"They might never get to do it if we can't get David out from under these murder charges." Madeleine sunk into a chair, a look of despair on her face.

I was tempted to cheer her up by telling her what we knew about Mr. Warren, but I wasn't sure how any of this would turn out, so I kept the information to myself.

I dropped to my knees in front of her and grasped her hands. "You know this will be over and soon. Alex is working on it."

Her face brightened for a moment. "He's discovered something? What? Tell me."

"Well, nothing for certain yet, but he's working on it."

The sunny look on her face faded back into sadness.

I missed her bright smile and the twinkle in her eyes. Would my friend never be happy again?

"And Nappi's going to the ranch on Sunday," I reminded her.

Madeleine got out of the chair, and with a resigned sigh, reached for one of the bags of consigned clothes. "I know. Now let's get this stuff tagged and ready for Saturday. First we sell, then we take on Elvira Reed."

I didn't like the angry look on Madeleine's face. Did she have an agenda of her own to run with Elvira tomorrow, something she wasn't sharing with me? Because Madeleine's mood shifted in a flash to her usual outgoing and upbeat persona, I wondered if I'd just imagined her rage.

"Are you thinking of doing something, uh, rash tomorrow at Elvira's?" I asked.

"What do you mean by that?" She didn't look at me, but continued pulling clothes out of the bag and tossing them onto the table.

"Madeleine, what are you planning?"

"I don't have to share it with you. You're always scheming and concocting plans with your friends, and I get left out. And, when something important comes up, you don't tell me. You hide it, like you think I can't handle the truth or I should be protected from ugly stuff. Well, let me tell you, Eve Appel, I'm one tough cookie. I may be small, but I'm made of steel." She stood up and flexed her arms. "See? Muscles."

It was such a humorous image. My Madeleine dressed in her usual feminine ruffles and flounces, looking as if she was competing for a body building contest.

I opened my mouth to say something, but she interrupted. "And my mind is sharp as steel too."

"I'm hurt that you think I think you're a wimp," I said. If she knew I'd been keeping things from her, it might be best to put her on the defensive, find out if someone had spilled the beans about Mr. Warren/Hunter.

As suddenly as she had turned into Wolverine, she plunged back down into the couch, sheathed her claws, and once more became the Madeleine I knew.

"Oh, I'm sorry, Eve. I *am* kind of a wimp in ways, but you know how resilient I am. I learned how to drive the rig, didn't I? And I know you'd never keep anything really important from me, anything that might have to do with David's case. I guess I'm so mad at Elvira Reed I can't think straight. I'm dead certain she was responsible for our shop burning down. Don't you agree?"

Well, perhaps it wasn't Elvira's well-manicured hand that lit the fire, but I still pictured Hunter's arm tossing that Molotov cocktail into the Warren house last night. Elvira might have had help.

I nodded. "Maybe you shouldn't go to the grand opening. I've never seen you so angry before. You might—"

"Trip over a mannequin into a counter full of jewelry which would plunge to the floor causing other customers to fall into one of the clothing rounds tipping it into the display windows breaking the glass which could let in the wind and rain soaking all of the silk dresses and fur coats..." She paused to take a breath.

"You do have a plan, ya little minx!" I giggled at the images Madeleine's story evoked.

"You know how clumsy I am. I can't help myself."

Madeleine demonstrated her klutziness by beginning a pirouette which ended in her spinning off balance toward our one-armed mannequin. Before she could crash into it, a hand reached out and grabbed her. I hadn't noticed Sammy enter the rig.

"Sammy. And just in time too. I haven't seen you since…" *Oh, oh.* I'd been about to reveal Alex's and my trip to the Reed ranch, something Madeleine didn't need to know, especially after her outburst claiming I kept things from her.

"I thought you might like to know that I spotted Mrs. Warren and her friend Moses hitchhiking on the road toward the casino. I picked them up and gave them a ride as far as the turnoff to Clewiston. They wanted me to tell you thanks for the place to stay but they felt safer getting out of town. I was surprised to see them. The story going around is that they died in that fire last night."

Madeleine's earlier playful mood was gone. "Is there something you want to tell me, Eve?"

No, I did not want to tell her anything, but I knew I had to. Perhaps more important than updating my dear friend was finding my house guest/escapees before they blew the story Frida and I had concocted to keep them safe.

"Leave the clothes for now." I grabbed Madeleine and pulled her out of the rig and into my car. I tossed the motor home's keys to Sammy. "Turn off the lights and lock up, would you? Jerry should be by soon to keep an eye on things. I'll explain later."

"Where are you off to?" Sammy asked.

"I've got to get those hitchhikers off the road before someone sees them."

I stomped on the accelerator and threw gravel as we sped off.

"You got your seatbelt fastened?" I asked Madeleine.

She said nothing, crossed her arms over her chest and stared arrows of anger and disappointment at me.

As I swerved to avoid a large turtle in the road, I explained about the identity of Hunter and the fire at the Warren house last night.

"So you can see why it's important to keep those two out of sight, for their own safety."

"I see that, but why did you think you should keep all this from me? I wasn't the one threatening their well-being."

"Well, of course not. We just didn't want to get your hopes up."

"Why not? It seems pretty obvious to me that Hunter is Warren and that he set up David to get back at him for shooting his son. Frida should be arresting him and letting David out."

"It's not as simple as that. We don't have any proof Hunter is the one who shot that hunting client of David's."

"But you did see him set fire to the Warren house," Madeleine said. "Why doesn't Frida arrest him for that? His role in setting up David would come out when she questioned him."

I wished Madeleine's view of justice was correct, but I suspected Hunter would simply ask for a lawyer and keep his mouth shut. We needed more people than Hunter in jail. I wanted to get Hunter, Reed, Elvira, and Sheriff Leopold in for questioning so that they could spill the beans on one another. They were somehow involved in two murders aimed at setting up David and his foreman for the crimes. I could see Hunter's motive—to destroy David's life as payment for his son's death—but there was something else going on, something that involved kidnapping Sammy and then releasing him. Oh boy, my head hurt trying to figure this out. I shared with Madeleine my thoughts, at least the ones that made sense. She was quiet for a few minutes, then spoke.

"So what's our plan?"

Okay, there was that plan thing again, as if I had one or should have. I'd need to come up with something. I usually had some kind of plan, even one that didn't work. Today I had nothing. I was depending on Nappi's visit to the ranch on Sunday to do something, I didn't know quite what. Until Sunday, it was important for Hunter to believe he was safe. To do that, I had to get Mrs. Warren and Moses Ermlich back where they belonged in the land of the recently deceased.

"Isn't that Frida's car?" Madeleine pointed to a vehicle stopped alongside the road.

The sun had gone down, making it difficult to identify the person outside the vehicle, but that person was a woman and she was talking to two others standing with her.

I slammed on my brakes and pulled over behind them. Frida leaned toward the other two people, and her body language told me she was furious at them. I caught the tail end of her comments.

"What the holy heck are you two doing here, out in the open? You're supposed to be dead. Not only are you risking your lives, but you're jeopardizing any chance we have of arresting Hunter for murder."

I joined in. "To say nothing of what you're doing

to Frida's career. She stuck her neck out by covering up for you."

"But Maimie," Moses gestured toward Mrs. Warren, "received a call on her cell from Hunter. He knows we're still alive."

TWENTY-THREE

IT FELT AS if everything we'd found out the last few days and all the work Alex, Frida, and I had accomplished in tracking down Hunter's identity had just blown up around us.

"You answered the call or did it go to voicemail?" asked Frida.

Maimie Warren shook her head. "I didn't answer it because I didn't recognize the number. He left a message saying, 'I know you're still alive.'"

"He was bluffing, trying to smoke you out if you had survived the fire." Frida delivered this assessment with cop-like certainty.

My heart, which I was certain had stopped when Mrs. Warren told us about the call, began to beat once more.

"Let's get out of here," Frida said. "It's really too dark for anyone driving by to recognize us, but I don't want to take any chances."

"What if it wasn't a bluff?" asked Moses.

"Trust me. It was. Now, back you go to Eve's place." Frida shoved them toward my car.

"I'll give you a ride home, Madeleine, since there's more room in my car. Call me when you get them tucked in again, Eve." Frida's voice sounded reassuring, and Maimie and Moses needed encouragement, but when I looked into her face, I could tell she wasn't so convinced that Hunter was bluffing.

"ARE YOU HEADING back down south to see customers tomorrow?" asked Alex.

It was later that night, and I'd resettled Maimie and Moses into the guest bedroom and warned them to stay put. Alex and I were savoring some alone time on the couch.

I leaned into him. "I think we have everything we need for the upcoming rodeo. I'm going with Madeleine back over to Stuart."

"How about a touch more wine?" He held up the bottle of pinot noir we'd been sampling.

"No. I've got to get up early and meet Madeleine at the motor home. We still have clothes to inventory and tag before we head out. And—oh damn—I forgot Frida wanted me to call her tonight. I'm not certain she really believes Hunter was bluffing with that call to Maimie."

"How could he know they didn't make it out of the house alive?" asked Alex. "Frida worries too much. I mean, it's what makes her a good cop, but she needs to chill a little, be more like you."

"How so?"

"You plan all sorts of stuff, but most of your plans don't work out. Then you just punt."

I smiled. "And that's what makes me a good amateur sleuth, right?"

"No. That's what makes you so aggravating to be around."

I pulled back my arm as if to give Alex a playful punch, but he was too quick for me. He grabbed my hand and pulled me closer, then kissed me. Wow, I loved that guy's mouth. I forgot all about calling Frida, and we once again turned off the phones. It was one of the best nights we'd had in some time.

I FELT SO alive and happy the next morning—funny how a good man does that to a woman like me—that I let Madeleine drive over to the Stuart market. She did a fair job, taking out only one mailbox on the way. We pulled over, and I left a note on the box giving the owners our names and a number where we could be reached.

When we got back into our shop on wheels, Madeleine gestured toward the driver's seat. "I suppose you want to drive now."

"Nope. Accidents happen to a rig this big on this narrow road."

She gave me a puzzled look, settled into the driver's seat, and pulled back onto the road.

"You're in a good mood today. What's up?"

"You should be too. I've got the feeling that today we'll get a break in David's case. If not, there's always the afternoon hassling Elvira Reed at her opening to look forward to."

We smiled at each other and both joined in singing "It's gonna be a great day."

I interrupted the song only once to warn Madeleine of another mailbox that seemed about to "step into the road." She swerved around it and missed the bridge abutment on the other side by a good three inches. Yes sir. It was indeed a great day.

AFTER A LONG day of brisk sales, we buttoned up the rig and prepared to visit Elvira's. The problem was, as

I saw it, what were we going to wear? I'd been too distracted by running around trying to pin down Hunter's identity, keeping Maimie and Moses out of sight, and romping around my bedroom with Alex to give the matter any thought. Madeleine dismissed my concerns, deciding she didn't feel the need to dress up for her competitor's launch party, but I wanted to make Elvira's heart skip a beat with envy at the sight of my class and style and stop altogether with the realization I could outdo her personally as well as in business. So what outfit said all that?

Madeleine, Maimie, and Moses sat in the living room as I scoured my closet for the perfect ensemble. After rejecting most of what hung there, I threw myself onto the bed in despair.

"I need to be inspired." I ran to the kitchen and grabbed the Scotch, poured several fingers in a glass and tossed it down in one gulp. I waited for it to take effect. Aside from that warm feeling that comes with a good Scotch dancing in your stomach, nothing happened. Madeleine picked up the remote and began channel surfing.

"How long do you think this will take?" she asked.

I poured myself another finger of Scotch and held up the bottle with a questioning look on my face. "Have one?"

Everyone shook their heads. Madeleine chose a cooking show. "I wish you'd hurry. I had no lunch and my stomach's growling. Elvira's invitation said there would be food. If I don't eat something soon, my blood sugar level will plunge and I'll black out."

Black out?

"Madeleine, you're a genius." I ran back to my bedroom.

"I don't know what you're talking about, but this genius is going to raid your cupboards and refrigerator."

I heard the television go off and the sound of cupboard doors opening.

"Don't you have anything to eat in this house?" she asked.

"Never mind that. I'm ready." I walked back into the living room wearing the world's tightest knit sheath in basic black. I paired it with five-inch-high black leather pumps. My only jewelry was a pair of silver earrings that hung to my shoulders. I repunked my hair so that it stood up in spikes almost as high as my shoes.

"Ta da!" I said.

Maimie and Moses' mouths dropped open in astonishment, but Madeleine eyes twinkled with delight.

"You nailed it, Eve," she said.

"You want to reconsider your dress?" I asked.

"Are you kidding? This lets me off the hook. Who's going to notice me? Who's going to notice anyone but you? I could walk in stark naked and no one would take their eyes off you." Madeleine clapped her hands in delight.

"Naked, huh? Why didn't I think of that? Maybe—"

Madeleine grabbed my arm and pulled me to the door. "I said you nailed it. Don't spoil it now."

"Wait a minute. I forgot something." I ran back into my bedroom to grab the amulet off the dresser, then stopped. "Never mind. It doesn't go with this outfit anyway."

The late afternoon was perfect for having the top down on my convertible, and mussing up my hairdo only gave it more wow. Madeleine's red curls blew away from her face, baring her big eyes and pouty red lips. Two glam gals made more enticing by the warm evening wind. We sailed into the parking lot in front of Elvira's store in fine style. Madeleine was right. All eyes, even Elvira's, shifted to me as we entered the store.

"Where did you get a dress like that?" asked one patron.

I slid a business card out of my purse and handed it to her without a word. Other women gathered round, and Madeleine and I talked up our unique shop on wheels, giving out most of our cards and promising the women discounts on items to wear to the upcoming rodeo. I temporarily lost track of Elvira, then out of the corner of my eye watched her emerge from the backroom, seething with rage, eyes bulging, cheek twitching, and teeth grinding. She plunged into the crowd around me and waved her arms to get everyone's attention. In a loud voice, she announced a discount of ten percent for the next ten minutes, a feeble attempt to woo the crowd back to her merchandise.

"Stay longer and we'll have a twenty percent markdown coming up." She gestured toward a table set up with snacks and champagne. "Help yourselves."

The woman looked desperate. We had Elvira on the run, in her own store, at her own grand opening. I should have felt guilty. I thought about it for a minute, but swept the idea from my mind. She deserved whatever she got.

A few of the women wandered over to the food and drink table, but most of them remained near Madeleine and me. To my surprise, Madeleine did have something up her sleeve. I shouldn't have worried she would cause a scene or try something aggressive with Elvira. Not our Madeleine. It wasn't her style. Instead she extracted papers from her purse and began distributing them among the customers.

"What are these?" I asked her. She gave me a flyer, and I read it:

> Fifty percent discounts on Sammy's airboat rides, ribs at the Biscuit and bullwhip lessons at the Calm Dude Ranch. Just mention Madeleine and Eve sent you.

"Give me that." Elvira jerked the paper out of my hand, tore it in half, tossed it on the floor, and stomped on it. Her face went from bright red to blotchy purple. I worried we'd gone too far and given the woman a stroke or a coronary, but she got herself under control, albeit with difficulty.

I gave her a calm yogi-like smile. "Don't bother asking us to leave, Elvira. I think we're done here anyway."

Madeleine and I headed to the door, leaving behind a sputtering, cursing Elvira.

"Scary woman, huh?" asked Madeleine as she settled herself into the passenger's seat.

"Yeah, but wasn't that fun? Who says advertising your business has to be dull? What a great idea you had with those flyers." I shifted into drive and sped out of the parking lot.

The sun was dropping below the far edge of the lake, painting the sky in colors of purple and coral. Madeleine raised her arms above her head and let the warm breeze blow her curls into a whirl of red flames.

"I feel so good. Let's take a drive out the lake access across from that used car dealer and watch the sun set."

"Shouldn't we worry about Hunter still being out there?" I said.

Madeleine gave her tinkling laugh. "With Jerry, Sammy, Frida, and Alex on the case, I'm sure he can't make a single move without being observed."

Checking my rearview mirror and seeing no one around, I calmed my fears and decided we deserved to bask in our victory. What a wonderful ending that would be to a great day. I pulled onto the highway and drove south, took a slight turn right at the traffic signal, then turned left over the berm and onto the sandy area at the lake's edge. I nosed the car into a parking space and turned off the engine. Madeleine unfastened her seatbelt and leaned forward, her arms on the dash, chin propped on them. I stretched my arms toward the evening sky and heaved a deep sigh of profound satisfaction.

We sat in near silence, the only sound the soft lapping of the water against the reeds at the shoreline. After a time, I saw a pickup truck pull up. The tint of the windows was so dark it was difficult to see who was in it, but I assumed the driver and anyone else in the four-person cab was enjoying the same display of sunset colors as we were and experiencing the sense of serenity that the end of the day in rural Florida gives to its inhabitants.

After all, no one had followed us. I'd made sure of that. Hadn't I? Maybe they were just really good at following. With a jolt of terror, I briefly considered that Hunter might be the driver, but I quickly recalled what

Madeleine had said. Considering everything that had happened, he wouldn't be roaming about without a tail.

To the west, the sun still painted the sky with purple and coral. Once it dropped below the watery western horizon, night crept over the lake and into the parking area. We continued to sit at the lake's edge, not talking, simply gazing out onto the surface of the water and into the night sky until we could make out the planet Venus staring back at us. The truck behind us started up.

"I guess it's time we left too." I reached out to turn the key in the ignition when my car was hit with a massive *bang*, forcing it forward toward the water.

Madeleine screamed, then I heard her hit the dash. I looked over and saw her body crumpled between the seat and the dash.

"What the…?" I slammed my foot on the brake and the car stopped for a moment, until another *wham* from the truck pushed the front of my car into the water.

I heard doors open in the truck and the sound of footsteps in the gravel behind us.

"Sorry, ladies. I must have mistakenly hit the accelerator and not the brake. Here, let me give you a hand."

By now the night sky was inky black, so devoid of light that I couldn't make out the features of the man who spoke, but dread filled me at the realization of what was happening. How could we have been so stupid? He grabbed my arm and tried to pull me out of the car.

"No, leave me alone!" I tried to make a grab for Madeleine. Was she okay? Still alive?

He gave a quick glance toward Madeleine and shook his head, then he opened my door and lifted me out of the car. I looked up, confused and frightened, and gazed into the eyes of Hunter.

"Your friend can stay here. She's dead anyway." Hunter tightened his grip on me and dragged me toward the truck. He threw me into the backseat of the giant four-door vehicle. The other man, whom I recognized now as Reed, got in with me and restrained me by putting his arm around my neck. "Stop struggling or I'll cut off your air, and you'll die now and never get to see what the surprise is."

I guess I'm a sucker for lines like that, because I just had to ask. "What surprise?" I gasped for air.

"Well, we thought you might like to do a little hunting. We've got a special rate for you. It's free. And you're the game."

TWENTY-FOUR

THE RIDE TO the Reed ranch seemed long. All I could think about was Hunter's comment that Madeleine was dead. But he didn't know that for certain, did he? He didn't check to see if she were breathing or had a pulse. No. Madeleine couldn't be dead.

"Madeleine's not dead," I said. "She was just knocked out, and when she wakes up, she'll call for help. She saw who you were. I'm sure of it." Who was I trying to convince, him or me? It was the wrong thing to say out loud.

"Think we should go back to reassure Eve that her little friend is a goner?" asked Reed.

I wanted to take back what I'd said.

Hunter laughed. "No way. If she's not dead, she soon will be. The front end of that car will slowly sink into the lake, and she'll drown." He paused. "Or a gator will come along and have her for dinner." The two men laughed.

I shivered at the thought of a death far worse than dying of a concussion.

As if he felt my body tremble, Reed spoke. "As for you, my dear, you'll be spending a cold night. But you'll have every chance to warm up in the morning. In fact, I'm certain you'll want to warm up as fast as you can. As if it'll do you any good. We've got some eager hunters coming to the ranch tomorrow, and they expect something exotic to shoot. You're about as exotic as we could find."

"Except for those cape buffalo. Mean bastards. So you'll be dodging bullets and a cape buffalo's fury. It should be quite a day." Hunter turned halfway around in his seat and gave me an ugly smile.

"Who would be willing to shoot down a human as if she was game?" I asked. "That's just absurd."

"These guys coming tomorrow have done it before. This time we're offering them something a little more interesting, a blonde bitch rather than just some brown Indians." Reed reached into his pocket, extracted a cigar, and began unwrapping it.

"You're a monster. You'd offer your workers like animals to be hunted down by people who pay to kill them?"

"Oh you are so quick. You figured that out, did you? And I suppose you think your friend will help you out tomorrow?" Reed bit off the end of the cigar and spit it out. It landed on my bare leg, but he'd tied my hands behind me, and I couldn't brush it off. I could feel the dampness of Reed's spit on my skin. My stomach did a flip flop.

What friend was he talking about? "Friend?"

"Your mob boss friend. You think we're dumb, don't you? Out of the blue we get a big mob boss who's interested in hunting my ranch? We asked around town and found out the two of you knew each other. Whatever plan you've got cooked up to trap us won't work. Mr. Napolitani doesn't know that another mob boss, one of his old enemies, will be hunting tomorrow at the ranch, and he's gunning for Napolitani. Fingers Bonti says he's waited a long time to get back at Napolitani."

I saw Reed's teeth gleam white in the headlights of an approaching car. His eyes were obsidian. They appeared flat, incapable of reflecting any light, empty and cold. Looking at him was as frightening as listening to the evil acts he intended.

My brain was scrambling to put things together and to find a way to escape, if not tonight then tomorrow, but my thoughts were weighed down by my concern for Madeleine and now my worry that by soliciting Nappi's help, I'd set him up to be a target as well. Maybe if I kept talking I'd find out something that would help, some piece of information I could use against Reed or Hunter.

"You grabbed Bernard Egret and used him as game, didn't you?" I asked.

"I was tired of dumb illegals from Guatemala. I thought a bright college kid might be more fun." Reed flicked a lighter and lit his cigar. The smell of the smoke aggravated the nausea I already felt. He'd killed innocent men, men who wouldn't be missed because they were illegals or had no family to report their absence to the authorities. But Bernard was different, a hometown boy with family, even if they were Miccosukee. I was horrified by what Reed and Hunter were doing, but I was also enraged by it. I couldn't hold back my anger, so I continued to probe, to poke at them. It seemed the only thing I could do.

"You made a big mistake with Bernard, didn't you?" I had a moment's satisfaction pointing out their blunder. "He got away and was found by the authorities. And that brought in his Uncle Sammy. Now Sammy is one Indian to be reckoned with."

Reed sat back in his seat and exhaled smoke. "Hunter made the mistake, not me."

I could see Hunter's shoulders tense.

Reed sucked on his cigar again. Smoke rolled from his mouth when he spoke. "You were supposed to get rid of Bernard's body, and you didn't."

"I made that work for us, didn't I? I used Dudley's gun on him. It took Dudley out of the picture as well as David."

"Try to remember that this is not all about you and your vendetta against David. If you didn't have me, you'd be nowhere. Those gambling idiots dragged Sammy out to the ranch thinking we could use him. Leopold put a stop to that. I don't need no smartass big Indian trying to outwit my clients. They pay well, but some of them are bad shots. Scared Guatemalans are easy prey, but that Indian was another story."

Well, now, that gave me some hope. Maybe I could outrun or outmaneuver or outthink these guys.

Reed tapped me on the leg with his finger. "Don't get your hopes up, gal. The ones tomorrow are crack shots."

I tried to hide my fear by continuing to needle them.

"You sure were dumb trying to outsource how you got your game," I said.

Reed turned his opaque eyes on me. "You think so too? We'll have to eliminate our gambling friends before they begin to feel the need to talk. Even Sheriff Leopold won't be able to help us then. Let's tie up loose ends, and soon. What do you think, Mr. Hunter?"

Hunter's neck looked sweaty to me. Was he having second thoughts about Reed's game? Had he only signed on so he could get revenge on David by making him pay for a murder he didn't commit?

It was a thought I stored to be used later.

"I can take care of that for you." Hunter didn't sound eager to do the job, but I heard no reluctance in his voice either.

"You'll buy David's ranch, won't you? Hunter gets his revenge, and you get to expand your operation," I said.

Reed tapped cigar ash onto the floor. Most of it landed on my shoe. "I will buy his ranch for nothing, and he will sit in jail and watch me succeed where he failed."

"And he'll have time to think about what he did to my son. For a while. Until the state puts him to death. It took time coming up with this plan, but it was worth waiting just to see that man sweat and then fry," Hunter said.

"Yeah, yeah," said Reed, as if dismissing Hunter's agenda.

I again noticed Hunter's shoulder and neck muscles tense.

These two were a matched set of monsters, but how long could this foul bond hold?

There was one last detail I was curious about. "I guess Elvira sent you to get me tonight."

"Yep. She finds you and your friend annoying. My wife is one smart lady, noticing your partner's preference for turquoise ink and suggesting we write the phone number on the back of one of Wilson's cards and plant it on Bernard's body. She said the authorities would connect the dots and think the ink was from a pen Wilson borrowed from his girlfriend. Nice touch,

I thought." Reed again spoke through an exhalation of smoke.

"And one of you burned down our shop."

"Mr. Hunter is good with fire," said Reed. "And now that you have found out all you need to—not that it will do you any good—I suggest you rest up. You'll need all that sass for tomorrow's romp through the swamp."

"He's not that capable as a fire bug. He was seen setting fire to the Warren house." I wanted to bite back my words as soon as I said them.

The sudden quiet in the truck indicated neither of them knew this. *Oh, Eve, you dope*, I said to myself.

"Who saw him?" asked Reed.

I shook my head.

Reed leaned back into the seat and blew out a smoke ring. "No matter. I'll take care of it after we wrap up things tomorrow."

I could read his thoughts. He didn't care who'd seen Hunter. Hunter was expendable. Hunter had to be removed. Did Hunter see this also?

Reed reached up and patted Hunter on the shoulder. "Big day tomorrow, good buddy," he said.

I was wrong to question it. The bond between the two seemed unbreakable. At least until one of them was dead.

REED AND HUNTER shoved me into a shack on Reed's property. As near as I could tell from the route we took onto the ranch, the building was located a short distance from the waterhole where David's client had been killed. My accommodation for the night wasn't much of a shelter—its walls made of boards running vertical to one another. I could see dim light between them. The floor was rough wood also, with gaps in the floorboards. The roof was tin. When I looked up I could see places where the tin had peeled back and the night sky was revealed. It would provide little protection if it rained. I imagined all sorts of bugs and other crawly things coming to visit in the night.

They left my hands tied and slammed a roughhewn door behind me, leaving me alone with my imagination and anxiety over Madeleine and Nappi's safety. From Sammy's description of his night of captivity, this had to be the shed where they'd held him also. It was probably where Bernard had spent his last night.

I was horribly thirsty, to say nothing of hungry, but I knew better than to ask them for water before they left. Why slake my thirst when they intended to kill me in a few hours?

With no source of light and the moon hidden behind the clouds, I could see little outside once the truck lights receded into the distance. I walked the length and width of the building to get an idea of its size. I paced off only ten feet by six. I sat on the floor in one corner and with my back braced against the wall, tried to kick through the boards. For once I wasn't worried about ruining my shoes. Despite its crude construction, the side and door of the shack were solid. I managed to loosen the heel on one of my stilettos and made no impact on the wall.

I leaned my head against the wall and laughed. Here I was fashionably dressed with nowhere to go except to my own death. I should have worn Grandfather's amulet, regardless of whether it complemented my attire. He'd be so disappointed in me.

I closed my eyes. There was no way I would get any

sleep here. Not only was it cold and the floor unyielding against my back and sides, but I needed to keep watch in case something came a-slithering my way.

I must have dozed for a time because I came awake with a jerk. Something was out there. I could hear a sound from the other side of the wall. I sat up and pushed my face against the side of the room and looked out from between the cracks. The moon had come from behind the clouds, washing the open area beyond the shack in silver light. A shadow moved out of the palmetto and emerged into view. A wild pig. It warily approached the shack, grunting and sniffing the air as it got closer. I could see its tusks, top and bottom, long and sharp and lethal looking. I was grateful for the safety of my shack.

Tomorrow would be different. Tomorrow I'd have men with guns, cape buffalo and wild pigs to deal with, perhaps even an alligator or two. I felt a tear slide down my cheek. *You need to be brave, Eve*, I told myself. *You always have a plan. Get some sleep now and in the morning you'll find a way out of this mess.*

By the time the sun rose over the palms to the east and the light slipped into my prison, I still had no plan, but my tears had dried. I clenched my teeth in determination. I intended to go down fighting.

HUNTER AND REED came for me soon after first light. I knew I was becoming seriously dehydrated, and while my body shook from the cold for much of the night, the tremors had stopped now. I worried that hypothermia was setting in. The pleased looks on my captors' faces told me they knew my physical condition and applauded it. I'd present a challenging target for the hunters, while still being too weak to escape them.

When Hunter untied my hands, I went for his face with my nails. I knew it was a futile gesture. He slapped me, and I went down.

As he bent down to pick me up, I shook off his hand and whispered to him, "Why do you think Reed is so uninterested in who saw you set fire to the Warren house? Because you're next. You're the guy who's gonna take the fall for all this."

I wasn't certain if Hunter heard me, or if he did, whether he believed me.

"Hear that?" Hunter nodded in the direction his truck had come from.

I heard the sound of several engines.

Reed stepped in front of me, a sneer on his face. "My pals are on their way. And they aren't going to like shooting their prey while she's cowering on the ground. Oh, they'll do it, but they won't like it. Still, you'll be dead."

I got to my feet, leaned down and took off my shoes.

"That's better." Reed smiled. I hated that smile. How I wanted to claw it off his face.

Last night I had watched the pig move through the clearing where the shack stood and then make its way east. I remembered the condition of the waterhole the day we found David's client dead nearby—how the wild pigs had torn it up. I assumed it was a favorite place for pigs to gather, and I thought I heard the croaking of frogs and maybe the call of a gator coming from that direction.

"You'd better get going, Eve," Reed said. "Run."

Shoes in hand, I took off, my long legs pumping as

fast as they could go, heading east toward what I hoped
was the waterhole, closer to David's ranch and maybe
closer to Sammy. Sammy might be at the ranch, and
he might be patrolling the area. It was a wild chance
and a risk. I knew that most animals would be coming
to the water to drink in the morning before they went
off to do their own hunting for the day. I might have
company, but if I got that far, I thought I knew my way
from the waterhole to the main buildings on David's
property. Reed couldn't chance taking his men off his
property onto David's, could he?

The sound of the vehicle engines faded into the
morning, replaced by the voices of men and the sounds
of them moving through the brush, coming closer despite my attempt to put distance between us. But they'd
probably had a full breakfast and a good night's sleep.
The adrenaline rush I was experiencing was from fear.
Theirs was from excitement. I was fleeing. They were
sportsmen hunting an unusual prey.

I broke through some dense brush and into the
muddy area surrounding the waterhole. I stopped and
scanned the surface of the murky water and the torn up
bank. It looked as if several pigs had visited it recently.
I could see their hoof prints in the soggy ground. And
there were other prints, larger ones, like those of cattle
wandering away from their herd. I stood for a minute
listening, but could only hear my pursuers behind me.
I took a step into the open and waited.

"Sammy!" I yelled. "Sammy. I need help."

All sounds behind me ceased for a moment, then the
scuffling began again. To my left from among the reeds
growing high near the water, a dark shape emerged,
its curved horns lethal looking, the broad plate of ma-

terial across its forehead bulging like armor. It turned toward me, grasses hanging from its mouth. It swung its head as if enraged at the sight of someone invading its domain. Saliva swung in long slimy strands from its nose. It stopped chewing and pawed the earth. *Wow, it's huge*, I thought, and then it began to move toward me. I could almost hear the earth shake as it gathered speed. The blackness of the beast's eyes reminded me of Blake Reed's, devoid of all that was human, intent upon killing.

I knew I could not outrun it, but a few feet behind me loomed a giant live oak. The lower branches hung near the ground, close enough for me to grab one and swing onto it, then leap from there to a higher one. And yet higher. The angry beast came to rest under me, bellowing as if challenging me to come down and fight. Fear made me giddy, and I laughed.

"I'm staying right up here, fella." As if to underline my intent to stay far out of reach but not to let the challenge go unanswered, I threw one of my lovely black stilettos at him. The shoe ricocheted off the horn plate and fell to the ground. The buffalo lowered its head, sniffed the offending object for a moment, then began to stomp on it. I watched in horror with the realization that it could as easily have been me beneath those huge hooves. The buffalo tired of its game, raised its head and shook it, then ran off into the brush. I breathed a sigh of relief, but the ping of a shot hitting the tree branch next to my face started my heart racing once more.

Blake Reed moved into the clearing and his eyes came to rest on me. "Now that's not much fun for anybody. The prey up a tree, just sitting there, waiting to be shot. Get down from there, Eve, or the next shot will wound—not enough to kill, but it will hurt, I guarantee you."

I shook my head and pointed to what was left of my shoe. "The buffalo did that."

Reed threw back his head and laughed.

"I've got business to attend to so if you insist on sitting there in that tree, maybe I'll leave you to it. The boys will be here soon. They got sidetracked by a wild pig they decided to pick off before they finished with you. So sit there and think about it. There's no place you can go anyway."

I heard his laugher as he made his way back into the brush.

Soon the area grew quiet with only an occasional shout from far way, but I knew Reed wasn't lying to me. I'd be an easy target for the hunters soon enough. Did I dare come down from the partial safety of this limb? I was puzzling that one out when I heard someone or something making its way through the brush. Hunter emerged from behind a stand of palm trees and moved toward me.

"You think Reed's going to get rid of me, don't you?" he asked. "You think that's why he didn't care who saw me set that fire."

"Duh, Hunter. That one's easy. Why don't you help me get out of here, and I'll see to it that the authorities view you as a pawn in Reed's game. I'll bet you could make a case for PTSD as a factor in all of this."

Before either of us could say anything more, the cape buffalo came charging out of the brush to the right of me. At the same time Reed emerged from where he had previously entered the wooded area. Hunter swung around and raised his rifle to shoot the buffalo, got off a shot that went wide. He spotted Reed to his right and yelled at him.

"Shoot him," shouted Hunter.

Reed remained unmoving, and for a moment, I thought he was paralyzed with fear. Then I saw a smile etch his lips.

"This will work," he said. I don't know if Hunter heard him, but Hunter shot again and again missed. The buffalo was on him in a second, butting him nearly across the clearing and sending him into the reeds. The beast moved toward him, and Hunter crawled into the water and behind the reeds at its edge. The last I saw of them, Hunter had his arm raised as if it would be sufficient to fend off the buffalo's oncoming attack. I heard yells and the sounds of man and animal struggling, and then it was quiet once more. The buffalo did not reappear, nor did Hunter.

"Shame, isn't it?" Reed said. "Now it's time for you to come down from there, Eve. Since the hunters couldn't get to you, I think I'll bring you to them. Unless, of course, you don't want to see your friend, Mr. Napolitani, and say a few kind words before he dies."

What choice did I have? If I stayed up in the tree, Reed would simply shoot me. Going with him to Mr. Napolitani meant I had another chance to save Nappi and me. Maybe together we could deny Reed his kills. I climbed down, my one stiletto still in my hand. I glanced back at the other one, embedded in the mud.

Reed marched me off to my death.

TWENTY-FIVE

REED PUSHED AND prodded me along the path leading back toward the shack. Sounds of firing could be heard, but they came from the other direction. I wondered if his other clients were killing pigs, buffalo, or humans. I couldn't think about that now. I had Nappi to worry about.

As we entered the clearing where the shack stood, I spotted Nappi decked out in hunting garb that looked as if it had been recently purchased from a men's outdoor clothing catalogue. He was standing a few feet away from another man, also dressed in hunting paraphernalia, but his was camouflage wear—pants, shirt, and jacket like the ones I'd seen in the local sportsmen's emporium. This man was shorter than Nappi, about the same age, with a swarthy complexion. Where Nappi's outfit said "mob boss and gentleman," his said "mob boss and ruthless killer."

A rifle lay on the ground near Nappi. The other man, who could be no one else other than the rival boss Fingers Bonti, held his gun leveled at Nappi.

"Ah, good," said Reed. "I see the two of you have come to an understanding."

Fingers flashed one of the ugliest smiles I'd ever seen on a human. I could detect neither fear nor anger at being betrayed on Nappi's face.

"And now, Mr. Napolitani, since Mr. Bonti has told

you he is holding your family hostage and will kill them unless you do what we say, you will shoot Ms. Appel here. Consider it your finest hunting experience. Too bad you won't get to talk about it to your friends."

Nappi didn't blink, didn't change the expression on his face, didn't move. "I will not do that."

"Mr. Bonti, you can call on your cell now and tell your men to begin shooting Mr. Napolitani's family, one by one, until he kills Ms. Appel."

Bonti raised the phone to his ear, said something, then slipped it back into his pocket. His smile widened.

"It's done, then?" asked Reed.

"I don't think my good friend would do that to me, would you, Fingers?" Nappi smiled.

"You betrayed me?" Reed's face turned purple with disbelief. In the time it took him to recover from his shock and shoulder his weapon to fire at Bonti, Nappi snatched his rifle from the ground, rolled into position and fired. Reed's shot went wild and he dropped to the ground.

"I could have done that just as well, you know," said Fingers.

"I know, but I wanted to show off for the lady." Nappi shrugged and his smile grew. I rushed into his arms.

"The two of you are friends?" I asked.

"Always have been," said Nappi.

"Except for that one time years back, and we settled that by having his oldest daughter marry my son. We're family." Fingers' smile seemed less malevolent now, more like that of a kindly father.

"Is he dead, do you think?" I asked looking down at Reed.

"No. I aimed for his shoulder, and I never miss," said Nappi.

"Well, he's shot in the leg." I pointed to the hole in his thigh and the thick stream of blood that poured from it.

"I meant that I aimed for his leg then." Nappi gave me another hug.

I heard vehicles in the distance. "That might be the other hunters. What should we do?"

Both Nappi and Fingers exchanged looks.

"Not to worry, my dear. They're all family members out for a little hunting experience—dove and quail, not people, buffalo, or pigs." Nappi waved to the men in the SUVs as they pulled up near us.

Reed groaned and held his leg. "I'm gonna die, bleed to death. I need to get to the hospital. Now."

"What do you think we should do with him, Eve?"

"Leave him here. Either the pigs or the buffalo will get him." I pointed skyward. "See those buzzards circling overhead? They'll clean up the mess. When we come back tomorrow, there'll be nothing left."

For a brief moment, I thought I saw fear in Reed's black eyes.

MUCH AS I thought Reed should have been dinner for the buzzards, Frida—back on the job after informing her boss of the fire and who set it and turning over information on Warren's change of identity to Hunter—took Reed into custody. She told me that deputies from the sheriff's department found what was left of Hunter's body at the far edge of the waterhole. Everyone at the scene was on high alert, having seen what a cape buffalo could do to a human, but the animal didn't put in an appearance. Sabal Bay's police chief tried to contact Sheriff Leopold when he called for back-up at the scene, but the sheriff was missing—home with the flu, according to his secretary. The undersheriff for the county directed the operation at the waterhole.

Alex was allowed to pick me up from the shack, and I ran to him when I saw him get out of a police cruiser. It felt good to be in his arms, but I was worried.

"What about Madeleine?" I asked. "Hunter said she was dead. Is she—"

"She's just fine now. She was in and out of consciousness, but aware just long enough to recognize who took you. Bad concussion, but there seems to be no permanent damage. Your airbag didn't deploy when you were hit. That's why she flew forward into the dash. Someone came upon the scene probably only minutes after Hunter and Reed took off with you. They called the EMTs. Early this morning Madeleine convinced the hospital to call Frida. She told them who hit the car and took you off."

"Well, I always knew she had a hard head." My words were the usual plucky Eve stuff, but I was so relieved tears filled my eyes.

"What about Elvira? Reed told me she called to have me carted off to the ranch."

"She's in custody, has been since around six this morning, soon after Reed and Hunter took off to get you. Frida said she got a call from headquarters, and now Elvira is singing her head off. When she was picked up, she refused to tell Frida where they were holding you, so it took some time before we could find you. Sorry about that, babe. I wish you hadn't gone through all this." Alex squeezed me to him even harder.

I almost thought my ribs would snap, but I didn't want him to let go.

"Let's get out of here and let Frida sort out the mess," he said.

"I need to go back to the waterhole."

"You don't want to see Hunter's body. I wouldn't recommend it. The deputies said it's pretty grisly."

"No, no. I just need to pick up something." I held up my lone shoe.

"Not another shoe thing, Eve." Alex sounded a bit annoyed, but resigned.

THE SUN SHONE down out of a clear blue sky, salt spray hit my face, and I drew in the sweet smell of it as David's boat flew down the waterway toward Nest Key. I tucked Grandfather's amulet into the top of my bikini. I was taking no chances. Besides, I decided it went with every outfit I owned. I was the fashionista of the Florida swamps, wasn't I, and I should know these things.

Madeleine relaxed in the chair on the boat deck, an expression of pure joy on her face.

"Not worried about sharks then, I guess." I patted the amulet as I spoke.

"Nope. After the past few weeks, don't you think what walks on land seems more dangerous than anything in the water?" She raised her arms over her head as if to embrace the sky.

"Frida did wonderful work on this one. I heard that Reed and Elvira tried to blame everything on Hunter, but after Sheriff Leopold was picked up at the West Palm airport boarding a flight with connections to South America, he was willing to rat them out. I guess there was a lot of finger pointing, especially when the gambling guys told their side of the story about kidnapping Bernard and Sammy for Reed and Leopold." I sighed. "Have they found that cape buffalo yet?"

Alex heard my question and left David in the cockpit to come back to join us.

"Sammy tracked it down," he said, "and it was turned over to a zoo. The authorities also found the source of Reed's exotics, and arrested them for importing banned species."

"Here, take my chair." Madeleine got up and went to stand at David's side. She leaned her head against his chest and looked up at him.

"Talk about love," I said. They were a beautiful couple.

"Yes. Let's." Alex's tone was light, but underneath I knew he was serious.

I reached out and pulled him down into the chair. "Not now. It's too soon."

He nodded. "So are you going to try to put in a bid on Elvira's shop?"

"We can't sell out of the rig forever, but it's a new building and a lot of money. Elvira might consider a deal to pay for her defense. Reed's ranch was mortgaged to the hilt, I understand, and they both will need megabucks for lawyers."

"I'll bet you could get a loan easily." Before his eyes could meet mine, he looked away toward the thick mangroves lining the shore. We both watched as a cormorant used the water as a runway, gathering enough speed to go airborne and flying off toward some distant mangrove island.

"If you mean a loan from Nappi, I'm certain my partner would not allow that."

Madeleine heard me. "Your partner would not allow that. Much as I like Nappi, it's still hard for me to want to do business with someone who earned his millions by doing stuff that's illegal."

"I think we can approach the bank for a loan. We've been in business long enough and we've got the profits to show we know what we're doing. And here's an idea: we could operate both the rig and a store."

"Are you serious? Doesn't that spread you a little thin in terms of personnel?" Alex asked.

"We've got people who would work for us."

"Like who? Sammy's thinking of turning the airboat business over to his nephew Eddie and taking over David's hunting ranch, since David's still determined to get out of the business."

David turned his head and said, "Sammy would be good at it too. We're talking about it now."

"Sammy's not the only member of the Egret family who's entrepreneurial," I said.

Alex looked confused. "Who's left with some selling experience?"

"Grandfather. He loved working in the store before it burned down, and the ladies loved him. He's a draw on his own. I'll bet he'd be great."

Alex looked doubtful.

"Don't give me that look."

"He's an old man," Alex said.

"Jerry could help him."

"Oh, God." Alex hit himself in the forehead as if he thought hiring Jerry was the worst idea since my decision to marry the man.

"Hey, we're coming up on that old sailboat wreck. I've got to go below and grab something." I ran past

David and rushed down the steps, grabbed a bag, and then went back to the stern.

I pulled a pair of stiletto heels out of the plastic bag. One was badly worn, leather split and scuffed, heel loose. The other shoe hardly looked like a shoe. The heel was gone and the rest of the shoe flattened and covered with dried muck, much of it buffalo spit.

"My shoes from the waterhole. I loved these shoes." I held them up and gazed at them, feeling sad. "I thought I'd give them a burial at sea." I tossed the pair over just as we sped past the sailboat. The skinny, dirty man living onboard stood and watched us for a moment, then held his hand up, the middle finger pointing skyward.

I returned his salute.

* * * * *

Creations in Fotografia by Rafael Pacheco

Lesley A. Diehl retired from her life as a professor of psychology and reclaimed her country roots by moving to a small cottage in the Butternut River Valley in upstate New York. In the winter she migrates to old Florida—cowboys, scrub palmetto, and open fields of grazing cattle—a place where spurs still jingle in the post office, and gators make golf a contact sport. Back north, the shy ghost inhabiting the cottage serves as her literary muse. When not writing, she gardens, cooks, and renovates an 1874 cottage with the help of her husband, two cats and, of course, Fred the ghost, who gives artistic direction to their work.

Lesley is the author of a number of mystery series and mysteries as well as short stories. *A Sporting Murder* follows the first two books in the Eve Appel mystery series, *A Secondhand Murder* and *Dead in the Water*.

For more information, go to www.lesleyadiehl.com.